AND NO QUARTER

Surgeon and adjutant of women in O'Cahan's Irish regiment, warring in Scotland with Montrose, is Martin Somers, better exponent of sword play than of surgery. In his adventurous wardship of this ill-fated company of women, in the strengthening of the line against the forces of the Covenant, his dexterity and toughness of sinew is often decisive. Here is a tale of keen endeavour, of fury and of tenderness—ingenious and thrilling enough to win thousands to the company of Walsh admirers.

AND NO QUARTER

BY

MAURICE WALSH

W. & R. CHAMBERS, LTD.

LONDON AND EDINBURGH

Latest Reprint, 1952

Printed in Great Britain
by T. and A. Constable Ltd., Hopetoun Street,
Printers to the University of Edinburgh

DEDICATED TO MY FRIEND

SEAN O'HOGAIN

COLEPARK HOUSE, COUNTY DUBLIN

IN TOKEN OF THE HISTORICAL AND GAELIC SCHOLARSHIP
PLACED SO GENEROUSLY AT MY DISPOSAL

CONTENTS

CHAPTER I

THE BATTLE OF TIPPERMUIR

I

THIS half-chronicle of certain things that befell some of us in the broken kingdom of Scotland I am writing at the request of my wife, and at the request of Tadg Mor O'Kavanagh, who is my foster-brother; and I am writing it at the command of ten or twelve—or even fifteen—of my grandchildren. And as I sit here at the start of it in my own house at the head of the Pamunkey River in Virginia of the New World I am wondering where to begin. It will be mostly about myself, Martin Somers, Englishman and Adjutant of Women in O'Cahan's Irish regiment, and I can begin where I like.

So, after due thought and for a reason of my own, I will begin it with a small account of the lowness of our state at the start of a most marvellous year, and of the frightened man I was before I struck a blow at Tippermuir. In the first place I should not have struck a blow at all, for, as a sort of half-surgeon, my place was with the wounded and the women; but our straits were so desperate that day that every man who could wield a sword had to wield it in the line, and face, steel-fronted, the imminence of death.

I will begin then, and God be good to me.

I am an old man now, but, even yet, after more than thirty miles on the hunting trail with Tadg Mor O'Kavanagh or, maybe, a finger more of laced brandy-wine than is my nightly due, I suffer bad dreams of Tippermuir, that bloody onset of Tippermuir that we drove home fifty years ago.

That was on Sunday the first day of September, in the year of 'forty-four—sixteen hundred and forty-four to be exact—three miles out of the town of Perth, where the moors begin to make the first great swell into the hills of the Clans. A grand fine Sunday morning in the fall of the year, and it looked to be the last day for all of us on top of earth. And we were all so young; young, young, and not yet tired of living, but weary to the bone of marching and of hunger and of fear in this aloof hostile mountain-land of Scotland. Montrose himself, our Captain-General, was only thirty-two; Colkitto, the great Alasdair MacDonald, for all the weight of killing behind him, was no older; Manus O'Cahan, our Colonel, though his black bullet head carried a band of white, was younger still; Tadg Mor O'Kavanagh, my foster-brother, was an ancient of six-and-twenty, and I, Martin Somers, the rawest, most frightened man of all, was one year younger. And we knew, as sure as our feet—and many of them bare feet—as sure as our feet stamped the heather, that all of us, every last one of us, sixteen hundred men of Ireland, would face death that day, and death not relenting.

We had, every one counted, down to the horseboys —and we had no horse—two thousand and eight hundred men drawn up in a lean line, three deep instead of six: our three Irish regiments; one thousand men of the clans, Clan Vuirich out of Badenoch, MacDonalds of Keppoch, Clan Finlay of Mar, the Atholl Stuarts, Clan Duncan of Struan; and a company of two hundred bowmen from Kilpont. Only ten days before, these tall Highland men had contemplated cutting our Irish throats, but now we were united under the King's Captain-General Montrose, and we were all going to die that morning.

For there were seven thousand men under Lord Elcho and the Kirk facing down on us six deep out of Perth; hard-praying, covenanting men whose terrible rallying cry was, "Jesus and no quarter." Seven thousand men of Fife and the Midlands, six deep, the blue banners of the Covenant flaunting over them, two musketeers to each pikeman, every man with a corselet and an iron headpiece; and a flurry of horse guarding their flanks. And we were in rags, raw-hide brogans tied to our feet, a few flintlocks and arquebuses in Randal Oge's regiment with one bullet for each piece, and the rest of us armed with spears, claymores, sparth axes, and a handy cornered stone in the breasts of our tunics. That is how we were equipped to die.

For months we had been hearing of the terrible fighting qualities of the Covenanters, their dourness, their steadiness, the sheer unshakable weight of the conviction that drove home their charge and reaped without mercy. Now at last we were facing them, and we could only hope to die not badly, and that the Lord Christ would judge mercifully a poor fighting man who had done his best. But when I heard that first savage peal of that abominable gathering cry, "Jesus and no quarter," my mind shook and I wondered if the

11

Solemn League was not right after all, and the Lord Christ on the side of the strong and merciless.

There I was now in Manus O'Cahan's regiment, mostly men of the Route and the Lagan and the borders of Tyrowen. I was in the front line with my foster-brother, Tadg Mor O'Kavanagh, who leant his heavy shoulder against mine to hold me firm in my place.

"I am thinking," said he in his slow, sardonic way, "there will be a blow or two struck in a small while. Are you frightened, Maurteen?"

"I am," said I.

"Good man!" said he. "I'm frightened myself."

"And I'm thinking," said I, "that Slaneyside and Preston's regiment's a safer place than this."

"The thought in my own mind, brother," said Tadg Mor. "A pity I did not think it before I landed you here."

"There is room for only one thought in a man's mind this day," said a strong voice behind us.

"And what thought is that, O'Cahan?" asked Tadg Mor.

"That you will kill your man out there after choosing him, and a second man if you can."

"Very well so," agreed Tadg Mor mildly. "But what'll I do with my third man?"

"Leave that fellow to me," said O'Cahan.

"You are welcome to him, Manus," said Tadg Mor.

That was Manus O'Cahan, colonel of us: a smallish man with a round, white-banded, black head, and blue eyes almost black in a colourless clean face above blue-shaven jaw; a cool, steady man that never lost his temper, never broke his word, never did a mean hand's turn. He was the only man could face Colkitto, and

Colkitto in one of his tempers, and calm him with his own calmness. Now, cool as on parade, he went up and down between his lines, saying a word here, making a joke there, straightening a man's shoulder with a friendly handclap, driving his own strong spirit over ours. But he said afterwards that the only hope he had that day was that, when the word went back to Ireland, Ireland would not be ashamed of our last fight.

Seumas Graham of Montrose and his Major-General, Alasdair Colkitto, walked slowly down in front of our line and talked to each other. Lame Sir William Rollo, that faithful man, hobbled along behind them. Montrose looked a small man by the side of Alasdair—Alasdair MacDonald of Clan Ranald, Coll Gillespick of Dunveg, son of Colkitto of Colonsay—but most men would look small by the side of that giant. He turned his back to us, did Alasdair, set his legs wide in the heather, his claymore, point off the ground, in his right hand—he was not left-handed despite his nickname of Colkitto—and thrust his dark-red head forwards towards the line of the enemy advancing down on us so slow, so sure. He was wearing the red-and-green barred philabeg of Clan Ranald, and his legs were like towers. Never anywhere were there legs like Alasdair's, so mighty, so shapely, so springy. Though he had great shoulders and great arms, the terrific drive of his swording, so it was said, came out of his legs.

Montrose turned and looked us over, a small quiet smile, as always, about his deep-grey eyes, but his face lacked its usual fresh colour this morning. He was not a tall man, but he had good supple shoulders and a lean flank. He was not in armour—there was not a scrap of armour in our whole force at that time—but wore a belted tunic over plaid trews, with a green-and-blue tartan hanging from one shoulder, and his blue bonnet carrying his badge of oat grass and green laurel: a gallant brave figure of a man, and young to die.

He looked us over slowly, his face never changing, and then slowly turned to talk quietly to his friend Rollo; but we had read the doubt behind that smiling eye. Well, he had no reason yet to put much faith in the Irish or in the Clansmen. He had seen the daring fiery horsemen of Rupert, the stark buff troopers of Cromwell, the steady Scots pikemen; our regiment, beyond a small tulzie at Lochaline with a weak force of Clan Diarmid, had done no fighting on Scottish soil; and back in '39, Montrose at the head of a covenanting army—these men now facing down on us—had gone like a wind through the Highlands, and found the Clans with no stomach for fight. And here he was at the end of the road, staking his life and his King's cause on ragged Irish and long-shanked Highland cateran.

So little faith had he in us that that very morning he had sent an envoy to Lord Elcho and the Kirk to point out that he was their King's and a Scots King's Captain-General, and that they should be on his side and not against him; and as a second clause—he was always the great one for secondary clauses—he urged that, if fighting it had to be, it should not be forced on him on the Sabbath day. And the ministers, fixing on that second clause, sent word back that the Lord's day was the proper day for the Lord's work, and the Lord's proper work was the extermination of the barbarous Irishry. They were as sanguine of victory as that. They were sure of it. They had prophesied it. So it was, "Jesus and no quarter."

14

But when all is said and done, Colkitto's Ulstermen had no great reason at that time to put their faith in Seumas Graham, the Marquis and Captain-General of Scotland. They had sailed from the Wexford coast to add no more than two thousand to his twenty thousand. He was to come up from Oxford way with a thousand of Rupert's horse; and all the hardy Border men would join him—Nithsdale, Annandale, Morton, Roxburghe, Traquair, Carnwath, and Galloway thrown in for good measure; and all the great Clans of the Highlands would host to his standard; and the Ulstermen might get a flank to hold in some small battle. To-day they held the centre.

We had kept our tryst at any rate, but Montrose was long in coming; and the clans grew tired of feeding us; and we marched and we marched, and raided when we had to, through cold and hostile mountain-lands: Morven, Kintail, Lochaber, Badenoch, and the highlands of Perth; the Grants and the MacIntoshes blocked the Spey and the fat lands of Moray against us; the MacKenzies were coldly hostile on the line of the Ness; Atholl and Struan looked doubtfully on ragged men speaking a strange Gaelic and reiving black and dun cattle; and we had got to the very edge of throat-cutting when, at last, Montrose came. But he brought no army. He brought himself, ragged as ourselves in his pedlar's disguise, and he brought Black Pate Graham of Inchbrakie and an English captain and three horses, and no more and no less. Rupert's cavaliers had been scattered at Marston Moor, and the Border chiefs had purchased peace at its own price— and later on they double-paid that price with bloody interest under the heel of Cromwell.

But Seumas Graham was a resolute, honourable,

tough man. He came and, against all prudent judgment, did not forsake us. Easy enough for him to leave us to our fate amongst the dirks of the clans or on the gibbet of the Covenant; easy enough for him to jink back the road he had come to his King Charles at Oxford; and he would lose no credit for refusing to lead a shoeless, cannonless, ammunitionless rabble. But, instead, he made peace between us and Atholl, made our Colkitto his Major-General, and marched us, bold as brass, down to Perth to throw dice in the face of death and abide the issue. But *Dhia!* he had little hope in the game, and his grey eyes that smiled and smiled could not deceive us on this fine, fateful autumn morning.

We could hear now what he was saying to Sir William Rollo.

"They are sloping their left to outflank us."

"To cut off our retreat belike."

"If retreating we'll be," said Colkitto easily.

"Will your Irish stand to the onset?" Montrose wanted to know.

"But not standing," said the bold Alasdair, who had a way of his own in meeting onsets.

"If they do," said Montrose, "I will swing the Stuarts against their right. If we can disarray their line we might break their centre with cold steel."

"Cold steel it will be, one way or the other," said Colkitto. "Let the Atholl men be in a hurry."

Alasdair had, maybe, one or two bad faults and three or four not so good, but he had the confidence of the god Jove. He would face the gates of hell sure of himself, claymore in hand and his Ulstermen at his back. He was the only confident man facing the enemy that day.

Montrose turned for one last look at us and started.

As he and Colkitto had talked our line had slid forward right up to their shoulders. He did not know then that the Irishman at the full stretch of waiting has that strange trait of slipping forward inch by inch towards the enemy.

Alasdair laughed. "My cocks will fight. You will have to be in a hurry, Seumas Graham."

And Montrose went off down the line, lame Rollo hirpling after.

Alasdair turned to us, his arms thrown wide and his targe making a smooth winnowing motion. "Easy, children, easy!" His voice was deep croon. "I will give ye the sign, and I will know when to give it." He was a strange, wild man, Alasdair, but many a reason had the Ulstermen to love him. Then he grinned over my shoulder at O'Cahan. "Manus *avic*, young Seumas Graham thinks it safer down there with the Struan Robertsons."

"Small blame to him," said O'Cahan. "Struan and Atholl are namely fighters, and his royal standard in the middle of them."

"We will carry that red standard many a day yet," said Alasdair.

And so we did, and so we did. It was the only flag we had flaunting that day, and I have been at Kilsyth where every company carried its colours. It was made for Montrose out of silk by Struan Robertson's ladies, and the three golden leopards looked like wolfhounds.

The scene was set now and the deadly play about to begin.

3

It was a fine stage and far flung. There was our lean line strung out in the heather, and the long, strong, steel-shining, flag-flaunting line of the Covenant creeping forward on it. That line was in fact coming at a brisk pace, but the length of it made it seem slow. High overhead in the aloof pale sky of autumn, the white clouds of morning drifted before the breeze, and the same breeze shivered across the blowing purple of the heather. Far and far away the austere peaks of the Highlands stood up in a great half-circle and looked across to see us die. Three miles in front of us, over a low ridge of woodland, the roofs and towers of Perth took the sun greyly, and smoking vents sent a blue plume eastwards before the breeze. A grassy knowe, right-rear of the advancing line, was black with people; the sober-clad burghers and council of Perth come out for a Sabbath holiday to see the Loyalists cut to pieces; and the cutting done, they would go back to their kirk for the afternoon sermon, and listen to the ministers extolling the vengeance of the Lord.

Behind our own line, on a slope of heather, were our women, and they were silent this morning. But they had more need of courage than their men. We had two hundred of them with us—mothers, wives, sisters, sweethearts—a gay, laughing, skirling, faithful clan. But deadly silent this morning. They had to trust their men for all things, and there was no one else they dare trust, and if their men were broken, as they were like to be broken this very hour, the women would have to thole with the dealing of the Covenant, and it not namely.

That was the scene set.

The time was near now. The onset was at hand. Not a hundred paces separated the steel-clad Covenant line from the waiting Gaelic one. Waiting, but not patiently. A man would stamp the heather, setting his feet as for the push, a man would shake a shoulder free to give himself another inch of sword room, a foot would slide out amongst the tussocks and the other foot follow it, and Alasdair, his face to the enemy, would move a quieting hand behind him and take one easy step to the front. I looked aside down the line. Grim lean faces every one, tanned by the sun, blenched beneath the tan, but with the cheek-bones massive as stone and the eyes hard-set and unflinching—men prepared to die, but not easily.

"Drive in with the point," Tadg Mor whispered grimly, "with your shoulder behind it, and keep on driving till we hit Heaven's gate."

And then, in that last tense moment, a sudden silence shut down over all that place. In another moment the shots would go dunting and the clamour shake the sky, but there in that moment before everything snapped, there was no sound at all. And then, sudden as a clap, a sound broke it that stirred us to the marrow. Our women knew that the time had come, and, like the clang of a bell, their voices pealed in one wild skirl, lifted and held and broke in one savage, shivering, taunting whimper.

"Wolves, wolves, wolves of the North! Let the fangs bite."

And great Alasdair chose that time well. Not looking behind him, he threw his broadsword up, slashed it forward at the full point and leaped out towards the enemy, his voice, wordless, swallowing all other sounds.

He did not gain one inch on his men of the North. They were at his shoulder. As ever in all their battles, the Gael made the onset. I heard nothing, the shots dunting, swords flashing, men falling; and I saw only one thing, a man in front of me. A thickset man he was, flinging his buckler up and bringing pike to the attack. Him I saw. To me he was the only man in that wall of steel. It looked like a wall, and I had to shatter a way through it over that man, or lie shattered at the foot of it. Never pausing I drove in, point forward, with everything that was in me. There was a crash like the clang of brazen gates, and there was no man and no wall in front of me.

And that was the battle of Tippermuir.

I have with travail, put down a good many words, not expressive, about that battle, but it could be adequately described in less than a hundred. Look! The enemy marched down on us at Tippermuir six deep out of Perth, and we waited for them till we could see the whites of their eyes; and then we charged so furiously home that we lifted them off the heather like blown thistle-down, and the terrific drive of that charge never slacked till it reached the gates of Perth; and one might walk on dead men all the way back to Tippermuir. That was that battle.

But Montrose stood alone in the heather watching that red rout, a great wonder in his eyes, and his hand holding his chin after a habit he had. And then, after a while, he spoke in a whisper to himself.

"Now that I lead men I will make a war in Scotland that will be remembered."

And that war we made for him will not be forgotten as long as men are stirred by a song or a tune or a lost cause lost nobly.

CHAPTER II

THE GIRL IN THE STOCKS

I

IT was the second day of the sack of Aberdeen, and I have jumped a fortnight to the real beginning of my story.

That was the first time, but not the last, that we were angry to the core. At Tippermuir we had been frightened, and had fought as desperately as rats in a trap; but here in Aberdeen we were eager to bite hard and bite often.

We were all angry, friends and enemies alike. Aberdeen was angry and thrawn, and, for a beginning, a soldier of its garrison had wantonly shot down a drummer boy of ours coming back out of the town under a flag with one of our heralds. That was our first experience of the Covenant's strange disregard for the rules of war, and it roused us every one. Montrose was angry and cold, Colkitto angry and hot as flame, and the Highland and Irish fighting men angry and grim as death. That drummer boy was not yet fourteen, and his mother, Sorcha MacNeill, head of my nursing staff, wailed over his pitiful dead body for all the camp to hear. So the time was ripe for blood-letting, and we had the will and the means to assuage bad tempers.

Aberdeen was aye thrawn. There was never a

thrawner town in all thrawn Scotland. It had a name
for being at cross-purposes with a strong cause or a
strong man that it could hurt or that could hurt it, and
it dealt and bore the hurt with the same dour spirit.
Here now, at last, it had chosen the right cause and the
right man to the reaping of the full harvest; for the
cause was the cause of Charles the King, and the man
was Seumas Graham, the great Marquis of Montrose.

Aberdeen decried and despised the King for his
vacillation as well as his episcopacy; and it was on the
leash to avenge itself on Montrose for the bloody comb
he gave it away back in 'thirty-nine, when he was for
the Covenant and Aberdeen was not. And so, when
our three thousand came fast-marching up from Perth
after the astounding victory of Tippermuir we found
an army four thousand strong drawn up against us
beyond the Dee; and the town close behind was
buzzing like a wasp's bike.

Aberdeen was confident as well as angry. It remembered Harlaw where it had worsted the best of
the Highland clans, and as for the wild Irishers they
were only mad dogs to be slaughtered. In truth, the
Aberdeen burghers were so eager to cut our throats
that they would not mind losing a finger or two in their
hurry. They lost a finger or two beyond a doubt, but
whatever throat-cutting was done that day was done
by the clansmen of the Highlands and of Ulster.

Colkitto's men drove in so sternly fierce that the
Covenant line, five deep, gave way at the first push,
and O'Cahan's regiment, with a few horse under that
great soldier of fortune, Nathaniel Gordon, actually
broke a charge of cavalry, a thing that had never
happened before. They were hacking down the High
Street before evening, and Montrose left them to it.

For the first and only time he treated a taken town as taken towns have been treated since Troy fell. He turned his back and rode off to a friend's house, and Colkitto's men had their own way with Aberdeen for three days.

Angry men and hungry men and thirsty men can be doing their share of harm even in three short days. Not that they were very terrible when all is said and done. No man was killed unless he had arms in his hands, and the whole tale of dead inside the walls did not reach one hundred; and if twenty or so women were missing out of Aberdeen at the heel of the hunt, most of them came willingly. Many of our men were still half-naked after the Highland campaign, and it is related that some of Alasdair's Irish made the townsmen strip before dirking them so that their clothes would not be soiled for the new wearer. That is not true. I saw no stripped dead men anywhere when I went down into Aberdeen.

I did not go into Aberdeen until the second day. I was busy with the wounded, was not much of a fighting man, and some things that take place in captured towns did not appeal to me. I went down then looking for my foster-brother, Tadg Mor O'Kavanagh, to whom all things appealed. In three hours I found him with a mixed company of Clan Vuirich and Clan Finlay in a drinking-shop facing the harbour inside the river bar. There were women there too, our own as well as some Aberdeen hussies.

Tadg Mor had been in rags yesterday morning, now he had repaired his wardrobe uniquely. He wore a seaman's long boots big enough even for his great feet, a knitted blue body-vest up to his chin, a knitted cap that hung a red toorie over one ear, and a great leather storm-coat hanging to his heels. And every pocket bulged. He was not more than half drunk, but that means little, for no quantity of the hardest liquor could make Tadg more than half drunk. Sober he had an ironic humour and a warm temper, but half drunk he was the pleasantest man living, smiling ever to himself, laughing heartily at the poorest wit, singing songs of his own rhyming and of doubtful character, and refusing all quarrel unless hit hard in the face; and if I grew stern with him he wept. He was a fine tall, red-haired, sanguine-complexioned man, with a long nose hooked at the end, and I do not think that Alasdair Colkitto himself was any stronger. He was and is the best man I ever knew. Let that writing stand.

He was glad to see me in his pleasant, strangely dignified, half-drunken way; his Highland friends shouted a welcome, and Ranald Ban MacKinnon, who was one of the few Clan Ranald men with us at that time, singing with all his might a song in praise of Mull of the Mountains, pushed a wooden mug of liquor under my nose, said hastily, "Drink that, Martin," and went on roaring in good tune. But Tadg Mor placed one big hand round me, so as to make my ribs crack, and with the other waved aside the spattering mug.

"No, Ranald Ban," he shouted. "Drink goes to his head in one lepp, and makes him loose in the tongue. I have heard him argue the point with an iron pot that had one leg missing and wouldn't stand up for him."

"You are coming home, muttonhead," I said.

He looked down at me, affection in his drunken blue eyes, and again crushed my ribs. "I knew 'tis how

24

you'd come looking for me, Maurteen, and I will go home with you or to the world's end with you when you say the word. But first"—again he squeezed me—"but first, for the sake of old times and the mother that suckled the both of us, you will drink one small mether with me. You will so, Maurteen Somers. It is a new French wine, buzzing in the mug, and it lifts your head up above the moon. Two new songs it has put in my head already and I will sing them to you on the road. There! Drink it up now, small brother."

I drank that big mether of wine because I knew I must, with Tadg Mor standing over me like a mother watching her bairn finish the last drop of his senna brew. The wine frothed over the brim of the mether, and I suspected from the taste that there was a strong lacing in it of that new liquor out of the Americas distilled from the sugar plant. We forged for the door then against hospitable holding hands, Tadg Mor shouting over his shoulder, "Drink while ye are able, my brothers, for to-morrow will be hell's sober day, with Seumas Beg Graham down on us."

Ranald Ban MacKinnon wanted to come with us, but Tadg Mor turned him back from outside the door.

"Whisper, Ranald *avic*! One or two of the Far-quharsons in there are looking crooked at three or four of the MacPhersons. If you are amongst them 'tis yourself will get belted, and that will be the best thing could happen."

"I would like to see the bastard out of Badenoch that would cock his bonnet at me," said Ranald Ban, and went back into the inn.

"I like the peaceable way of doing things," said Tadg Mor; and we went off arm in arm.

In five minutes or less I found that I was no less

drunk than my foster-brother. I knew that because my mind lit up and grew clearer than any crystal, and I had a great desire, while that clarity lasted, to reason mysteries out for myself but more especially for all my friends. I stopped Tadg Mor in the middle of the causeway.

"You will tell me now, Tadg Mor, the sort of the world's fool you made of yourself the last two days, and the reasons for it. And if you cannot tell me the reasons I will tell them for you, and if you are not satisfied I will belt you with the flat of your own sword from here to Bridge of Dee."

"Very fine and good enough!" agreed Tadg Mor pleasantly. "And whether or no I will deserve the hardest belting you can give me, so long as you do not hit me on the nose. Come on now, *aviceen*, up this quiet lane and listen to me."

Whatever the discourse that Tadg Mor made I had forgotten it next morning. But sometimes, to make his point clear, he threw back his red head, making the toorie swing, and bellowed a verse of a doubtful Gaelic song, and if the tune pleased me I joined in the chorus.

We had that narrow way to ourselves. The close-set grey houses were like houses of the dead, doors shut tight, windows barred and blinded, and never a wisp of housewifely smoke from any chimney cowl; though, indeed, a small drift of grey smoke floated down the air from where houses still smouldered in the High Street. No doubt, men frowned and women paled and children whimpered behind the barred windows, listening to Montrose's savage soldiers roystering up their lane, but, if they only knew, there was not a finger-nail of harm in us that time—or most times.

We took a quiet way out of the town by a narrow

twisting close that the fighting had not touched, and presently came amongst buildings that looked like schools, with tall narrow windows and patches of green lawn through round arches; and two pointed squat towers of red stone stood up against the evening sky. And it was there we came upon a young woman, ankle-locked in the public stocks—an iron frame three feet off the ground with a narrow cross-plank for seat and no back rest—outside the round-arched door of a kirk of the stern God of the Covenant.

2

She was sitting forward, her hands lax in her lap, her head down and her blown linten hair hiding her face. But when our feet struck the cobbles in the gateway her head jerked up, and she flung the hair out of her eyes with a fine womanly gesture.

"Mother o' God!" exclaimed Tadg Mor. "The people of this place breed a cruel marrow."

"There is reason in most things," said I, "and in this thing too, it could be. Let you and I look into it."

"I will look at the woman, whatever," said Tadg Mor.

And like two sedate judges we stalked side by side and slowly across the cobbled close. She sat up stiff as a rod facing us, her hands across her breast and her wide-open grey eyes unflinching, but I noted that her shoulders were shivering and that her jaws were clamped to keep her teeth from chattering. But the cause might be cold, not fear, for autumn evenings are wersh to the skin on that coast, and all that this woman had on was a white shift close at the neck and tied with a string at the ankles; and the strong shapely bare feet

27

of her, thrust through the cruel circles of the trap-bar, were blue and saffron. Yet, still and all, what her eyes looked on might well make her tremble. Tadg Mor in his looted garments looked as outlandish and savage as a boar, a red stubble of beard all round his big hooked nose, and the basket-hilt of his broadsword thrust forward in the opening of his leather coat. My appearance would be even worse. Above the sound pair of shoon I had taken off a Lowland trooper at Tippermuir I was in rags, but my raggedness was little compared to my dark leanness and to my long devil-slit chin that had not been shaved for three days; and the black eyes that damn me are the sort of black eyes that seem to hide murder or worse when they hide only dreams and the thought of a lark soaring.

Aberdeen smoking and booming below us, we stood swaying shoulder to shoulder looking down at her solemnly, and she sat straight looking up at us, her eyes wide open and unwinking.

"Wha be ye, ye drunken gangrels?" That was her greeting. Her voice was husky, and I noticed now that the whites of her eyes were streaked with red.

"We are two poor Irish sojering men," Tadg Mor told her, grinning pleasantly and leaning to her.

"Not so," I protested. "I am an Englishman myself and a sort of a surgeon."

"In a way that is true," agreed Tadg Mor weightily. "There is a small spark inside of him that is Sassenach, but in blood and bone and flesh he is Irish, and my mother's milk still wet in his mouth."

"Also," I went on reasonably, "some hold that I have Indian blood in me, for my father, God rest him, was in Virginia with Captain John Smith, and my mother I never saw."

"No man should miscall his father," reprimanded Tadg Mor, "for I have learned to my cost that a man's father is a better man than his father's son, drunk or sober."

"That is a mixed saying, Tadg Mor," I said, "but I will think about it some other time."

The young woman looked from one to the other of us, her eyes blinking now and her mouth open a little. She might know rough men and their ways, but here were two men, ugly as sin, speaking strangely for devils.

"Young woman," said I, with a short bow that finished abruptly against Tadg Mor's supporting shoulder, "is there anything we could be doing for you?"

"Na, na! dinna let me keep you," she said quickly. But, then, she had another thought and pointed with her hand. "There's a drouth on me. The water is yonder, and the wimple o't in my ears the lee-long day."

Where she pointed, near the gateway, a jet of spring water spouted from a carved madman's mouth into a white granite basin sunk in the red wall. I walked across with the held steadiness of a pikeman and looked down into it. A clear cool basin of water, but the tinkle of the falling streamlet was as lonely as a linnet's song. "All the live-long day," I murmured, "and she lonely too, and a drouth on her."

There was an iron cup hanging from the lip of the basin by a small-linked chain, and this cup I rinsed and filled and raised to my lips. "No, it is not you who want it," I protested, emptied the cup, filled it again, and tugged softly at the staple holding the chain. "There is some way out of this if I could think of it," said I. "I hope that the burgess-council of this place will not mulct me in damages." And there I jerked the chain so sharply that it broke below the cup, and the water splashed over me. I was half-way across the cobbles before I noticed that the cup was empty, and, shaking my head, I stalked slowly back to the basin.

When at last I reached her with the nearly full cup she smiled for the first time.

"Bairn, bairn! but you are fou," said she, emptied the cup in one draught, and looked regretfully into the bottom of it.

"You did that well, Maurteen," commended Tadg Mor. He was sitting on the side-bar of the stocks, watching her drink greedy as a child, and now he dropped his head between his knees and covered his head with his hands so that only his long hooked nose protruded.

"I will be crying salt tears in a minute, Maurteen Somers," he mumbled. "Is this not the cruel bad world we have landed in?"

"Cry away, brother," I comforted him, "if that will help, and I will clout you when I want you to stop."

He shook the soft tears out of his eyes and looked over his shoulder at the girl sitting so straight on her narrow board.

"You are a bonny, bonny girl, as Ranald Ban would say," he praised her, "and if I was sober I would kiss you. Will to-morrow morning do as well?"

Her grey eyes flared at him. "Gin ye put yer muckle ram's neb anigh me, I'll brak my fast on it—and nane the worse ye'll be for the loss."

"*Dhia*, Maurteen!" cried Tadg Mor in admiration, "hasn't she the very tongue of my aunt used leather us and we so high?"

"Silence will become you, Tadg Mor O'Kavanagh,"

I said sternly, "if your tongue cannot keep a decent hold on itself," and I turned to the girl. "What is your name, young woman?"

"Meg—Margaret Anderson, if you maun ken."

"That is a Norse name and not Gaelic, but, nevertheless, I am sorry to see you in this hobble. Where is the man that should be standing by your side?"

"Whatna man?" Her eyes were grey on me.

"The man that wronged——"

"Ye ill-thochted gangrel!"

I was not so drunk I could not get my head out of the way of the metal cup as it flew. I caught it in the air as if it were a shinty ball, and handed it to Tadg Mor.

"The girl has still a drouth on her. It is your turn."

"To be sure." He clattered across the cobbles in his huge sea-boots, and from the fountain shouted over his shoulder, "She is my aunt back in the flesh. Keep your ear out of her way, I warn you."

I stood looking down at her and touched my leather bonnet.

"Your pardon!" said I, my eyes on her clean mouth. "The man who would stand at your side would be an honest man, I think."

"So you stand—but I hae my doots," said she.

She drank that second cup of water more continently, and her shoulders shivered as she drank.

"*Mhuire!* the girleen is cold," cried Tadg Mor, and forthwith lumbered off his leather storm-coat and bundled it round her. "There, little one!" And he patted her shoulder.

I looked at him. "You are a fine big figure of a man, Tadg Mor," I said, "and kindly too, even if you are a robber."

And indeed he was a grand, stripped-for-fight figure,

his mighty shoulders straining the knitted vest, his sword-belt narrowing his hips, and his sinewy arms hairy as a boar's hide.

Margaret Anderson looked from one to the other of us, her eyes perplexed and a frown between them.

"Ye twa mad loons frighten me," she whispered. "Are a' the Irishers like you?"

"Most of them are middling honest as well," Tadg Mor told her.

"Wait ye!" I cried impatiently. "Let us be orderly in this. Tell me, Margaret Anderson, why are you hobbled here?"

"Do you mak' it your business?"

"Girl, girl!" cried Tadg Mor. "It is a way he has and he with drink taken. Answer him or we will be in this place and night on top of us."

"And a gey foolish way." And then suddenly: "I called Andra Cant a snivellin' ranter."

"And who is this Andrew Cant whose retort has been so dolorous for you?"

"He's our kirk minister."

"I can understand," said I, "that you could not call a kirk minister a name that would get more under his skin. But——"

"There was mair tae't than that." And then some control in her gave way and she went on impulsively. "I said that it was rank unhalesome of him, at his age —twa score an' mair—to be speirin' a third woman for wife, an' his second nae cauld aneath the sod, an' that it was no' a wife he wanted but something waur."

"It is better to marry than to burn," I told her. "That is in King James's Bible."

"Are ye anither o' they ranters?"

"Now and then he is, and that's no lie," said Tadg

32

Mor. "Like his father before him he belongs to that new church set up in Ireland by bloody Queen Bess. Tell me, colleen, were you the third woman this lad Cant had in his eye?"

"Ay was I."

"He has some of the qualities of a sound husband," said I. "Is that all, Margaret Anderson?"

"There's waur to come. I telt him I widna sit under him anither preaching, an' him ding-dingin' Sabbath after Sabbath—two score and three as I kept count—with havers o' sermons all on ae text."

"That was a notable text surely. What was it?"

"Dinna ye be makin' fun o' me, black laddie. I didna gang to the kirk for three Sabbaths, and himself and the session hae put the joogs on me for three days. This is the second. But I'll thole it, and, what's more, I'll nae gang three more Sabbaths, and thole three more days o' this, and three after that. Ay will I! till the wind and the snaw blaws atween my bare banes."

Her voice had lifted into a skirl, and her grey eyes flared into a flame. I patted her shoulder and she shrank away from me. That woman hated any man to touch her.

"Hush, hush!" I quieted her. "But was it not a notable text that held two score and three discourses in it. You were saying it was——?"

"Go and speir! Yon's his hoose, and him, nae doot, gleekin' thro' the pane for ye to take dirk tae me." She shook her blown hair and recovered control of herself. "Am I no' the gowk to be tellin' a'thing to twa gangrel tykes."

"Speir him I will," said I, and turned on my heel. The house she had pointed out, at one corner of the

33

quadrangle that made the kirk close, was tall and narrow with a doorway recessed under an arch.

Tadg Mor called after me. "Hurry, brother! She might be clouting me with the iron mug and it gripped under the new coat I paid dear for."

"What did you pay for it?" I called back.

"A keg of ale that Ranald Ban stole out of a tavern."

"That was fair enough," said I.

The clamped door was tight closed at the back of the recess, and I wondered dimly why any man of God had need to hide himself behind bars. I gave the sound oak the heel of my fist, the iron toe of my shoe, the hilt of my father's sword, the drive of my shoulder, but that stout door did not as much as groan. Then I put my head out and called:

"Your ox shoulder here, brother."

But I had barely spoken when the door creaked open behind me, and I jerked round, hand on hilt, at the man that had opened it wide.

"Slay me then, O man of Belial!" was his greeting, and his head was up for the blow.

He was a lean, middle-sized man of my own build, not yet old, but well grizzled. His hollowed cheeks below the strong eye-bones were whiter than the thin beard on his chin, and his steel eyes gleamed defiance under a dome of brow that carried no hair; and the bands of white at his neck made the pallor of his skin the colour of the belly of a salmon two weeks in river water.

"Are you the minister, Andrew Cant?"

"Such is my name, and I serve the Lord humbly."

"I might question that last statement if I had time," said I, "for I am thinking you are what my father would call a theocrat. Is it true that you have housed two score and three sermons in one text?"

"Mock thou the servant of the Lord," he boomed, "and the law bonds of the Lord shall crush thee. Get thy work over, thou bloody Irisher."

I was tired persuading men that I was not Irish.

"I fear me," I said regretfully, "that that notable text will evade me. There is one other request I have to make. The key of your parish stocks."

"I have it not. My grave-digger had it, and I fear he has died under barbarous swords in the streets below."

"An apology is due you," said I politely, "and this your busy season in his trade."

He lifted up his voice. "If I had the key I would not yield it, for though you make my flesh carrion, I will never be the outgate to lead that foolish and stiff-necked woman towards the charnel house of lust."

"Lust surely! The thought of it is in your own mind."

I stepped forward and laid my hand softly on the lapel of his dark-grey coat, but he never flinched.

"Man," said I, "that is fine cloth"; and I felt the smooth dark texture of it. "My father brought a bolt of that broadcloth out of Bristol five and twenty years ago, and my elder brother, who is a fool in many ways, was wearing a coat of it last time I saw him. Do not quote the Bible to me, new priest, for I have called my brother a fool any time these ten years at the risk of hell fire. Come with me now, for I like peace, but if you will not come with me I will like that too, for at this minute peace tastes like dust in my mouth."

He came with the draw of my hand quietly and

without a word, his strong face composed but his eyes looking strangely at this strange drunken man. So we came to the side of the stocks, and Margaret Anderson gathered herself inside the leather coat.

"Is that the man himself?" enquired Tadg Mor, trying to look fierce.

The kirkman looked at Tadg Mor and lifted up his voice in the glory of the coming sacrifice.

"Cut ye and pierce deep, for the blood of the martyr shall be his assurance against hell's fire."

"You are orthodox as far as you go," said I, "but instead of blood let us speak of spring water. Look at that young woman there, her mouth wan and her eyes bloodshot, and terror in her heart all day at the sounds of war, and tell me if you never read in the Bible of the father of the King whose place your Kirk has usurped of the charity of a cup of spring water?"

"My hand, Maurteen!" cried Tadg Mor. "That was well put and not a stutter down the length of it. Answer him if you can, grey badger."

"I will answer him," cried the man, and he was no saner than we were. "Had I the key I would have freed her till another day, and my sinful flesh grieved that she should thirst; but better thirst now with hope of repentance than thirst for ever in the furnace house of hell. For lo! as the psalmist sayeth: He shall rain snares upon sinners; and fire and brimstone and storms of wind shall be the portion of their cup. Better she be snared now straight and narrow in these irons than bound like a faggot amongst the damned of the Pit, where fire shall be her chain and her tether. Ye have challenged and ye are answered."

"There is an answer in it," I agreed.

But Margaret Anderson cried out: "Fause ranter!

36

Ye wad hae me commit The Sin under the cloak o' the Kirk."

Her hand came out from the leather coat with the iron cup clenched in it. But before she could throw I took it firmly from her and flung it against the far wall, where it dinged clear and clattered.

"Good man yourself!" commended Tadg Mor. "She might do the poor man a hurt. Will we have to slit his tongue for him?"

"That is a road too," said I.

I went round to the front of the stocks and bent to the iron trap bar. The hasp of it was held down by a big, rough, hand-forged padlock, that rasped obdurately to the tug I gave it. Tadg Mor bent over my shoulder.

"It might not be as strong as it looks," said he.

"Is it stronger than you are?"

"Give me room at it."

He crouched down and patted the lock, tugged at it softly, tugged at it again and listened, nodding his head.

"I know where the weakness lies, if you could call it that. Watch me now."

His hard broad hands grasped the lock at each side of the shackle-loop, and his shoulders hunched. "Pray now to the locksmith that forged you," and with a smooth steadiness that looked easy let the strength pour down into his hands. His knuckles whitened, his forearms ridged into rods, a vein came up in his neck, one shoulder slowly hunched sideways; and when I thought that all the strength was out of him he gave one explosive jerk, and there was the lock in his hand, the shackle-loop open. He straightened up, all his muscles relaxing, and dropped the lock at his toes.

"I knew where to put the strain, for no matter how big a lock is, its weakness lies in the bolt that threads the shackle. And mark you, Maurteen, there was a small barrel of strength left in me at the end."

He flung up the trap bar on its hinge and reached a hand to the prisoner. "Out of your snare, little one!" But indeed she was not little.

She shook her head. "I canna. There's nae life below my knees."

Suddenly then she was in his arms and off the stocks, his leather coat bundled about her.

"Dinna haud me," she protested. "I canna thole to be held."

"Childeen, childeen!" his voice soothed her. "Let your uncle hold you till the blood runs."

And she leant against him, his arm round her, her feet fumbling on the cobbles with the uncertainty of a child's, and her face twisted into that smile of agony that is caused by *culla greefeen*—the pins and needles.

Andrew Cant was mouthing words in a whisper as I came to his side. "Lost—lost—lost! Damned and lost!"

"Patience! You will have your time to think whose the loss and where the damnation lies," and I unbuckled my sword-belt and pulled the torn tunic over my head.

The man made no protest, no struggle when I stripped him of his dark-grey broadcloth coat. "I would take your fine bandle-cloth lindershirt as well," I told him, "but I would not expose your nakedness and mine to a young girl's eyes."

I fitted on the coat and it was warm and snug about my shoulders, and I belted my sword over it. Tadg

Mor's mouth was open, and he clumped Margaret Anderson's shoulder with his free hand.

"Man, Maurteen! it fits you like a glove, and what harm if you look like the devil's own chaplain out of bottom hell! Have you any other bit of devilment in your mind for us?"

"And the last bit," I told him, laying hold of my victim.

He looked as tough and wiry as woodbine and could have made a pretty struggle if he wanted to, but he was like a bag of meal in my hands as I lifted and set him on the cross-bar of the stocks. I placed his ankles in the half-circle of the bottom bar and brought the trap down over them.

"Why could not myself think of that?" lamented Tadg Mor. "This story will go the length and breadth of Ireland if God spares me to see its pleasant shores. Girl dear, why are you not laughing?"

Indeed she was not laughing, for, already, a thought of the future before her had come into her mind. She had recovered the use of her feet in some degree, and was loose from Tadg Mor's arms, supporting herself instead by the side-bar of the stocks.

"Ye are just, I think," said she, "but dinna spoil it."

"Wait ye!" cried Tadg Mor. "If I have no great head, I have something near as useful."

He fitted the lock back in the staple of the hasp, and, this time using all his strength and a grunt to help, twisted the shackle into an overlapping loop.

"There now! It will take a blacksmith to unravel that, and I am thinking there are not many left in this town, being quarrelsome men by nature."

I stood in front of the stocks and looked at our prisoner. But he was not looking at me. He had eyes only for the tall young woman holding the side-bar of the stocks, her tossed linten hair about her face, and her eyes unafraid of the devouring light in his.

"Raise up your voice against us in your four and fortieth sermon, and prove your God stronger than mine," I said solemnly.

And he did it. He was as mad as I was drunk, and entirely without fear. His mouth opened, his eyes flamed, and his great voice poured out of him. And at last I learned what his text was. It was from Isaias: "Hell hath enlarged her soul, and opened her mouth without any bounds." His words boomed back from the walls of the quadrangle.

But suddenly Tadg Mor clouted his breast and cried aloud: "Mother o' Grace! am I listening to heretic preaching?" And forthwith he picked Margaret Anderson up, coat and all, and clattered out of the quadrangle by the gate we had entered.

I turned on my heel and followed them slowly. And there Andrew Cant's preaching stopped, and his voice, shrill as a woman's, made a prayer to me:

"Slay me! Slay me! Slay me!"

But I left him there. I never set eyes on him again, nor do I know if the barbarous and lustful conduct of two Irishers is recorded in the session-book of the Kirk.

Tadg Mor and the young woman waited for me round the corner, but Tadg Mor had no arm round her now. She stood facing him, her strong feet gripping the cobbles with wide-spaced toes, and he stood leaning away from her, one hand at an ear. And ever and again as the breeze veered and drifted, the sound of Andrew Cant's voice lifted faintly and died away. He was again at his mad preaching to the empty quadrangle, unless the jackdaws and the pigeons and the sparrows had come down to listen to a new and sterner Francis.

"I know at last," said I weightily, "why the great John Knox persecuted Mary of Scotland. And another thing I know, Tadg Mor——"

"Only a brother's kiss I was giving her," said he, "and here I am deaf for three days."

"You were her uncle also a short time ago, but what I know deals not with kissing but with death. Your death and mine, brother, for now indeed I know that we, all of us, Gael or Sassenach, can never beat these men and the men they lead."

"Twice already——"

"And many more times yet. But they are strong with the strength of their stern Jehovah, who only chastises them with defeat for the sins of the people, but must lead them victorious in the end. And we, poor soldiering men, shall be hunted down like wolves and slain without ruth to the greater glory of that stern deity. And there's an end of us."

"And of puir Meg Anderson," said the girl, a sad irony in her voice. "What's to come o' me in this toon o' Aberdeen after this day's work, and what's to come o' me out yont it among Montrose's sojers?"

"Anything you like and nothing you do not like," said I.

"And nae use to a puir weak lass."

"With a fist of iron." Tadg Mor rubbed his red ear.

"It could be that our meddling has done you an ill-service," I addressed her. "Is there no place of refuge for you inside or outside this town?"

She shook her head. "My father's deid, and my mother new marrit. I have an Uncle Alick, a shipmaster, a guid and kindly man—he was aye guid to me—but he bides far frae here at Maviston of Lochloy."

"And where is that?"

"A wee bit fishin' place near Nairn in Moray."

The glow of a good deed well done lit a new road for me.

"Ah, Moray! The fat Laich o' Moray. That is not far for us. In ten days or less we will be going through it like a hot wind. Look you, Margaret Anderson! We will take you to your uncle at this Maviston of Lochloy."

"And a richt pleasant greetin' he'll gie me out o' your hands," she said dryly.

"You are hard to please. But you need have no fear. There are fifty women in the regiment already, and no weak ones as far as I know. You can be strong or weak as you like, tall girl—the choice will be yours. The choice is yours now too, and we will not press you. O'Cahan's regiment as far as this Maviston of Lochloy, or Andrew Cant and his stocks there in Aberdeen."

"I kent you had a cruel drap in you, black laddie," she said, a little dolefully. Then she threw back her head, her linten hair leaping, and her lustrous grey eyes met mine fairly. "The choice is gey poor, but I hae made it. I'll just come, and the Lord have mercy on me."

"There is my fine one!" praised Tadg Mor, patting her shoulder. "And you need not be one wee small bit afraid of your old grandfather, Tadg Mor."

"I wish," said I, "that you would decide on your kinship and stick to it."

"We will be leaving that to the bit of a girl herself —and who knows?"

42

"You puir gomeril!" she said, jerking away from his hand, " of you and a' the ither gowks that'll be like you I hae nae fear, but of this black lad wi' his wicked black e'en and his hidden black thoughts ahin' them I hae fear in my banes already."

"Let that fear abide," said I. "Come then. To-night Sorcha MacNeill of Ulster will take care of you, and to-morrow we will replenish your wardrobe."

"We will so," cried Tadg Mor and lifted up his voice in an old song:

> " And she shall swing a silken gown,
> A milk-white steed to ride upon,
> With silver buckles on her shoon,
> And silver belt her waist to span."

And that is how we, two half-drunken men, took Margaret Anderson out of Aberdeen to our own honour.

CHAPTER III

EVE OF BATTLE

I

I HAD just been hit on the bone under my left eye by a slitter ball. Thirty men of us picked from O'Cahan's regiment were playing a bout of hurley against thirty picked men of Clan Ranald on a green park of level grass before the demesne house of Boath outside the hamlet of Auldearn. That was about two hours after noon on Thursday, the eighth day of May, in the year of 'forty-five, the eve of the battle of Auldearn, which battle is the only thing, and a great thing, that that small place is famous for.

It will be noted that I have this time jumped a full eight months in my chronicle. In another place I may write of those great months, but now I have made a jump, so that, without weariness, I might come to the day that at last sets my story full-march on the road.

Our Captain-General, Seumas Graham, and his staff were looking on at the game from the portico of the house of Boath, and Montrose was laying wagers with his Major-General, Alasdair Colkitto MacDonald. This game that the Irish call Hurley is the same game that the Scots call Shinty, and is played with a hooked stick or caman and a small ball called a slitter, but it is not a game unless war is a game. I have seen

44

battles that were mild in the onset by the side of it. The Irish were used to play stripped to the trews and barefooted, while the Highlandmen, more circumspect, wore kilt and crotal shirt; but when the contest took on heat the clansmen had a habit of shedding their kilts, and when that happened, our women, skirling on the lines, hardened as they were to life in all its nakedness, fled the field.

The slitter ball that hit me under the eye was only a knot of pine wrapped in the foot of a worsted hose, and it had more corners than any ball should have. I was reasonably quick on my feet, though not strong, and I was credited with a good eye for a flying ball, so my post was to hold the Irish goal, which was no more than two piles of tunics with ten paces between. My foster-brother, Tadg Mor O'Kavanagh, from the Nore side of Kilkenny, was guard in front of me, and if there was a better man with a caman he was not of my acquaintance. He was fast and sure and with the heart of a lion, and if he sometimes missed the ball he never missed his man or his four or five men.

We had been fighting it out a matter of two hours or so with the score of the game three hails or goals each, and the master of the field, Angus of Glengarry, proclaimed that the next hail would decide the victors for that day. The fight raged up and down the field then, and it was shortly after that the ball hit me, struck close in by Ranald Ban MacKinnon of Mull. Indeed I might have cleared my goal if Tadg Mor had not deflected the ball with the boss of his caman fairly into my face as I leaped in the air. He broke its force but the blow was shrewd enough to stagger me, and that was enough, for, before I could gather myself, I was flat on my back with hard bare feet trampling over

45

me and hard bare bodies flattening the last wind out of me.

The next thing I knew I was sitting aside on Tadg Mor's knee, and he was holding a cold stone under my eye, and I was crowing like a cock to get my wind back. Out of one eye I could see the young, eager, eagle face of Ranald Ban MacKinnon leaning down to me, a pulse beating hard in his fine brown neck, and his flaxen hair dark with sweat about the temples. He was patting my shoulder and telling me how sorry he was.

"Sorry how are you!" growled Tadg Mor derisively, "and you after trampling on top of him as well."

Ranald Ban lifted Tadg Mor's hand from my eye, and I found to my satisfaction that the sight was not scattered in it.

"*Dhiaoul!*" [1] exclaimed Ranald Ban, disgustedly throwing Tadg Mor's hand aside, stone and all. "The skin is not even broken, and I hoping to leave my mark on him after what he did to me that day on the Haugh of Balvenie."

"You Mull robber!" roared Tadg Mor. "A nice plover's egg he'll have under his eye by to-morrow's morn."

"And he ugly enough as it is," said Ranald Ban.

I had my breath back now. "I did nothing at all to you at Balvenie, Ranald Ban," I protested.

"You did so, Maurteen. You put your knee and your hurley in the small of my back, and I not able to walk straight for a week."

"Was it a goal that time?" I asked them.

"And a foul one," said Tadg Mor.

"Yourself and the ball and thirty men with ye went

[1] Devil.

through the goal," Ranald Ban told me, "and you can call it what you like."

"We are beat so," said I.

"Have it your own way, Ranald Ban *avic*," said Tadg Mor. "It was time for ye to win something—since we win all the battles."

I got to my feet and felt the skin already tightening under my eye. But in that hard-bitten small army of Gaeldom that had gone like a flame through Perth and Aberdeen and Argyll and Moray we thought little of bruised eyes or slashed scalps in a friendly game amongst ourselves. The players were already scattering off the field, buckling tunic or kilt, the MacDonald lads crowing it gaily over the Irish, who in turn reminded the Highlandmen of a certain great game at Balvenie in the days before General William Baillie and Sir John Hurry tried to nip us between their Covenant armies. I was belting on the dark-grey broadcloth coat I had taken off the Aberdeen kirkman that bloody day of September; and there Tadg Mor swore heartily, his hand up to his ear after a fashion of his.

"Here comes our Meg! Here she comes now! And it is me that will get the blame for that black eye."

"Stand this side of me," I told him, "and she might not see it."

The woman he named, Margaret Anderson, came straight through the scattering men, and any man in her road got out of it as quickly as he could. Her head was up, her fine linten hair free about her clear brow and in two long plaits on her breast, and she came down on us gallant and easy as a schooner before the wind. A bonny young woman and tall, and suppler than a blown birch branch, with hair lighter than flax and eyes greyer than the blue flax flower. That was Margaret Anderson.

I stood back of Tadg Mor and looked at her sideways out of my good eye, but she pushed the big man out of her way disdainfully, caught my long chin in her firm fingers, and brought my face full forward. Her grey eyes flashed straight into mine, for she was equal height with me.

"Gin you had sense, Martin Somers," she cried in her high coastwise tongue that I can only hint at in this writing, "you wouldna be at this bluidy game with they red-shanks." That is the name she had for the kilted brown-legged Highlandmen.

"True for you, Margaret," I agreed mildly. "It was Tadg Mor made me."

"Oh! the traitor!" cried my foster-brother.

"Didna the Lord give you a mind of your own?" She grimaced at my purpling eye. "Sakes alive, laddie! gin a lass was to meet you in the gloamin' she would run a mile."

"She would have her reasons," said I, still mildly.

"And the wrong ones," said she, "for you are a puir harmless loon."

"Meg Anderson," boomed Tadg Mor, "if you belonged to me I would skelp you day and dark and in between whiles to make sure."

"And weel I'd deserve it if I let you own me, you muckle ram's neb," she gave him back, and caught him neatly, but not too hard, on the ear with her open hand.

He yelped and jumped clear, bringing one hand to his ear and the other over his head with the caman stick threatening her. But the grin on his face was entirely amicable. Tadg Mor O'Kavanagh would sooner cut his hand off than touch her in anger; and he would cut another man's head off no matter how that man might seek to touch her.

In Aberdeen I had promised Margaret Anderson that she would be with her uncle at Maviston of Lochloy in ten days; but nearly eight months had gone by and she was still with us. The truth is that we found Moray a hard place to come by. The Covenant put strong forces in the field, and MacCailien Mhor, the red earl of the Campbells, forced us into the hills: the great, upheaved, far-flung tangle of the Grampian Mountains that Montrose grasped within his clear mind and wound and rewound his secret roads through. Instead of a raid on Moray we made that terrible winter campaign into Argyll, and dealt finally with the Campbells on the red beach of Inverlochy. That slaughter was away back in February, and here now it was May at the beginning of a dry summer, and we were at Auldearn in the heart of the Province of Moray, and awaiting our fourth big fight.

And Maviston of Lochloy was only two miles away.

But Margaret Anderson said nothing about taking refuge with her uncle at Lochloy, nor did we; though that was a time when prudence might think seriously of safer quarters than Montrose's camp. Many prudent men did forsake us, and were sorry for it later. We were between two Covenant armies. General William Baillie was behind us at the other side of the Spey, not too sure in his own mind, but with feelers out for us, and Sir John Hurry, not much of a Covenanter in personal habit, was luring us forward towards Inverness, hoping to finish us on his own chosen ground. And here we were resting at Auldearn not knowing whether Montrose would turn us against Baillie or against

Hurry, or whether the two would clamp down on us. We did not care. We were in such grand fighting fettle at that time that we did not mind any weight of odds. We were used to odds as to our daily meat.

Margaret Anderson by this time was part of the camp and had her own importance. She had found early on that the Gaelic women who followed their men —husbands, fathers, sons, brothers, sweethearts—to war were no ordinary parasitic camp-followers. They were an important part of a Gaelic army on campaign: the camp-makers and shelter-builders, the providers, scavengers, cooks, baggage-bearers, nurses—in truth nearly everything that is represented in continental armies by the quartermaster and surgical corps. Amongst such women Margaret Anderson found her feet firmly on the ground. She had character and a great well of spirit; she was entirely fearless, had capable hands, and an ability for organisation that can be found only in her nation; she had a fine easy-going contempt for men; and amongst the women she was frank and kindly and understanding. In a short time, herself and one Sorcha MacNeill, a middle-aged mother of soldiers, were mistresses of the camp; and when I pause to consider, I do believe that she, and not Tadg Mor, was my second in command amongst the women.

I was "Adjutant of Women" in O'Cahan's regiment. But indeed it was no small post, and I might well be proud of it. It was after Tippermuir that Montrose found me with some knowledge of wounds and medicaments. Before joining General John Preston's regiment at Kilkenny I had spent two years at Micael Breatnac's medical school at Callan, and could set a bone, stitch a wound, tie an artery, use a moss dressing, administer the simpler drenches, and look wiser than I felt.

Montrose immediately took me out of the line into the doctoring corps, and that placed me at once amongst the women. Tadg Mor came with me, though he was all a fighting man, but the tie between us was so close that where one went the other followed.

Montrose had the genius for choosing men. His command was entirely personal in our small army of Gaeldom, for we were not professional soldiers and not subjects for the harsh military discipline of the period. We followed only where there was love and loyalty, and we gave Montrose his full share of both. He knew us all, gave each man his post, and so went about his own business, a smile about his eyes. Thus he would consider the strategy of a campaign, instruct his leaders, and with sheer dare-devilry play a noble game of chess up-and-down and back-and-fore and in-and-out among the wild Highlands until he got the enemy where he wanted them; and then he would lay down his tactics of battle, and there was the great Alasdair Colkitto to drive the plan to victory. If there was ever a better man than Alasdair to do that I have not read about him.

Margaret Anderson was no longer afraid of me, or she did not show it, and of Tadg Mor O'Kavanagh she had never been afraid. As a kind of ritual she used to clump his ear when she got near enough, and he used to yelp with mock pain and threaten her with mock ferocity. We were fond of her and she trusted us. Between us there grew a strange and close tie. Margaret Anderson and myself and Tadg Mor. She went freely and gaily amongst her gay rough Irish laddies, knowing that the man who troubled her would have to deal with Tadg Mor and with me, or even with Manus O'Cahan, our colonel. Our friends made fun of us, but very carefully, for if one of them went too far in sly or open allusion he had to run for it or eat his words. We provided her with all she needed, and more, and I think that Tadg Mor, outside the regular foraging of a campaign, did some plain stealing, so that she be equipped as fine as any of the gentle ladies that sometimes visited the camp from the houses of the loyalist lairds. She had silver buckles on her shoon that Tadg Mor polished each morning, and a silken gown, and a Spanish comb for her hair, but he had not yet succeeded in looting a silver belt for the span of her waist. She had a baggage-pony of her own and a boy to lead it, and she could have had a pony of her own too, only she preferred to march with her women on her own long legs. And she was happy; we could see the happiness growing on her and a lovely white bonniness with it. And on the Sabbath, when she was fully adorned to go up with me to hear Montrose's chaplain preach—she remained always a staunch Calvinist— she was finer than an earl's daughter. Montrose himself was proud to see her there. And she would look at Tadg Mor and at me, the soft lustre in her eyes, and she would say: "Loons! am I nae the proud one."

2

Margaret Anderson had clouted Tadg Mor on the accustomed ear, he had yelped and threatened as was the ritual, and Ranald Ban MacKinnon was laughing at him; but young Ranald was careful to stand well out of reach of both Tadg Mor and the tall girl.

"You did not see that one coming, Tadg boy," he mocked. "My soul! but she reminds me of a girl I

52

knew once over in Moidart, and a bonny, bonny girl
she was moreover, with a raven's wing for hair and eyes
like the sea, and a skin milk-white—are you listening
to that, Meg Anderson? Donald Oge himself, Clan
Ranald's son, was courting her and making a poor hand
of it, for she had a habit of using her own hand in a
fashion we are accustomed to, especially Tadg Mor.
One evening she heard him coming up to the corner,
the short light step of him, and he whistling his own
tune, 'Maire van oge,' and she stepped back and let
him have it fair on the ear as he came round. And
look ye! it wasn't Donald Oge at all but his father,
Eoin of Moidart himself. 'What is the gift for, Eilidh?'
says he. 'Your pardon, Mac Vic Ailein,' she says,
giving him his title bold as brass, 'I thought you were
Donald Oge.' 'Very well,' says the old hero, 'if I
have to take one gift my son has to take, I will take the
other he is afraid to take.' And he gripped her hard
by the two shoulders and kissed her hard on the mouth
I dare you to that, Tadg Mor."

"Quit your haverin', Ranald Ban," Margaret chided,
"I hae business with Martin Somers."

This Ranald Ban MacKinnon out of Mull, sept of
Clan Ranald, was a remarkable young man, for,
besides being by-ordinary with caman or claymore, he
had the loosest-hung tongue in the most talkative small
army in the world. Anything at all, word or incident,
reminded him of something he had seen or done or
heard, and out that something had to come to the
nearest listener. He would talk round the camp-fire
the night long, and wake one of us up in the cold dawn
to share a laugh with him. All he usually got at that
hour was a blindly-aimed kick that more than once
ended in a turmoil amongst the hot ashes. But for all

53

his lightness he had a heart of corn, and an iron steadfastness in fight or friendship.

"What is this business?" I enquired.

"You ken it. If our lads maun hae meat, ye maun
go reive it. We hae only ae stirk by us."

The Irish and Highlandmen were ever notable meat-
eaters, and notable fighting men as a consequence.
Fish, even salmon, they despised, a thing that Margaret
Anderson could not understand; in hard times they
could do with brose and oatmeal cakes; but for a
ruthless do-or-die campaign they must have meat and
plenty of it, beef, mutton, venison, pork, kid, or even
an occasional lifted fowl. For three weeks now we had
been living from hand to mouth, with Baillie pricking
at our tails and Sir John Hurry clearing the country
ahead of us as he lured us on; here at Auldearn we
were down to our last beast, and it takes a good many
to make a meal for near three thousand meat-eating
men.

"O'Cahan will be attending to it, but I will say a
word to Colkitto," I told Margaret.

"Here comes the big lad then, wi' bonny Montrose."

Montrose and his Major-General, Alasdair, strolled
across the field towards us. Alasdair was a huge tall
man and yet very shapely in shoulder and leg below
the black and green and red tartan of Clan Ranald. By
his side Seumas Graham of Montrose looked slim and
young: a slender man of middle height, with flowing
darkly-fair hair, dark-grey eyes, a smooth fresh com-
plexion, and there was aye a queer, aloof, half-wistful
smile about his eye-sockets. To-day he was neat in
a belted light-blue jerkin, and, a habit with him,
carried his bonnet swinging in his hand. He was a
gallant dresser always.

A few of his gentlemen walked behind him; faithful Sir William Rollo hirpling lightly on his one sound leg; Nathaniel Gordon, that iron soldier of fortune, with the gash on his leather cheek that had blinded one eye; leal young Lord Gordon, heir of Huntly, not long for this life; old Maormor Ogilvie of Airlie, who would never forget the loss of his gallant son at Inverlochy; and others that I do not now recall. Our colonel, Manus O'Cahan, was not there, I know. That small adequate man would be about his business, and that business his beloved regiment.

"You did not save the day for me, Maurteen," shouted Alasdair in his burly voice, "but small blame to you this time."

Montrose paused in front of me and I saluted him. He shook his head at me, and his fine hair swung on his shoulders.

"Clan Ranald left its mark on you, adjutant," he said, "and I am sorry, but not too sorry, for that last goal won me ten pounds Scots from MacDonald."

"Have you it in your pooch, Montrose?" Ranald Ban enquired.

And Montrose laughed. He was courtier and Lowland bred, and proud as Lucifer of caste and station, but amongst us he fell readily into the customs of the Gael, amongst whom a man, knowing the pride of race, talked to his chief on equal terms and did not hesitate to use the keen blade of wit. Montrose liked that life.

"I am glad you reminded me, MacKinnon," said he, "I will keep on asking it."

"Captain-General," said I then, "the camp is short of meat."

"I know, adjutant. That is why I am here. I had a right tough piece to dine on. I have three thousand pretty men in my hands and heart—beside five hundred women not so pretty, but some prettier "—he gave his courtier bow to Margaret—"and I will not have them go hungry in a teeming land. Look round ye, gentlemen."

We were low down here in front of the house of Boath and the horizon was not a wide one: a swell of wooded land eastwards over which we had marched yesterday, slopes of wood and pasture southwards into the brown hills of Cawdor, a round knoll carrying ruined walls eastwards and hiding the town of Nairn, and northwards a spread of cultivated land lifting and falling towards the sea. A peaceful, fat land, and used to peace these many years: that was the thought in my mind. And in Montrose's mind.

"Our e'en are tired of heather, and of mountains leaning to fall on us," said he, "and here at last is a land of plenty. Once, my gentlemen, not once but many times, this land of Moray was the buckler of Scotland against Dane and Sassenach, ay, and against your Eireannach too, Alasdair. Now it is dour against a Scots King. Very well! If the Brodies and the Roses and the others will not help us with their swords, they maun yield us their cattle to nourish the King's army. We camp here, gentlemen, and we strike from here, and here even my Ulstermen shall have meat in plenty. Let the women build up the fires, Mistress Anderson; to-night there will be meat to cook."

There was the decision crisply made for us. And that was why a party one hundred strong went raiding for a *creach* [1] of cattle into the lands of one Brodie of Lethen. And Destiny sent me riding with it.

[1] Herd.

56

CHAPTER IV

THE PRISONER IN THE BELL-TOWER

I

THERE was Tadg Mor O'Kavanagh with half a
company of O'Cahan's regiment, and Ranald Ban
MacKinnon with some two score men of Uist and Mull.
Nathaniel Gordon rode with them to see what fun
might be going; and I went too, to be rid of women
for a space, as I thought, though now I know that
Fate had something else in mind for me on that jaunt.

The Irish and the men of the Isles had, and still have,
I am told, a bad name in the lands of Moray and
Marechal Keith, because Montrose, like the canny
man he was, had learned to pick them for his foraging
parties. He knew by experience that the men of the
Mainland—Strathbogie and Badenoch and Lochaber
—could not resist the temptation to run a good *creach*
of cattle home to their own glens. Not that the Irish
and Mull men were one whit honester than the rest of
his army; indeed, given the chance, they would out-
rogue any body of men this side of Caithness; but Mull
and Uist and Ulster were far away across the sea, and
no booty of cattle might be reived that far. So they
brought it into camp, regretfully enough sometimes.

I was mounted on a tall bay saddle-horse that Tadg
Mor and myself had lifted out of Laird Brodie of

Brodie's stable two days before. Tadg Mor, for some reason, never liked a tall horse, but preferred to have his feet near the ground on a broad-backed Highland shelt; Ranald Ban MacKinnon rode a like beast, and Nat Gordon, a famous breaker of horses, was mounted on a stallion of the Huntly cavalry. Most of the others padded afoot, but that was no hindrance, for they were as tireless as hounds, could outrun any pony, and hold a two-year-old stirk by tail or horn. We had a man of the Grants of Cromdale to guide us, a light and wiry rogue, with the fleering Grant eye and red hair, who had spent all his life reiving cattle in these lowlands, and deserved hanging for other things as well.

Southward we went then at a jog-trot behind Colin Grant, slung targes and flintlocks slapping on broad backs, and broadswords gripped under oxter; and like all companies of the Gael there was talk and laughter and snatches of song and bouts of sly horse-play. Ranald Ban was riding close ahead of Tadg Mor and me, telling some queer story to Nat Gordon, who had heard queer stories and made a few as far away as the banks of the Elbe; and Tadg Mor talked to me.

"Did you see Colkitto whispering to me back there?"

"About some woman?"

"What else? He wanted to know if Meg Anderson belonged to you."

"And you lied as usual?"

"I did not. 'If she does not belong to Maurteen,' says I, 'she does not belong to anyone else.'"

"Why did you not tell the whole truth?"

"I had my reasons. And, anyway, how do I know which belongs to which?"

"You know well."

"Which then?"

"What else did Colkitto say?"

"'Find out for me, Tadg,' says he. 'I would like to know.' 'Why would you, Col?' I gave him back. 'Because,' says he, 'I would not like to offend Maurteen and he the only Sassenach amongst us.' He has his hot eye on the girl. 'You would not like to offend me either, Alasdair,' I coaxed him. 'That would not trouble me,' he says, laughing, and off he went. And mind you, he would not be an easy man to put in his place."

"Margaret Anderson will do that for him as she has for you, Tadg Mor!"

"Do I not know it?" said he, his hand up to his ear. Ranald Ban reined back to my side, laughing.

"Whenever I see him rubbing his ear that way," he said, "I know the thing in his mind. That girl——"

"What girl?"

"Meg out of Aberdeen. She reminds me of a girl I knew one time in Barra——"

"I warn you, Ranald crooked-tongue," said Tadg Mor, "that I am not going to laugh at this one."

"You will so. She was a girl of the MacNeills, and her father was a proud man, a half-bit of a half-sir; and if he had one hate in the world it was for the Harris MacLeods. And lo and behold you! if a gallant lad of that gallant breed did not set his eye on the daughter Ellen and his heart after it. I do not know anything about the wooing, but if it was warm it was not long, for in less than a month the bold MacLeod came slipping across the ford one dark of night and back again before morning, and Ellen was with him, and she willing. I was there myself when MacNeill heard the news, and my hand! but he had a bitter tongue.

First of all he wept before us outside his own door, and
then he gave us the full and honourable genealogy of his
race from Barra to Gigha, and then he wept again for
the black slur that was now on it; and after that he
raved and recalled every bad thing he had ever heard
about the MacLeods. Indeed that clan is no worse
and no better than the rest of us, but a bad and a
bloody thing here and there could be named against
it, and he named them all and invented one or two.
Dhia! but he was worth hearing that day. And at
the very end he gathered all his powers, and he threw
his hands and his face up and roared with all his might
into the face of the sky: 'But shamed as I am this day,
I thank the great God Almighty and all His Saints
that that bastardly MacLeod has got hold of the
laziest, idlest, dirtiest, worst-tempered bitch in all
Scotland.'"

He stopped and waited for our laughter.

"Well?" said Tadg Mor.

"Is that all?" I enquired.

"That is all."

I pulled my horse round to his other side and we had
him close between us, our feet under his stirrups, and
with Nat Gordon ahead blocking his way. He looked
from one to the other of us and cried out:

"What have I said against the girl this time?"

"You will tell us," said I, "why Margaret Anderson
reminded you of that fly-away girl out of Barra?"

Ranald Ban rubbed his flaxen toss of hair desperately.
"Meg has a hot temper, has she not?"

"Warm but sound."

"Was she lazy the day she carried your targe in the
snowdrifts of Glen Roy?" Tadg Mor wanted to
know.

"She was not, but I was carrying a gralloched hind for your supper."

"Was she dirty," I persisted, "the time she fed you the juice of beef, and salved the head-wound you got at Inverlochy?"

"And it was the back of your head, moreover," roared Tadg Mor. "Who was your face turned from that time?"

Ranald Ban rubbed the back of his head where the healed wound was. "I am thinking I had hold of the wrong girl," he admitted lamely.

"Pity for you that you did not remember that earlier," I said. And with one concerted heave we had him somersaulting over his pony's head.

He was as active as a cat, and landed neatly on his feet, but his pony dunted him with its muzzle and knocked him flat against the hocks of Nat Gordon's mount, that, like a well-trained cavalry horse, danced sideways without kicking. He scrambled to his feet swearing as fast as he could remember.

"You bloody Irish Sassenach!" he yelled, and shook his fist at me. "Wait, Maurteen! till I get you with a hurley in your hand and I'll blacken your other eye for you."

"You will not be able," said I, "if I get your back turned first."

He laughed then, bearing no ill-will. "Have it your own way this time," he said, and remounted his pony between us; but in the saddle he flared again. "Your souls to hell! I would put my hands under her feet any day, and you know it."

"In that case," said Tadg Mor, "forget that you ever left your saddle." And we all laughed. Ranald Ban MacKinnon was a very lovable man in those far-off days when we were all young and made fun in the face of death.

Nat Gordon was half turned to us, his scarred cheek twisted with laughter.

"Take due notice, gentlemen," he said, "that if any one tells you I miscalled your long-legged she-bairn, I here and now proclaim it a lie."

He stayed turned in his saddle, but he was no longer looking at us, but at something far behind us and below. "See that?" said he excitedly, and we turned to look.

We were at the head of the long slope that we had been steadily climbing all the way up from the hamlet, and a marvellous view was spread out below us and away. It was a cool early evening in May, with filmy clouds sailing thinly in a high thin sky, and the air was clearer than rock crystal. Auldearn was hidden in its hollow behind the woods of Kinsteary, but there was Nairn Town close-set on its green carse, and blue plumes of smoke drifting eastwards from its huddled chimneys. A shallow river curved by it on our side, and a new bridge spanned across in two arches. And beyond Nairn was spread the lifting floor of the northern sea, a stronger green than the sky, veined with the paler green of currents, and splashed with islands of purple. In that clear air the bold coast north of the firth seemed near enough to shout to, though it was a dozen miles away; the great whale-back of the Black Isle flowed in a clean curve crowned with the green of pasture and the dark of woods, and behind all was the strung welter of the northern hills, blue and fainter blue to where far and far away stood one lonely peak a blue thinner than smoke.

"Ay! but she is bonny, bonny," murmured Ranald Ban.

The bonny thing and the thing we thought Nat Gordon was pointing to was a ship in full sail coming down the coast from the narrows of Chanonry. She was the biggest vessel I had ever seen, bigger by far than any of the vessels that had brought our two thousand from Wexford to Scotland, and every sail was set to catch the faint draw of western air. A lovely sight that great tower of canvas against the green of the land and the blue of the mountains, with a white plume flowing backwards from the shearing prow.

"Not that, though she is bonny," said Nat a little impatiently. "See that smoke in the sand-hills west of the town."

We saw the smoke then, many plumes and drifts of it, lifting over the dunes that fringed the shore. One would say that down there was a good-sized town, sending up its evening smoke, but we knew that there was no house, other than a few fishing bothies along that shallow coast.

"That is a camp, and no small one," said Nat Gordon.

"Sir John Hurry and his army!" exclaimed Ranald Ban. "But——"

"I know. Hurry camped last night at Dalcross of Petty—so our outriders reported—and that is ten miles from here."

"That smoke is not five."

"Whatever it is we must look into it," said Gordon, and reined his horse round. "Montrose must be told about it, if he does not know already. Sorry, comrades, to miss any ploy that may be going." And he gave his horse reins and spur. A gallant, prompt man, and cunning in war and ambuscade. He shouted over his shoulder: "Bring in a good *creach*; we might be needing a sound lining under our belts the morn."

63

We went down the back of the ridge into a country of pine groves, with a rough track winding between, and out across thin pastures and patches of young corn greener than grass. This was one of the old droving roads to the south and we followed it for a mile. But there were no cattle to be seen, not as much as a ewe and her lamb on the whole heathery curve of a round solitary hill on our right. Colin Grant, our guide, was none disappointed.

"The warning bell of Ardclach was ringing last night," he told us. "The beasties will be in their hidy holes, but myself will find them for you."

He swung us well westward of the strong house of Lethen, at that time garrisoned against us, and led us streaming down into a hollow on a small township of black houses scattered about a stone mill straddling a stream. Whether they had warning of our coming I do not know, but there were no men about that small place, and the only women that we saw were a few old crones that came fearlessly to the smoking door-ways and cursed us warmly and at length. Other than a pleasant curse or two in return and the shaking of cattle goads, our lads took no notice. We left women alone. That was Montrose's rule since Aberdeen.

We found no cattle in that township nor in the stony fields about it, but Grant and a score of trained reivers scattered wide, reading the ground with knowing eyes, found a not too old cattle track here and there, followed them up, made a few false casts, and finally came to where one, two, six, ten beasts had moved in the same direction. It was skilled work, and in a short time we were streaming full pelt across an upland moor, and even I, unused to tracking, could see that a strong herd had passed that way not so long before.

We ran the herd down in a fenced valley on the edge of a pine wood in a strange country of small round detached hillocks. Half a score of ragged men in trews tried to scatter the beasts as we came, and an arrow flew amongst us here and there. But we were too quick for them, throwing our net wide, and frightening them like conies into the wood with the explosion of a flintlock. There were all of eighty head, mostly small but meaty beasts, black and dun in colour and shorter in the horn than our Irish beasts.

"Another beat like this, Colin," said Ranald Ban to Grant, "and we are not asking too much."

"Indeed that is right," the Grant agreed. "A man should be leaving something on the ground for a hungry fellow coming after. There is a place I know below Carn Achagour that I never drew blank these twenty years."

We detached some third of our party to hurry this herd campwards, and the rest of us followed Grant's leading. We were even more successful this time, with no herdsmen and no arrows to trouble us. We tracked down a hundred head of cattle—some shaggy Highland beasts among them—a flock of sheep with lambs, and a scatter of goats, hidden inside palisades on the edge of a wood called Dulsie.

"A right kindly people," remarked Tadg Mor, "to save us the trouble of gathering the beasts."

"But you would need a man like me to find them for you," said Grant cunningly, "and that man would deserve his reward. If ye will give me my pick of twenty and two lads to help I will be safe home in Cromdale with them before the morrow's morn."

"That would be robbery," said Tadg Mor.

"And what is this then?"

"This is the King's enemies feeding the King's men," Ranald Ban told him.

"The point is too fine for me."

"It would be—to a Grant," said the Clan Ranald man, old enemy of the Clan Grant.

"Am I no' gettin' my pick then?"

"The pick of a bone, the same as the rest of us," Tadg Mor told him.

"I thought you would be refusing me," said Grant cheerfully, "but there was no harm in trying whatever. Let us take the road then."

He led us out of the wood and on to a track along the head of a gorge with the strong stream of the Findhorn River brawling in the bottom.

By this time it was within an hour of sundown and the lads hurried the beasts to get into camp before dark. Four or five of us came behind at our leisure, and the drove gradually drew away, the men circling and hallooing on the flanks. There were Ranald Ban and a body-servant of his—a solid hulk of a red man— Tadg Mor, Colin Grant and myself. I cannot call to mind any others. Our road for a time paralleled the river curving widely below us in its widening valley, a great and lovely valley of woods and green haughs opening away before us to the distant sea golden in the sun beyond the town of Forres. Down in the bottom of the valley was a cluster of thatched houses, with a grey kirk and a grey manse standing apart; and a treacherous swinging foot-bridge sagged from one crag to another across the river where there was another cluster of black houses.

"That is the parish town of Ardclach," Grant told us, "and it is famous for having the highest bell-tower in all Scotland. There it is up there for you."

Up the slope above us, on the summit of a round hillock, stood a tall square stone tower roofed with flags, with one door facing us and one barred window high up under the eaves. It had a smoking short chimney at one end, and at the other a squat belfry arch with a big bell of dark bronze filling the mouth of it.

"They say there is gold in the brass of that bell," remarked Grant, "and that could be, for the clap of it is as tuneful and far-flung as the middle reed of the pipes. I have heard it of a calm morning as far away as my own haugh on the Spey. It is only rung for two things: to warn the people to kirk on Sabbath mornings, and to warn them that cattle reivers are on the road. Ye heard it last night, and here are we the reivers."

"Some one bides up yonder by the smoke," said Ranald Ban.

"It could be. Lethen and the Kirk use it for a prison on occasion."

"Were you ever in it yourself, Colin my robber?" Tadg Mor questioned.

"Ay was I. For one night, and I thought it my last night—but twenty of my friends from Ballindalloch rescued me in the morning with the rope round my neck."

We were directly below the tower now, and Ranald Ban checked his pony.

"If the Kirk has a prisoner up there," he said, "the same might be a friend of ours. Let us take a look."

He turned his pony up the brae, and I turned with him; and I often wonder since why I had no premonition of the thing I was turning to.

3

We had reached the foot of the knoll on which the tower stood, when a man came out of the single door, clapped it shut, turned the key in the lock, and made a run for it slantwise down the hill towards the township.

"Round him!" cried Ranald Ban, his pony's hooves slithering and clattering on the stony ground.

The fleeing man had no chance from the beginning, though he bounded nimbly enough on his short legs. The nimbler ponies cut in ahead of him, and he saw that he could never make the shelter of the houses. He checked himself in the middle of a leap, hesitated, swerved round and back up the brae to the tower like an unwieldy hare. But before he could unlock the door we were up with him, and Ranald Ban's cattle goad touching between his shoulder-blades. At once he turned his face to us, his broad back to the door, and his hands spread wide against the wood.

"Give it to me in the breist," he cried, his voice brazen against death.

"Patience, black brother!" said Ranald Ban, dropping his point. "Yon was not well played. You should have kept your locked door between us."

The man looked around at the half-circle of us, his black eyes glowering under black brows. He was a powerful figure of a man in trews and ragged shirt, short in the leg, long in the body, and his black bullet head looked solid as a culverin ball. His eyes stayed on the man of the Grants.

"Is it yourself, Red Colin?" said he, his voice only surly now.

"Myself it is surely, Black Rab Fraser," replied that man half-tauntingly. "The trade is good in stirks these days."

"I promise you, Colin, that you will never see the inside of this tower again if the Hieland *bodachs* leave life in me."

"Kind, kind, Rab."

"For I will hang you myself outside the door of it."

"This boar has a tusk," cried Ranald Ban, laughing. We were all laughing. "He reminds me of a man I knew in Uist—but remind me to tell you that one when we have time. Now, black lad, who have you at the back of that door?"

"How would I know?" growled the black lad. "I am no' the gaoler."

"There are prisoners then?"

Black Rab hesitated and then blurted, "Hugheon Rose of Belivat has one prisoner here—that is all."

"Do not you believe him, MacKinnon," advised Grant. "Hugh Rose of Belivat never put a lad in prison, with a dirk or a rope handy."

"Whoever is in it might be a friend of ours," said Ranald Ban.

"The prisoner is no friend of yours," put in Black Rab, but too hurriedly.

"We could decide that after seeing him. Will you open that door, stubborn man."

"You might as well kill me without more talk," said the stubborn man.

"I see that you have the key at your hip," said Ranald Ban patiently, reaching out his hand. "I will open it for you."

"Not while I have a drop of blood in me," said the other dourly, and then his voice lifted in challenge. "There are five of ye, and me without a weapon, but I dare ye to come at me one by one, weapon or no weapon."

Ranald Ban's body-servant—the hulking red fellow —stood at his leader's stirrup, and Ranald Ban clapped him on the shoulder.

"I want that key, Hector—without blood on it."

"You will have it, *avic*," said Hector lightly, his spear heeling into the ground and his targe slipping down his back.

He walked forward slowly, his red head down, and his arms hanging loose; but suddenly he came alive, his feet spurned the gravel, and his arms flung themselves for the grapple. Black Rab Fraser was as quick, if not quicker, for he caught a flying wrist with one hand and a hunched shoulder with the other, and the two heaved out on the packed gravel before the doorstep in a tight clench. That grapple did not last long. The man Hector was strong as a mastiff, but Black Rab was as strong as a boar. In half a minute or less they were on the ground with the Fraser safely on top. They fell close to Tadg Mor's pony that shied away from the tumble, but, as it shied, Tadg leant from the saddle-pad, and cleverly plucked the key from Black Rab's hip.

The man felt the tug, and, twisting his head, saw the key in Tadg Mor's hand. There he grunted like the boar he was, tore himself free from the Highlandman and launched himself at Tadg Mor. Tadg threw the key and I caught it in the air, and in the next instant he was torn off his pony, swearing through his laughter. He came down on one knee, but he drove his shoulder into the Fraser and heaved himself upright.

"We will see what you know of this game, my hardy man," said he, and he grappled the hardy man at collar and elbow, lifted him clear of the ground and swung him in a clean half-circle; but the black lad came down on his wide bowed feet as sure and as squat as a toad, and in turn swung Tadg, who landed on his feet just as surely.

"Neat!" said Tadg Mor. "We'll do that again." And so they went at it like a pair of clumsy dancers in the swing of a reel, and Ranald Ban nearly fell off his pony laughing at the weighty antic.

But I knew what Tadg Mor had in mind. He was giving me time to open the door. I had seen him wrestle often enough and knew him for a master. Indeed I never knew his better at anything requiring sinew—or, if it comes to that, at anything calling for loyalty.

So I slipped off my horse on the far side, threw the reins to Grant, and mounted the wide flag that made the step of the door. The lock clicked smoothly as one well used, and the heavy oak slab yielded quietly to press of shoulder. A couple of paces inside the door a flight of steep stone steps led upwards between unplastered walls, and at my right hand a blank doorway opened into darkness. I put my head carefully inside and sniffed the dank darkness of an unused room.

"Anyone here?" I murmured, and only an echo murmured back from the stone walls and the stone roof. It was in fact the dungeon room, but there was no one in it.

I mounted the stairs, and in the gloom at the head of it I was stopped by a door on the very last tread.

It was locked, but the key was in the lock, and I turned it gently and tapped on the wood.

"*Tar isteac*—come in!" said a voice inside. And the voice was a woman's.

I opened the door out of the gloom and leant to look into a room that, by contrast, was full of light. There were two barred windows high up, one that we had seen from the slope, the other facing the west, and through that westering one the levelling sun poured its reddening glory in one widening beam in which motes danced. That room occupied the whole top storey of the tower; it was floored with stone and the hewn rafters of bog pine supported the unrendered flags of the flat-pointed roof; there was an open fireplace with peat sods smouldering and scenting the air, a cover-leted couch, a rough table carrying a ewer; and a big armed chair of twisted wood faced me from the ingle-nook.

In that big arm-chair sat the woman that had called to me in the Gaelic. She was young and dark, and, though she was sitting down, I saw that she was not tall. She sat there leaning back very still and very calm, her dark head against the tall back of the chair, her hands resting lightly on the arm-rests, and her ankles crossed at easy stretch. Her hands were brown and shapely, and her square-toed small shoon carried silver buckles like Margaret Anderson's. The splay of sunlight from the window just touched those silver buckles. She had firm black brows above dark eyes and her face was softly dusky. She was wearing a dress the colour of red wine cut square at the neck, and a long cloak of dark-green tartan with a red line was thrown over the back of the chair. It is possible I did not notice all these things at the time, though now I remember them very well. But most clearly I remember the soft duskiness of her face below her dark brows, and her hair that was not curled yet waved faintly.

"Who are you?" Her voice was low and cool, and her lips scarcely moved.

"Adjutant Martin Somers of O'Cahan's regiment," I told her, and I took two paces inside the door.

"You are near enough now. One of Graham's Irishry?"

"I am an Englishman," I said wearily, tired to the bone of telling people that.

"That is worse," said she, "but I am not afraid of you. And yet I fear my heart is not as quiet as I would want it. That is why I am sitting still—to hide its beating."

The beat of her heart was not in the strange slow quietness of her voice, that had in it sometimes a soft remote husky note.

I looked round the bare room. "Are you the prisoner of this man—this Hugh Rose?" I could not believe it.

"That man is my father," she answered, "but you are welcome to say the worst in your mind about him."

"The thing in my mind is that he might have his own reason for making a prisoner of his daughter—if she is a prisoner."

"She was till you opened that door."

She was so calmly sure of herself that I found nothing to say.

"I heard cattle lowing and reivers ho-hoing past my window—my father's beasts, I hope. Are there many of you?"

73

"There are four or five below."

"Are they all as ugly as you are?"

"I am not sure about one or two, but you will be able to judge."

"Is that a threat, I wonder? Was it Black Rab Fraser closed your eye so neatly?"

I must surely have looked ugly with my black eye and long devil-slit chin.

"He would if he had time," I answered her.

She sat up at that and her brown hands tightened on the arm-rest.

"He is not hurt—you have not killed——"

"At this minute he is having a pleasant wrestle with an Irishman in front of the door—collar-and-elbow."

She loosed the strain, but did not again lean back.

"I am sorry for your Irishman," she said.

I laughed at that, and I think she was nettled though her voice did not show it.

"No Irisher in the world could put Rab Fraser on his back—in a fair wrestle."

"Fair collar-and-elbow. He will be on his back surely."

"I do not believe it."

"Why not come and look for yourself?" I thought that was a right clever way of getting this strange young woman off my hands and on to Ranald Ban's. In my own mind I was cursing him for not coming to my rescue. Rescue was the word in my mind, for the coolness of her and the cut in her tongue had a defeating effect on me.

"I will do that," said she and was on her feet. She plucked her tartan cloak off the chair-back and held it up for me to see.

74

"I will wager this against that old cloak of yours that Black Rab is not thrown."

I shook my head. "I need only one cloak."

"I will exchange cloaks with you then if Rab is down. This is a good new cloak."

"Mine is better," said I, "but I will take that wager if you insist."

The cloak I was wearing over my old broadcloth was the famous hooded Irish war-cloak, ankle-long, double woven of the finest worsted, dyed dark green with the berry of the rime, and lined with red silk. There was no more serviceable cloak anywhere—and I ran a good chance of losing it.

She walked across the floor to me, shoulders braced and head at full height, but that was no higher than my shoulder. She was short, but she was not slim, nor was she squat, and her neck was rounder than it was long. She had the shoulders of a boy, but her breast and the easy soft flowing lines of her were all woman. I stepped aside to let her pass, and she went by me to the head of the stairs without a tremor or a turn of the head. But I heard a small hard intake of breath as she stood with her back to me, and for the first time realised that here was a girl of very great courage. She was about to face men of an exceeding savage reputation in this countryside, and one of them stood behind her.

"You need have no fear, Mistress Rose," I said gently.

"How did you find that out?—but it is not fear, I think." Her voice was again low and softly husky. "But the tales they tell of you make me wonder, and, looking into your eyes, I am not sure that the tales are all lie."

75

"Not all," said I, "but we do not kill men or hurt women in cold blood, saying our prayers at the same time—like some."

She turned then and went down the stairs, and I followed her slowly. Sure enough we found the wrestling match at a finish. Black Rab Fraser was securely on his back, his arms spread and held and Tadg Mor's great knee across his thighs. He could neither heave nor wriggle. But suddenly Tadg Mor loosed his grip, sprang to his feet, and jerked the beaten man to his.

"You have the root of the game in you, black lad," he commended, patting the thick shoulder, "and if I had time to learn you one or two clips you might puzzle the best."

And here Ranald Ban MacKinnon threw back his flaxen pow and laughed his high and merry laugh.

"My soul to God! Here is Martin Somers at his old game of rescuing ladies. A dark queen this time, and no Meg Anderson."

He opened his mouth for further laughter and shut it again, his eyes fixed on the dark queen. I smiled to myself. Without speaking she had already impressed herself on this quick-minded Gael. She stood very still and straight on the step of the door and looked them over, and I, standing behind her, could not tell whether her glance was cold or scornful. And then she turned her head and spoke to me.

"You were right. There are one or two I am not sure about myself."

Black Rab Fraser shambled across the gravel and faced forward by the jamb of the door. He was still prepared to defend his lady.

"Was it a fair throw, Rab?" she questioned him.

76

"He had a trick or two beyond me, Mistress Iseabal," he admitted surlily.

"And there goes my fine tartan plaid on Sassenach shoulders." But she still kept her plaid over her arm.

Ranald Ban MacKinnon was off his pony now, his bonnet in his hand.

"At your service, my lady," said he.

Again I was smiling to myself. I could not see her face but I could see theirs, and already there was something diffident and embarrassed in their eyes. This was no ordinary wench facing them, and the limber tongue of Ranald Ban had a knot in it.

"So young, so young," said she in that quiet, remote, prophetic voice of hers, "and one of them bonny with his flaxen hair, and all to die so soon."

Ranald Ban started, and Colin Grant, holding my horse, turned his head and peered fearfully down into the slowly darkening hollow of the valley.

"Not too soon, I am hoping," said Ranald Ban at last.

"To-morrow or next day—or next week—when the men of Moray meet ye."

Tadg Mor looked over his shoulder and rubbed his red head grinningly. "Maybe it would be as well for us to start running now," said he.

"Indeed and indeed," said Ranald Ban, "one should stand up for one's own as long as one can, even if the men of Moray have been boasting a long time, with little to show for it since Bannockburn."

She turned her head and spoke softly to me. "I am showing poor manners, I know, but that is fear. Will they know that I am afraid?"

"They are too much afraid themselves to notice, O terrible one!" said I, and she gave me a quick glance

77

out of her dark eyes before she faced round again.
"You and I might be well matched," she murmured.

"If this is your prison, my lady," hinted Ranald Ban,
"you are now outside it."

"That is my difficulty," said she.

"No difficulty at all," said he quickly. "It would be
no trouble to lock the door on you, and give the gaoler
back the key."

"I am no' her gaoler," growled Black Rab.

"That would be a tame ending," said the lady.
"Now that I am out I am afraid to show that I am
afraid to be where fear is."

"I know," said Ranald Ban wisely. "It is fear that
bares teeth. Where would you be now?"

"I am not sure yet, and I only know that I am afraid
to take my courage in my two hands. But here comes
a man who might help me to decide—if ye do not kill
him before that."

The man was coming up the path from the riverside
hamlet. The brae was stiff but he came on steadily,
in no hurry, yet with purpose in his firm striding. He
was a tall and bony man in an old hodden-grey suit,
but already I could see that he had the white bands of
the Calvinist minister at his neck. He was a bold man,
too, but, then, not many of his calling were anything
else. Still, not many of them would be willing to stride
forthright into danger as this man was striding. Not
that he was in any danger, but he would not know that.
All that he would know was the reputation of Montrose's foragers for harrying men of his cloth when
Montrose was not there to curb them. The sun, low
in the west, was shining full in his face, and, as he
came nearer, I was surprised to see that he was a
young man in years. He had a strong and rugged

face, clean shaven, and there was no hat on his tossed fair hair.

"I am no uglier than that man, I think," I whispered at Iseabal Rose's shoulder.

"But that is a just man."

"He has the advantage of me there."

"Perhaps I did not mean that," she said, "but I may find out how just you are."

The man was in our midst now below the shadow of the tower, and halted, his hand coming to a brief salute. We waited for him to speak. His face was grey and stern, and, remembering Andrew Cant of Aberdeen, I wondered if he would begin by calling us sons of Belial doomed to the Pit. But all that he said in a low voice with a Lowland twang was:

"I am John Balfour, minister under God of this parish of Ardclach."

And the Highland gentleman that we knew as Ranald Ban replied:

"I am Ranald vic Ailin vic Eoin vic Donald vic Fingin of Mull and Clan Ranald, and these are gentlemen out of Ireland."

"I have met gentlemen of Clan Ranald," said the other.

"But not of Ireland," murmured Tadg Mor.

He waited for us now, and, no doubt, was wondering what cat-and-mouse game we were going to play with him. His eyes had not rested at all on the young woman, though he had given me a quick and curious glance where I stood behind her shoulder.

"I hope," he said then, "that this lady is safe—that she is not your prisoner?"

Ranald Ban thought he saw a road. "Is she prisoner to your Kirk?"

"God forbid that the Kirk have any part in this imprisonment."

"Then," said Ranald Ban quickly, "can we do better than place her in the hands of you and your Kirk for protection?"

"My choice man!" said Tadg Mor.

This John Balfour at last faced the young woman, and his deep-set eyes were steady on her. But, said she, her voice quiet as ever:

"If I am free, Master Balfour, what am I to do?"

"You can obey your father, Iseabal Rose."

"Always—in all things?"

"In all that is lawful."

"You will tell me what is lawful." There was a harsh note in her voice now. "You will tell me what is lawful, John Balfour, and you will think well before you tell me."

"Oh God!" said John Balfour, and it was a young man that spoke in pain, and there was pain in his eyes too.

"Think well, John Balfour. I did not withstand my father lightly. I have nothing now but my own soul, and the advice you give me may make me an evil woman of the Roses."

He did not answer her but turned aside to Ranald Ban MacKinnon. "Gentleman of Clan Ranald, might Mistress Rose and I speak together in private?"

"And welcome! Come, friends."

"Stay!" said the minister. "Mistress Rose and I will move the other side of the corner if it pleases her."

"Anything must please me this day," said that lady, and she stepped down on the gravel.

The two, the tall stiff man and the short, softly lined young woman, went together round the corner. Black

Rab Fraser went behind unhindered, and I heard him say: "I was running down to you when they grippit me, meenister."

I went across to my friends and we clustered close together and whispered, our horses close behind us. I smile now, thinking of us, hard-bitten men, whispering perplexedly there in the shadow of the tower, the sunset reddening the moors all about us, and lighting the sombre green of a pine wood on the breast of a great slope beyond the river. And the sough of the water came up and whispered about us.

"That small one frightens me," said Tadg Mor.

"Maurteen Somers," said Ranald Ban solemnly, "you are no safe man when women are about. What devil prompted you to unlock that door?"

"Tadg Mor," I told him.

"She is worse than your Meg Anderson in her own way."

"Leave Meg out of it this time," Tadg Mor warned him.

"Listen!" whispered Colin Grant anxiously. "Let us mount and make a run for it. This is no safe place, with enough broken men—mostly Roses—in Dulsie Wood to cut our throats in the dark. She is the daughter of Hugh Rose of Belivat, and he is a dangerous man to meddle with, as I know. Leave her to him, I say."

"What do you think, Maurteen?" Ranald Ban queried.

"They might slip away by themselves," I said. "But if you say the word I will be first over the brae."

"Will I say it then?"

"I am not sure that you will."

"Nor am I sure. This is no business of ours, indeed;

81

but what will my father, Ailin in Mull, say, when I tell him the story. 'You took a young woman out of prison and left her standing afraid at the door. That is not what the brother of your sister was taught to do.' Do you not see? I tell ye she is afraid, and not so much of us as of something on her mind. No, brothers. Here we stay, and if we can put her on a safer road than the one she is on, we will do that."

"I knew well we would do nothing else from the beginning," said Tadg Mor.

Ranald Ban grinned. "She reminds me of the story of the lad that waited for the *Leenawn Shee* at the gable end of the priest's house in Uist——"

I often wonder what the story was, for it was one of the few we never heard. The man and woman came round the corner of the tower, the man leading, his face set, and she with her head no longer in the air but turned thoughtfully on the ground. The man came to his business at once.

"I am going to do what a man of my race has not done these many years," said he, and he smiled, a whimsical smile that lit up his stern face finely. "I am going to put my trust in men of the Gael."

"Many bad things have been said of us, and some of them true," said Ranald Ban, "but the Gael has never been accused of breaking trust."

"I have lived with men of Clan Ranald in the schools at Edinbro, and I know that is true. My request is that you give this lady a safe conduct to the port of Lochloy below Auldearn."

Tadg Mor nudged me, and I nodded my head. Lochloy was where Margaret Anderson's uncle lived.

"Does the lady wish it?" Ranald Ban queried.

"It is what I wish," said the lady in a low voice, without lifting her head.

"To-night?"

"The sooner the better," said the man.

"We will take the lady safely to Lochloy," said Ranald Ban.

"I thank you, sir. Once there, no further demands will be made on your courtesy. And now ye had better hurry, for this is no safe place for the King's men." The tall, rugged, young minister turned to the lady, who still had her head down, and his face was so stern that it could be only a mask to hide his feelings. "God be with you, Iseabal Rose!" And his voice also was too stern for that prayer.

She never looked up, and he turned away, but at that she impulsively caught his sleeve and held him. It was the first impulsive thing she had done, and there was a new light in her eyes meeting his, and a new deeper note in her voice.

"I am sorry for you, John Balfour. This is not the place for you, this wild Ardclach full of broken Roses and men bickering over land and beasts and wives. Go back—come back to your own Lothians where men may listen to your gentle prayers and preachings and one here and there take heed. Here they love to be scourged with hell's fire and, sure of that fire, go out and make doubly sure of it. Come — come with me!"

But he was firm as a rock.

"No, my duty is here, amongst the poor ones that need me. I will go now."

He did not see the hand she reached him. He looked into her eyes and his own went clear and wide for a moment, telling their own story; and then he turned

83

on his heel and strode out from amongst us and down the brae into the darkening valley.

"There walks a man, by God!" said Ranald Ban MacKinnon.

"You get good men everywhere," said Tadg Mor, "and that is a strange thing."

"It is the first time that I am inclined to agree with a MacDonald and an Irishman," said Iseabal Rose.

Then she sighed wearily, and looked round us. "Ye will forgive me, I hope," she said simply. "It is only the bad Rose blood speaking in me."

"It is a brave blood," said Ranald Ban. "Will Mistress Rose take my pony?"

She looked at the horses. "Whose is the big one fit to carry double?"

"At your service, my lady," I told her.

"Then if I may I will ride pillion with you—if you will ask me."

"I will not do less."

"And only fair, if what your laughing friend says is true—rescuer of ladies."

"He is the sort of friend that gave me this black eye," I told her. "That is the sort of friend he is."

5

Iseabal Rose rode behind me down to Auldearn, my cloak well padded under her, her hand in my belt, and her head at the level of my ear. Her own tartan cloak was on her shoulders, and I hoped she had forgotten the exchange that I had won. I would not like to lose my Irish cloak. Her small satchel was strung at my saddle-bow.

The droving road we were on was a rough and

twisting one, looping round stony braes and dipping deeply into rocky hollows, and the sun was set before we got out of the watershed of the Findhorn to the head of the last steep pitch that opened the long easy northern slope to us. Far down that long slope the plain of the sea spread before us, not shining now and patched with light green and rich purple, but one smooth lonely level of leaden blue; and beyond the sea, the ramparts of the hills stood up peak by peak in a stark blue-black wall against the white glow of the west and north. At that hour there was no cloud in all the sky, and one or two stars were faint in the paleness of it. I knew it would rain before morning.

"Oh, sad and lonely—sad and lonely!" It was a small voice at my shoulder, but it was in tune with that wide-flung, sombre landscape.

Ranald Ban and the others, except Tadg Mor, were ahead of us down the slope. Tadg Mor was close behind, and I twisted my head to see how his pony was making the last stiff scramble to the head of the rise. There was a man at his side holding the stirrup-leather, and in the half-light I could not be sure who he was. And there the girl called out:

"Where are you going, Black Rab Fraser?"

"Where am I not going?" came up the surly voice. "I am going as far as my legs will take me from your father, Hugheon Rose."

"Will you be any safer amongst the Irish?"

"I could not tell you that, Mistress Iseabal, but for the time I feel middling safe with one of them."

Tadg Mor laughed, and the lady said to me: "A man is always safe with the man who has beaten him."

I considered the ironic wisdom of that, and marvelled where she had gathered it. All the way up from the belfry tower we had not spoken a word, but now, having again found her voice, she began questioning me in that strange quiet way she had.

"Martin Somers is your name, I gather?"

"That is it."

"A rescuer of ladies! Your friend named one?"

"Margaret Anderson, and the only one."

"Not a tame rescue—like this one?"

"We were drunk at the time, Tadg Mor and I. That is he, my foster-brother, riding behind, the best man in the world."

"He might not be a good man, even so. Where was this rescue?"

"Out of a ramshackle iron stocks near the kirk with two spires at Aberdeen."

"Ah! the tale of that has gone abroad. So you were two of the ten savage men that stripped the great Andrew Cant naked and set him in the parish stocks?"

"Only the two of us. You have your hand on Master Cant's coat the last half-hour."

"You cut his tongue out as well?"

"We had that in mind, but I was too drunk to make a good job of it, so Tadg Mor would not let me."

"I do not believe that, of course. But what did you do with this woman—this Margaret Anderson?"

"She is below in the camp that you will see over the next rise."

"It might be well for her that you had left her in the stocks," she said smoothly.

"I could not tell you that," said I, "but you could ask her, for you have a habit of asking questions that come close to the bone."

"And a bad habit. Have I offended you?"

"I will put it this way. You are going down to Lochloy in our keeping, and you may be sure that no one will put a hurting finger on you. But if you return to your own place next month or next year, you will, maybe, be hearing scandalous whispers of all the hurt that came to you at our hands."

She thought that over. "I see what you mean," she said then.

"We had drink taken, it is true, but we took a girl with bloodshot eyes and a dry throat out of the stocks, and put a cruel man in her place; and if I took his coat I needed it, and it was the only thing taken. He was using his tongue when we left him."

"I hope you will not hold a grudge against me," she said, "though I think you are a man that would."

"Margaret Anderson is my friend." I felt warm on this. "And she is noble too, and any man that says a word against her in my presence will have to fight Tadg Mor O'Kavanagh."

"But I am a woman and can say what I like."

"That is a habit of yours too, and I will never know you well enough to pick a rod for you."

"I would need one often," she granted. "But you would not do your own beating?"

"I am no fighting man," I told her. "I am only an Adjutant of Women."

"Adjutant of women?"

"That is my rank and my title, and if you were in O'Cahan's regiment you would know that it had its importance, and you might be sorry for yourself a time or two."

"No doubt of that. I am sorry for myself now. But will you tell me how it is that, being a captain of women, you have not a woman's curiosity?"

87

"I am bad enough as I am."

"But are you not wondering why I am here and why I was locked up back yonder?"

"You are here to go down to Lochloy, and you were back yonder because, I think, your father had a middling good reason of his own to put you behind a stout door with a lock on it."

"When it comes to frankness," said she, "I will take lessons from you, but meantime I will tell you the kind of man my father is, and the reason he had too."

"Our camp is over the next ridge."

"Ride slowly then. I have a reason for telling you. You may have heard of the Roses?"

"In passing only. They refused to join Montrose after Inverlochy. A clan half-Covenant, half-Highland, fond of land and fond of bickering."

"These are the Roses of Kilravock—the honest branch of the family. The Roses of Belivat are even more land-hungry and more quarrelsome, and to that family I belong."

"I can well believe that," I said.

"Three, two generations ago they owned much land and many houses in this county—Belivat, Fleenas, Coulmony, Levrattich, Lyne—and they were greedy for more; and that more they took by force or by fraud—they did not mind which—from their neighbours, Falconers, Dunbars, Tullochs, anyone weak enough. But they made a mistake with the Dunbars. The Dunbars of Moyness were not weak, and, besides, they brought in fighting men of the MacDonalds to help them, as well as the process of any law there was. We had war and sackings and law battles all to ourselves in this small county, and in the end the Roses of Belivat lost—lost everything but the small place of

88

Fleenas, and that place my father, Hugheon Rose, now holds, and ye, Montrose's reivers, are driving most of his poor beasts down there."

"If he had joined Montrose for the King last February, when the Moray lairds were invited, he would not be reived now."

"And he would have joined if he thought Montrose and his ragged army had any chance to win. And there you have him. He is no honest Covenanter like the Brodies or his kin of Kilravock, for what was won by force and fraud and lost the same way he would now regain by cunning and by alliances."

"You are hard on him."

"I have reason; in order to restore some of his power he would force me to marry Walter Dunbar of Moyness, grandson of the man that ruined us."

There was the kernel of the nut at last.

"It seems that you did not want to marry this man —Walter Dunbar?"

"I do not."

"You told your father so?"

"With all my might."

"You made him understand surely," said I. "And he locked you in prison to chasten you?"

"You have it all now."

"Your father did not know you very well," I said.

"You do not know my father."

"Did this man of the Dunbars know what your father had done?"

"He would know."

"Then I take it he wants to marry you."

"He says so."

"And you will not?"

"I will not if I can help it. He has red hair."

"That is not a good reason."

"His hands scunner me."

"That is a poor reason too."

"He is young and unwed, but he has two sons half grown."

"I will assume that you are not putting his faults in order of magnitude. Might I go on questioning you?"

"I need not answer."

"Is there a man that you would marry?"

"There is no man I would marry—that I want to marry—but there is one man that I like."

"Does he like you?"

"He is John Balfour, the minister, and he loves me," she said calmly. "That is why I am not sure that he is entirely honest in the advice he gave me."

"A man in love has his own dishonesty."

"You will know. He advised me to take ship secretly at Lochloy and sail to Edinburgh where I have cousins at Balbirnie of the Lothians."

"He was honest then, for he turned his back on your urging to go back with you to the same Lothians."

"He might change his mind in his own time. Men sometimes do at the touch of loneliness or the touch of desire. But what is there for me to do if I stay here? I am only one small woman, and since time out of mind women obey men in this land, and marry when they are told or when they are let. Even our Mary Queen found she could not do as she liked. Should I obey my father then and thole humbly what all the women I know have tholed?"

"Why do you ask me?"

"Because you have no interest but to judge honestly,

and you are frank—franker than the Gael. No, that is not the reason. I do not know the reason, but, as I have found out, by rude questioning, you have already befriended one woman—and kept her honest, I do believe."

And after a while I said: "There is one thing I know and it is this: you will do what you are doing."

"Must I?"

"You must because you will. Any road you set your feet on you will walk to the end, and any advice I might give you, you would only follow if it led your way. But will you get a boat at Lochloy?"

"Alick Anderson, the shipmaster, and a friend of John Balfour, sails a coastwise boat with hides and malt once a month to Leith, the port of Edinburgh. He is due to sail this week."

"Margaret Anderson has an uncle——"

"The same. That is how the tale of your exploit got as far as Ardclach, gathering force on the road. The Kirk in Scotland has a long arm, Master Somers. Aberdeen sent two of its elders to Lochloy to warn her uncle that the fallen woman—that is how they put it— that she must be returned to St Machars should she seek refuge with him."

"The world is a small place," said I. "Did you ever hear that said?"

"It is so small and so big that I am small and afraid facing it my lone."

And I thought in my own mind that though she was small she was brave, and that in taking this strange unchancy road into the big world she kept a sure hold on her calmness and her dignity. Dignity is the word.

"Fear touches us all at turns," I told her, "but you need no lesson to face it. One thing only I am sure of: you need have no fear while you are in our hands."

And she said in a low prophetic voice I barely heard: "That might be my greatest fear or all be done."

"There is Auldearn below us now," I said.

We had come over the ridge of Kinsteary and round the flank of a beech wood dark in new bloom above us. It was night by then with a black cloud lifting out of the west, and the lights of the village and the camp gleamed red and yellow, and sent shimmering reflections amongst the trees about us. The buzz and murmur of the camp came up to us too, with the anxious lowing of beasts and the ho-hoing of herders as our booty moved away eastwards towards our cattle pound in the Hardmuir.

We were coming down on the strung-out hamlet from the rear, and all the back doors were open and glowing warmly from the fires within. Beyond the kirk-mound of the village the square bulk of the house of Boath stood out against the dark, every window lighted. There was Montrose's headquarters. Camp-fires blazed all round the curve of the Castle Hill and all along the edge of Kinsteary Park, and dark figures moved busily about them.

"Why, it is a great army!" murmured Iseabal Rose in some awe.

"Three thousand and no more," I told her, "but Montrose and Colkitto handle it like a hooded goshawk."

Small fleering breaths of air betokening rain whirled about us and rustled in the young leaves; and one drift of air coming up from the village brought us a glorious smell of cooking meat. I heard Tadg Mor swear pleasantly behind us. The cooks had got early to work on the first *creach* we had sent in.

"I thought I should be hungry," said the young woman, "and I find I am."

Ranald Ban MacKinnon was waiting for us at the foot of the slope, and was talking, excitement in his voice, to a man who had come out from the camp to meet us. In the throw of light behind him I saw that he was a small man, and before I heard his deep strong voice I knew that he was my colonel, Manus O'Cahan. Manus or Magnus means great, and O'Cahan was not that in body, but he had a steadfastness and greatness of spirit that was not excelled by Montrose's and certainly not by Colkitto's. Colkitto was great but he was not steadfast.

"Battle to-morrow!" cried Ranald Ban. "The MacKenzies and the men of Ross have joined Hurry, and he is back at the other side of Nairn. Nat Gordon is just in from outriding."

Manus O'Cahan laughed pleasantly. "Has Martin Somers been at it again?" he wanted to know.

"He got away from me," Ranald Ban told him.

"This is Mistress Iseabal Rose, a lady of Ardclach," I said gravely. "And to-night she goes to the port of Lochloy under safe conduct."

"My duty to Mistress Rose," saluted O'Cahan, his hand to his leather basnet, "but she cannot have a safe conduct this night. The outriders of the Covenant are across the Nairn and strung by the coast to Findhorn Bar. No lady may get to Lochloy in safety."

"Is this the end then?" said Iseabal Rose, the intoned prophetic note in her voice. "Where will ye and I be to-morrow?"

"Where God decides," said O'Cahan, "and some of us indeed past all knowing."

"Most of us," said Ranald Ban, "will be trailing back to camp after drowning the last of the MacKenzies in Ness Water."

"Even if we are not as successful as that," said O'Cahan, "our women will have lines opened behind us. You will get to Lochloy in good time, Mistress Rose."

Like the gentleman he was he displayed no curiosity about this lady who had come riding into camp behind one of his officers.

"Mistress Rose will have to stay somewhere to-night," I said then, though I already knew where she was going to stay.

"I have a friend in the village," she told us quickly, "in the double-storeyed house at the corner of the Cawdor road."

"All the villagers were moved out three hours ago," O'Cahan told her, "and are now in shelter in Darnaway Forest. The houses are held by my men for the night, but you will be welcome to private quarters——"

"The best and quietest place will be with Margaret Anderson," I interrupted him. "She has a bothy of her own at the back of the kirkyard."

"It is a quiet place I want," said the lady. "Few people must know that I am in Auldearn."

"It will be known in all Moray," I told her. "We have burned your boats."

I had some fifty women under my own particular
charge in O'Cahan's regiment at that time, as well as
a few half-grown lads and one or two children in arms.
Thirty or so of these under Sorcha MacNeill were the
usual foragers, camp-makers, cooks, bearers, anything
they could put a hand to in that small army where
every man we could spare had to bear arms in the line;
a dozen, specially chosen, in charge of Margaret
Anderson, made up my nursing and medical staff, and
these, with two or three men wounded in the rearguard fight at Ford of Gight, were quartered in village
houses at the back of the kirk-mound. Margaret had
a bothy to herself, snug under the wall of the kirkyard
at the end of a lane running up from the Boath road;
a poor enough clay building of two rooms with a
scraugh roof and earthen floor, but with a drawing
stone chimney, and a brick hearth where food could
be prepared for herself or the wounded.

My feet clattered on the loose cobbles of the path
leading from the lane, and Margaret's high clear voice
came through the door.

"Come awa' ben, lads! I kent ye'd smell yer diet."

She never lost that strange strong Doric dialect,
though she could now string sentences in the deep-
throated Gaelic, the strangest Gaelic ever heard as she
rendered it in her Aberdeen tongue.

Iseabal Rose had not to bend her head under the
low lintel. Margaret Anderson turned from a pot at
the fireside, and slowly straightened and stiffened.
Behind her a fine peat fire, flaming under a bellied pot
hanging from a black crane, lit up the cavern of the

room, and, in addition, a lighted tallow candle was set in a withered old turnip on the rough table. In the gleam of that candle I saw Margaret's face go queerly still; and her grey-lit eyes widened and held on our dark young guest. I have seen the same look in the wide-open eyes of the horned owl at the time of taking flight at the close of the day.

Margaret's grey day-dress was kirtled for her cooking, and her short scarlet petticoat showed her clean ankles and her silver-buckled shoon; she had shed her outer jacket, and her knitted body-vest outlined her loveliness and left her neck and arms bare, and no earl's daughter had ever more shapely neck and arms: long arms white and slender, with no trace of that thickening below the shoulder that ill-fits many a bonny face. Her linten plaits were wound thickly about her head and held by her comb.

"Wha is it?" Her eyes never left Iseabal Rose, and her voice was lower than I had ever heard it.

"Mistress Iseabal Rose of Ardclach," I told her. "She will be your guest for the night, Margaret."

"I fairly ken noo," she said drily.

"She will be taking ship to-morrow or next day with your uncle at Lochloy for Edinburgh."

That was all I could tell her then, though I knew that later she would have the whole story out of me.

"You spoke of supper," I said, "and my nose tells me it is about somewhere."

The lid of the bellied pot on the fire tutthered, and a jet of steam perfumed the air to the watering of hungry mouths.

"The lady is welcome," said Margaret, her head unbending. "Will she tak' this hassock by the fire. Whaur's Tadg Mor?"

"Foddering. He'll be here in a minute."

The dark girl came to the fireside and her eyes went calmly over the tall fair one.

"So you are Margaret Anderson," she said softly. "I knew of course that you must be bonny."

"What div ye mean, young lady?" A small spot of colour came flecking into her cheeks.

"If your Martin Somers had drink taken it did not spoil the eyesight so eager to help his kindness."

"He's no' my Martin Somers."

"He is a fool then," said the other and sat on the straw hassock.

I sensed at once a strain between these young females and felt distressed about it, for I had expected them to be friendly, seeing that a fine spirit of personal integrity inspired them alike.

Iseabal Rose looked thoughtfully into the fire, her pose very still, and Margaret Anderson busied herself at the table.

"No' mony dishes among us," she said, trying to be casual. "Ae ashet and three beechen platters, but enough spoons to gae roond." She was silent then, and I missed her accustomed chatter of the day's doings. In the forenights when we three usually forgathered, Tadg Mor and I had ever to go over the whole day's work and listen to comment and criticism.

There was another clattering of feet up the path and Tadg Mor's red head came under the lintel, his eyes wary.

"Meg darling, would you be having the scrapings of a bone for a friend of mine?"

"Guid be here! Anither woman?"

"And bonnier than yourself. Let her look at you, Rab girl."

Tadg Mor crouched into the room, and the ragged bullet head and heavy shoulders of Black Rab Fraser appeared round the jamb of the door.

"Protect us!" exclaimed Margaret. "Is there life in it?"

"And a great emptiness."

"I didna ken there was an uglier loon in a' the warl' than my ain twa. Has it a tongue?"

"And the use of its hands and teeth."

"And its bit brain in its muckle shoulders like ithers we ken. Come awa' ben, laddie, an' lat's see the rest o' you."

Rab Fraser's sullen eyes went from her to his mistress where she sat by the fireside, her tartan plaid fallen loose off her boy's shoulders.

"Na, na," he said in his half-Gaelic, half-Doric way. "I will take a bite out here out of your way—an I get it."

Before he might draw back she had him by the collar and jerked inside the threshold, his head bumping the lintel.

"This is my hoose," she said, "and ye'll dae as ye're telt."

He looked at his mistress dumbly, and, for the first time, she laughed, a pleasant gurgle of laughter.

"You and I, Rab, are in a strange mad world of Irish and the women that own them."

"Noo than!" ordered Margaret. "Lift ye the skillet, Tadg Mor."

That was a welcome meal, but I forget what the viands were; beef or mutton fresh killed, with bannocks, almost certainly bannocks, for Margaret never failed to bake bannocks if we were camped near a mill. We were hungry, I know, and ate silently for a while, until Tadg Mor, remembering his Irish manners, began to make table-talk for us.

"Heard the news, Meg?"

"Ay have I. We'll be busy the heicht o' day, all of us. Will ye be lickit the morn?"

"Who is to lick us in all Scotland?"

"The men of Moray and of Ross," said Iseabal Rose.

"Moray and Ross and Kintail—or how is it that Ranald Ban puts it?—Loudon and Lawers and Lorn, it will be a great day whatever, if they stand to us."

"And if we be lickit, young lady," said Margaret, "the road to Lochloy will be an ill ane."

"I fear me so, but do you know, one grows used to fear."

"O'Cahan will keep the road open, as he said," I promised her, rising to my feet and reaching my cloak down from a deer's prong in the wall. "Whatever happens, there is a busy night in front of some of us, for the attack may come at dawn. While the camp-fires give us light, it might be well to see that our lines are open to our place in the Hardmuir. Margaret, you will have your women ready at peep of dawn, a hot meal cooked and a cold piece put aside for height of day. There is a broomy bank near the burn over the howe behind us that should make a first station, and we will go over it first thing in the morning. Come, Tadg Mor."

"Stay, Master Somers!" Iseabal rose also on her feet. "You are forgetting the plaid you won in exchange."

"So I am," said I reluctantly, "but I will not hold you to your bargain."

"A wager is a wager, and you have the best of it," said she, holding her cloak out to me.

That dark-green plaid with the red line was of sound, closely-woven wool, but not so weather-proof as my silk-lined Irish cloak. I knew that, but the exchange had to be made in good part.

And then Tadg Mor and I, with Black Rab at our heels, went out into the night, leaving our two young women to the obdurate ways women have.

CHAPTER V

THE BATTLE OF AULDEARN

I

The battle of Auldearn was fought on the ninth day of May in the year of 'forty-five, after a rainy night, and, though the forces engaged were not large, it is considered to be one of the greatest battles of that period, because of the new tactics Montrose employed. Before leaving Ireland, three years ago and near fifty years from that day, St Ruth, the French General of King James, questioned me at length about it, and I had to make a plan of the ground for him, and show him how Montrose hinged his army on its right wing under Colkitto, drew Sir John Hurry's attack at that point, and then, as with the clang of an iron door, swept the Covenanters off the field. St Ruth employed this very tactic at the fatal battle of Aughrim, but he was a jealous general and did not use the great Sarsfield as Montrose used Colkitto; and a cannon-ball lost him his victory and his head at the very moment he should have charged home with his cavalry. And that is why my eldest grandson is now serving a foreign king in Louis of France, and I am an exile here in Virginia.

I was already weary and sour-tempered before the fight started, and I was more weary when it was all over, but my temper had steadied by then. I had been

on my feet most of the night, and it a wet night, and
Iseabal Rose's plaid was sodden on my shoulders. I
had two hours' sleep before dawn, and then, with
Father MacBreck, our chaplain, Margaret Anderson
and Tadg Mor, established our first wounded station
at the rear of the Irish lines. It was in cold, wet, spirit-
sapping dawns like this that Margaret showed the great
heart in her. Then she was no longer fleering, but very
helpful and full of fine gaiety, and even tenderness.
She said no word of Iseabal Rose, nor did I.

While Margaret and the others went back to the
bothy to prepare some breakfast I went forward to
report to O'Cahan. His regiment, nearly six hundred
strong, were lining the woods immediately left of the
village below the slope of Kinsteary and screened by
the trees, so that Hurry should not see where our
strength lay.

The Irish were in a gay and laughing mood this
morning, and even the clansmen, usually dour before
battle, were not taking things too seriously. They were
confident, too confident to my sour mind—as confident
as the high gods. They were well fed, well equipped
at last, and well placed; and though Hurry had four
first-line regiments, five squadrons of Moray horse, and
all the fighting clans of Ross, still the odds were less
than two to one, which was no more than reasonable.
We were used to odds as to our daily meat.

The men had been in battle stations since dawn, and
it was now nine of the clock. No cooking fires were
allowed in the woods, but the women had cooked
behind the slope and brought up pots of meat and
brose, measures of new milk and oatmeal cakes. The
men, arms piled, headpieces and targes laid aside, and
corselets unlaced, were sitting about in groups among

the trees, careless of the damp ground and still dripping
leaves, eating busily and joking with the women.
Their good humour did not help to banish my sullen-
ness, and I was surly to O'Cahan's gay greeting when
I came upon him at the edge of the wood spooning his
breakfast out of a brose bowl. There was a hazel bush
growing in front of him and he could watch the open
ground through the leafage. That open ground was
little more than a quarter-mile wide, and the Cawdor
pony track wound across it between stony pastures and
small humplochs fresh with the young green of bracken.
Beyond it a wood of dark pine hid the town of Nairn,
but we knew that between the wood and Nairn
our fore-skirmishers were already in touch with the
Covenanters' advance-guard. No one would guess the
imminence of battle looking out across that empty
ground.

With O'Cahan at breakfast were Angus of Glengarry,
Black Pate Graham of Inchbrakie, and Owen Mac-
Andra MacPherson, captain of Clan Vuirich. A fifth
man was no longer there: the lovable Donald Oge
Farquharson of Clan Finlay, who had been foully slain
in a raid by Hurry's horse one night in Aberdeen a
few weeks before. These four officers were Montrose's
staff amongst the men of the Gael, and they kept the
Highlandmen and the Irish in close alliance, at least
on the field of battle. In camp and foray the two
branches of the Gael had their own bickerings and
horseplays and hurling matches, but in line of fight
they had a soldierly trust in each other and charged
home shoulder to shoulder. For instance, the usual
battle station of Clan Vuirich was between the regiments of O'Cahan and Seumas MacSorley of the Bann,
and often as not the clansmen were first into the

enemy's line. I do not belittle the qualities of the MacDonalds, the MacLeans, the Stuarts, the Robertsons of Clan Duncan, and others, when I hold that the Farquharsons of Clan Finlay of the Braes of Mar and the MacPhersons of Clan Vuirich of Badenoch were the most faithful, steadfast men in the Highland army. They were the first to join us in force in all Scotland, saved our throats from being cut by Clan Chattan and the Grants, and a remnant of them was still with us on the fatal brae of Philiphaugh.

"The first station all ready, O'Cahan," I saluted my colonel, "and our lines open to the Hardmuir."

"Good and better," said O'Cahan. "We are in order then. Sit in and put your hand in the skillet with us."

He laughed. "Man, Maurteen! You look as blue as your blue eye. You would think, to look at you, that you had buried most of us already."

"I might do that later in the day," said I, "if I have time."

"Has Hurry the beating of us, think you?" queried Glengarry.

"Will he ever have a better chance?" I queried back.

"True enough," agreed the half-Lowlander Graham.

"All the same," said the MacPherson equably, "we have the beating of him here about us this day—or any day. And then we will turn on Baillie and take our toll for Donald Oge."

A burst of men's and women's laughter at some broad jest came from the men's lines, and O'Cahan saw my hand jerk as it lifted a rib of mutton from the skillet.

"You do not like that, Maurteen?" he said quietly.

"I do not. Laugh in the morning and cry at noon.

There was not much laughter amongst us the morning of Tippermuir."

"*Dhia!* but there was not. I was afraid before and I have been afraid since, but that was the father of all fear." He slapped MacPherson's shoulder. "Do you mind, Owen?"

"I dream about it yet in a bad night," said Mac-Pherson.

"I dreamt about it last night," I said, and left them there.

All my dispositions for the wounded were made, and I had nothing to do now but wait. And waiting was not so easy, though I no longer carried arms in the line. I went back to my dressing-station on the banks of the burn, and talked for a while to Sorcha MacNeill. Margaret and the others had not yet returned, so, after a time, I followed the stream downwards to the back of the village. At the foot of the kirk-mound I came on a group of saddled horses held by Huntly horse-boys, and, on rounding the corner, I saw Montrose and some of the staff on the summit of the mound. The Kirk of Auldearn, a low whinstone building with narrow windows, stood on a sudden swell of ground close behind and overlooking the village street, and Colkitto's iron hinge was directly below it.

Margaret, Iseabal Rose, Father MacBreck, Tadg Mor and Black Rab Fraser had just finished eating as I bent head under the lintel.

"Ye are taking time to it on a busy morning," I grumbled at them.

"Lazy loon!" chided Margaret. "Ye dinna deserve the spoonfu' I kept warm for you in the pot. Sit in!"

"I broke fast with O'Cahan——"

"In that case," said Tadg Mor quickly, "Rab and

myself will put the last big spoonful on the top of the half-one that we got from her."

"Ay will ye," agreed Margaret, and she came and took the damp plaid off my shoulders, and spread it on a hassock before the fire.

"Your cloak was warm, Master Somers," Iseabal Rose told me. "I will lend it to you for the day while your plaid dries."

"Rain or shine I will need no cloak to-day," I said, "and you may see why."

She at any rate did not look weary this morning. Her darkling eyes were clear and the blood warm in her dusky cheeks.

"You slept, I think," I said.

"Your Margaret Anderson gave me her own pallet."

"Wha's Margaret Anderson?" said that girl crossly. "I'm my ain mistress in the hoose, and gang my ain gait ootside it."

"And where will that gait lead you, I wonder?" said the other smoothly, and closed her teeth on something further she had in mind to say.

"I think, my children," said Father MacBreck, "that we should go back to our posts now."

Margaret looked at the other woman. "Do you bide here, Mistress Rose?"

"Anywhere that I may be useful."

"Then you had better be wi' us. It will be safer—whaur no place is ower safe—if ye can stan' the sicht o' blood an' wounds."

"I have seen wounded men."

I had hoped that these two would have got to understand each other in the night, but, with regret, I noted that the strain was still between them. I do not know anything about the mental qualities of women, but I know that they do not get over dislikes as men do.

It was a fine, sharply-fresh morning outside, and the rain clouds had blown away before a veering of the breeze to the north. And, not for the first time, there came to me a hopeless kind of wondering that men should want to kill one another on a day like this; but after a time I felt that, deep down, most of them, like myself, did not want to kill anyone, but were driven to it by some cause or policy, or, indeed, by some cold-thinking power that was impersonal yet malignant.

Iseabal Rose touched my sleeve. "Who are those up there?"

"Our Captain-General and his officers."

"Which is the King's great man?"

"Can you not tell?" I wondered.

"Not from here. But does greatness shine out in any man? Can we go nearer?"

"Surely. He is an easy man to look at and speak to."

"I do not want to speak to anyone, but I would like to see a field stripped for battle—if it can be seen."

"You can see all there is to be seen. Come!"

We climbed the mound together between the leaning headstones of the village fathers, Tadg Mor and Black Rab behind us. Looking over my shoulder for Margaret I saw her halted and tapping the ground with her foot, her eyes down in some thought; then she threw her head and shoulders back and went hasting up the burnside after Father MacBreck.

2

We went round to the front of the kirk and looked about us. The kirk door was open and the two

MacBeth brothers, already stripped to the waist, leant against it. These fine clean bodies would be spattered red to the neck ere the day was done. Behind them in the porch some of the Keppoch women were plucking apart and fining a pile of peat-hag moss that we used for padding wounds. These two MacBeth brothers out of Mull were surgeons to the Duart MacLeans, and the ablest men of their trade in all Scotland. They could clean a festered wound and quell a fever better than any king's physician, and had secret simples of their own handed down from father to son since their forefather, MacBeth Finlaig, was King of Scotland in Danish times. That was the king that Will Shakespeare made a play about and strained the truth to make his drama. I gave the brothers good day, and the elder said to me:

"If the day is not hard on us here, Martin, I will send Fergus down to help you—if you need him."

Montrose and his group of officers were below us and to the right.

"I think I see your great man," whispered Iseabal Rose at my shoulder. "He is the smallest there—and the jauntiest."

"And the best."

Montrose was aye the gallant in his dress. He was now wearing a fluted steel corselet and thigh-pieces, but, as was his habit, he carried his plumed basnet in his hand, and the northern breeze had tossed finely his darkly-fair hair and brought the warm colour to his smoothly-brown cheeks.

"Bonny enough in plain company," remarked Iseabal Rose. "Is that your terrible half-Irish Colkitto—the tall man with the gashed cheek?"

"That is Nathaniel Gordon, captain of Huntly, and

the Gordons think he is as good a man as Colkitto any day."

"If he were as good," said she, "how much better would the Gordons think him?"

I looked down at her in wonder. Her face, below her faintly-waved dark hair, was young and clean, and there was no sardonic line yet bitten in the smooth darkness of it.

"You are not yet old," said I. "How come you to be so wise—and bitter?"

She shook her head so that the hair swung on her brow, and smiled at me a wistful smile that touched me strangely. "Not wise, and as for the other, that was the sour Rose blood speaking in me."

"And it could be that you are proud of that old blood too."

"That is the pity of it." She turned away from me to the scene in front of her. But almost at once her head was again over her shoulder. "But where are the armies in array? I see only a few men in the gardens down there."

And indeed to look over that empty peaceful spread of country between wood and wood no one might guess that in half an hour it would be a tangle of fighting men shouting and hacking at their deadly work. Our foot were hidden along the margin of the wood and our horse in the hollow of Kinsteary Park. The enemy was still out of sight over the ridge between us and Nairn, but the ridge was so low that we could see the towers and smoking chimneys of the town. Outside the bar, at the mouth of the Nairn River, the big ship we had seen on the previous evening was lying at anchor, sails furled; and so clear was the rain-washed air that we could see her crew clustered high up in the rigging. They were there to enjoy a peepy-show that few men had seen in such safety. Behind them the northern firth was as clear as bottle glass before a light, and small white horses ran and jerked before the whip of the northern breeze; and behind all, the great hills of the north were peacefully blue above the dark woods of Cromarty and Ross. A grand, fine, sunny spring morning, with the white clouds sailing, and, somehow, there was no weight of foreboding of the killing so soon to come.

I showed her where our lines lay and pointed out the strength of Colkitto's position below us and to the right. At the rear of the fenced village gardens a short slope ran down to a stream strong running after the rain but easily fordable. Beyond the stream was miry ground. Colkitto had broken down the side-fences of the gardens for ease of movement and had repaired the gaps of the tumble-down clay-and-stone wall at the rear with bushes and whins. The Royal Standard was fixed firmly on the summit of this wall, and it was so placed to lead Hurry to assume that here was our main strength. The right flank was guarded by the castle hillock with its stone circling wall.

It was a very strong defensive position, and Montrose had planned it all in two hours in the middle of the night. But would Colkitto be content to hold that defensive position until Montrose was ready to swing his iron door? Montrose knew Alasdair's impulsive nature, and that was why he was here now on the kirk-mound. He was doubtful if the raw Gordon levies with Colkitto would stand fire.

These young Gordons should not have been in the gardens at all. That was Colkitto's first mistake that morning. His own personal cohort of fighters, his bodyguard, the spearhead of many an onset, totalled about twelve score, mostly gentlemen of Ulster and the Isles, picked and fearless smiters, each equipped with breastplate and headpiece, targe, broadsword and two pistols. Their usual method of attack was to fire off one pistol in the face of the enemy and drive in with the broadsword. If they were compelled to fall back they kept the second pistol in reserve and locked their targes. They had never been broken or worsted in fight before Auldearn. Early that morning, because of some old friendship or pact between Clan Ranald and Clan Gordon, Colkitto, without consulting Montrose, had rashly exchanged one hundred of these veterans for three hundred Gordons from Strathbogie and the Bog-of-the-Winds. A good exchange, one might hold, for the Gordons were all swank lads and held themselves to be Cocks of the North; but in a generation of peace they had never seen the cold sheen of steel drawn for the kill, never heard the wicked whistle of a Highland arrow, the bark of an arquebus, the thunder of a culverin; and the very best of raw troops are subject to a sudden panic sometimes in their first battle. I could see that Montrose was anxious by the restless way he moved about, head forward and eyes searching the dispositions along the gardens.

"Look!" cried Iseabal Rose, and the beat of her heart was at last in her voice.

3

My own heart jumped too. At last the enemy was in sight. Outriders on the flank, the left wing of the covenanting army came over the swell of Kinudie brae less than half a mile away. A long thick line, a little uneven, five or six deep, the sun sparkling on its steel points. I looked at it under my hand.

"Kilted men!" I said. "The Northern clans— MacKenzies and Frasers."

"They are facing this way," she whispered.

"That is to be hoped."

"But why not swing round by the coast and come in behind your barricades?"

"Their backs to the sea! They have not forgotten Inverlochy." I touched her arm. "We had better go now."

"Is it not safe up here?"

"Safe enough if the front holds. No arrow will reach this far, though a spent ball from flintlock might. But my work——"

"Just a little while," she urged. "I am excited and frightened, but I want to see how men face each other."

"It will not be pleasant."

I looked at the advancing clansmen. A second body of men had appeared on their right, and though it was kilted too, I saw by the smooth dressing of its line that it was a regular regiment. I learned later that it was the first-line regiment of Lawers, one of the best in Scotland, and composed mostly of Campbell clansmen. The centre and right wing had not yet appeared and it was evident that Hurry was slanting his left to attack our right and outflank us, in which case my regiment would not be engaged for some time.

"You will not like this," I told her, taking her arm and leading her to a square-cut headstone four feet out of the ground. "There is your breastplate." I stood at her side, and Tadg Mor and Black Rab went to the kirkyard wall just below us. I noticed that the Fraser man had a scabbardless, rusted, two-handed claymore hanging from his left shoulder.

Sir John Hurry was a gallant reckless devil in his own life, and no Covenanter, but in war he was held to be skilful and not imprudent. His heavy-armed Lowland regulars could not manœuvre in the miry ground in front of the village, and so he manned his left wing with the light-moving Highland regiment and the active men of the North and Moray—MacKenzies, Frasers, Sutherlands, Forbeses, Findlaters, Roses, Chisholms, Hays, and a picked body of the MacRae bowmen from Kintail. The regular regiments of Buchanan, Loudon and Lothian made the centre against the Irish and the Highlandmen, and Drummond's horse were on the right wing.

But Seumas Graham of Montrose was an able man too, none abler, and he had imagination as well. He put himself in Hurry's place, and laid his lure in plain sight. That lure plainly said: "Here is a right wing, strongly placed, but weakly held. Come and take it!" And Hurry, looking over the ground, saw a reasonable chance. The chance was there beyond a doubt, and Montrose had to yield it as every great tactician must. Hurry would know from his spies that the Irish and Highland clans held the woods south of the village, and to attack such men across open ground and against the impetus of a down-slope charge was a risk he would hate to take; and his Moray horse under Drummond were not well trained. But if he could break through the right wing and turn the flank, there was every chance of driving Montrose's main force down into the open with the marshlands of the Nairn River to trap them.

There and then Hurry accepted Montrose's challenge,

threw his Highlandmen against Colkitto, and sloped back his centre and right. Colkitto, indeed, had much on his shoulders that morning. Already he had made one mistake and was to make another nearly fatal.

That battle began like all battles. The bark of an arquebus, and then a scattered barking, a shouting and piping growing nearer, the thunder from the Castle Hill of one of the culverins, the round ball of which could be seen hurtling out of the smoke-puff and falling short of the advancing line; a hard smatter of fire, the curving streak of arrows, slogan cries and gathering tunes lifting shrill and mad; and before one knew, the blended clamour of battle filling the air. That first thud, that first shout, that first shrill of the pipes strikes one as with a physical blow to the very heart, and one quivers with what is very near dismay; but the blended clamour not only deafens the ear but sets one in a new world, where one is dazed yet clear and has no longer a flesh shudder against steel or bullet. A haze of smoke began to drift down the field between the lines.

That first attack by the Covenant Highlandmen was finely delivered. They came sweeping in a good line, five deep, across the open, banners forward, pipes blowing, slogans pealing; and if the ground had been easier they might well have washed over the defenders. But the miry ground, the strong stream, the brief slope to the gardens slowed their impetus, and the manned wall brought them up short. It was touch and go for a long two minutes, and the fight heaved and swayed all along the wall. Some of the more active of the attackers actually flung themselves over the loose stones against the targes and died in the air. But the wall held firm after that critical two minutes, and they were critical. Colkitto's veterans fought coolly and very terribly, but they could not be everywhere, and the young Gordon soldiers had their one touch of panic; at every bark of shot and whiz of arrow they ducked their heads like boys at stone pelting, and their officers had to beat them with fist and sword-flat to keep them from scattering back to the apparent safety of the houses and the kirkyard. I had my hand on Iseabal Rose's shoulder to drag her away when the attack broke. Just in time the Gordon lads learned from the example of Colkitto's smiters that manning the wall was safer than anything else they might do; it gave them the advantage of the upper ground, and they saw how Colkitto's men held their targes slanting from shoulder over head against the MacRae arrows and gave the point downwards at men leaping for the wall. They gathered heart then like the sound men they were at bottom, struck lustily, and began to raise a shout or two of their own: "A Gordon! A Gordon!" "Strath-bogie!" "Remember James of Rhynie!" The attackers drew back from the wall at last, not because they were yet beaten, but to gather force and impetus for another rush.

Once again they came, but, the first attack having failed, there was less and less hope for any other. They hurled themselves against the wall in vain gallantry, their dead and wounded littered the brae-face, and again they fell sullenly back to the brink of the burn, while the defenders hastily reloaded pistols and flint-locks and arquebus. And now, too, the culverin from the Castle Hill began landing round-shot in the rear ranks. The Keppoch women were running down the mound past us to bring in the wounded.

Nat Gordon told me later that when Montrose saw

the steady, deadly defence made against the second attack he slapped his basnet against thigh-piece and cried out, "Well done, young Gordons! We have them now"; and was in the act of turning away to direct the next tactic of battle when Alasdair made his second and last mistake of the day.

Alasdair was an impetuous man and used to making onsets, not withstanding them. There was never in all the world a better man to lead a charge, but holding a stone wall was not in his mood. Not more than forty paces separated defenders and attackers, and at this juncture a big man of the Hays, a notable wielder of the broadsword, leaped in front of the line and flung a taunt in his great voice: "Cowards! come out and fight like men." And the taunt was taken up by the men behind and went thundering down the line. And then Hay walked three slow paces forward and clanged his targe. "Blade to blade, Alasdair *a cockagh*! Come out and fight me!"

That insult and challenge was more than Alasdair could stand. Impulsively he jerked a thorn bush out of an old doorway, leaped through, yelled his war-cry: "Gainsay who dare!" and charged down at Hay in great bounds. And like one man his own bodyguard, a hundred strong, leaped the wall and charged behind him. But the Gordon lads stayed where they were. They had a loving confidence in that defending wall; they had held it so finely and would keep on doing that, but it was beyond the power of their wills to force their shrinking young flesh to the sally beyond it. And I will not say they were wrong, for it is very possible that, if they had charged with Colkitto, the battle would have had a different ending.

It was then that Montrose left the mound. He left it

running, hair streaming, and thigh-pieces clanking, going in leaps down the slope, throwing himself on his horse and spurring. His staff clattered after. All but Nat Gordon. Gordon leaped the other way, over the kirkyard wall, his curses streaming out behind, and out into the gardens amongst his clansmen like a raging wind. But I hardly saw him, for the only man to watch was Alasdair.

And Alasdair was having his bad time. The first drive of his charge shocked the Covenanters back to the burn and into it, but he had not enough weight of numbers to break or drive them. One hundred men, no matter how impetuous, cannot drive a dozen times that number of fighting men in a killing humour. For a tense minute they strained against each other in a dead and deadly lock, and then the sheer weight of numbers lifted Colkitto's men backwards. And that looked to be the end. But it was then that that chosen hundred showed their quality. For they did not break. If they had broken, the enemy would have flooded over them and over the gardens. Instead, they fell back step by step, targes in line and pikes dunting on them, pistols spitting, broadswords shearing, men yelling, men falling. Alasdair himself did ten men's work. He slew Hay, some say by an underhand trick. That is not so. At the time Alasdair's broadsword was broken at the hilt, and he was warding off Hay's blows with his targe. It was then he said, "I will not deceive you. There is a man of mine at your back." Hay turned his head for one look, and Alasdair had time to snatch the sword that MacDavid of Ard-na-Cross reached him; and forthwith that blade shore through Hay's targe and shoulder. MacDavid died beneath the pikes.

Tadg Mor O'Kavanagh turned his face up to me, the flame of battle in his grey-blue eye, and his teeth bare under the strong hook of his nose.

"Alasdair needs us now," he cried, and leaped the kirkyard wall. Black Rab Fraser, tugging his sword over his shoulder with his two hands, tumbled after him. I caught Iseabal Rose by both shoulders and swung her round. "Run—run now!" I cried, and pushed her roughly towards the corner of the kirk. Then in turn I leaped the wall and down the brae.

My cowardly soul revolted against it, but I had to go. My foster-brother and I had an understanding—never put in so many words—that in danger where one went the other had to go, without question and without pause. The urge of that understanding was stronger than any cowardice. It was the thing that kept some manhood upright in me, and I had to hold by it.

My father's sword was back at the dressing-station and I was armed only with a black sgian, but there were swords to be had down there. Let me say at once that I did not need a sword that time. Alasdair and some seventy of his gentlemen won their way back to the gardens, and the Gordons, under the lash of their terrible Nathaniel, helped them nobly in the last difficult minute under the wall. The position was again secure, but near on thirty fine men were dead or wounded without need outside it.

The last man in was our Ranald Ban MacKinnon. Tall and strong, and with the lithe whip of a lance to him, he was as good a man as Alasdair that day. In camp he was light-headed, light-hearted, loose-tongued, a lovable, irritating youth, but in fight he was as steadfast as steel and as deadly. In the beginning I used to be afraid that Tadg Mor and he might come to blows, and I had heard men dispute as to which was the better man, but I soon got over my fears. They bickered often enough in camp, and played wicked tricks on each other, but when Ranald Ban was off on a ploy Tadg Mor was missing too, and, with drink taken, though Ranald Ban was inclined to take offence without being quarrelsome, nothing could disturb Tadg Mor's pleasant temper.

As I ran across the gardens Ranald Ban's back was in the doorway that Colkitto had charged through, and I could see his limber shoulders jerk and stiffen as the Campbell pikes dunted on his targe. And there Colkitto caught him by the belt and heaved him into safety. One over-keen pikeman, anxious for a final lunge, thrust head and shoulder inside the doorway, and I saw the terrific downward swing of Alasdair's blade. The man's head fell between Ranald's feet.

Ranald Ban turned to us, and I drew in my breath. The barb of an arrow and six inches of shaft stood out of one cheek and the feathered end stood out of the other, and his teeth were clenched on the wood. I leaped towards him, Alasdair caught him round the shoulders and thrust a strong thumb between his teeth, and I, breaking the arrow close to his cheek at the feathered end, jerked it smoothly from the wound.

Alasdair shook his bleeding thumb in the air and swore mightily. Ranald Ban had bitten it to the bone. "*Chreesta Tigearna!*" he roared. "There goes the first of my blood this day." Then he slapped me on the shoulder. "Good boy yourself, Maurteen! I knew you and Tadg Mor would be down to give us a hand." He thrust Ranald Ban into my arms. "Take him up to the MacBeth, and see if he has made a meal of his tongue." Alasdair was a rough warrior.

Ranald Ban looked at us with wild eyes, and for once had not a word to say. His lips were tight shut and a small trickle of blood ran down his chin. He was afraid to try his tongue, but he did not want to leave the field. He struggled in my arms till Tadg Mor came to his other side; and then we lifted him clear off his feet and rushed him up the mound to the kirk-yard. Fergus MacBeth met us at the wall and helped us over.

"I saw," said the surgeon. "Has he spoken?"

"Not as much as a whisper," said Tadg Mor in distress, "and how could he with his tongue in his paunch! Oh, wirra, wirra!" he lamented, "this will be the dull army now wanting his fine pleasant stories." Then he patted Ranald's shoulder. "But never you mind, my darling! Sure you have given tongue enough already to last you all your days."

Ranald Ban looked at him with eyes gone strangely wistful, and all the light of war quenched in them, but he kept his lips pressed tight and swallowed once.

In the kirk porch Fergus MacBeth faced him to the light and took hold of his chin.

"Let us have a look, *avic*! Open it—open it, I say! And if you bite me I will put my finger down your gullet. There! Fine—oh fine! But I do not want to jump in. Look, Maurteen!"

I had expected tongue and palate to be pierced and his teeth shattered; but there was scarcely a trace of blood in his mouth, and tongue, palate and teeth were whole.

"Like enough he had his mouth wide open and he yelling, 'Another for Hector!'" He chucked Ranald softly under the chin. "Say something, white Ranald,"

"Gug-gug!" said Ranald for a beginning.

"Ay surely!" said Tadg Mor. "That was your mother's black hen she got from the priest that used lay two eggs every day but Sunday. You told us that one often. Give us a new one this time."

"That bloody MacRae bastard!" said Ranald Ban.

"Now we have it!" said Tadg Mor.

"Did you see how I stood to them, Tadg Mor?" His words came in a rush now. "Did you see how I stemmed them and five pikes in my targe?"

"I did not," denied Tadg Mor firmly. "All you did was to walk backwards so fast that you cut a hole in the wind."

"I got one with my first pistol anyway, and if my sword had not stuck in its sheath I would not have got this wound. I dropped my targe hand to hold my belt and it was then the bowman got me. And *Dhia!* I missed him with the second bullet. A black MacRae in his red philabeg! Man, Maurteen! I thought I would never speak again!" And then he laughed, "I was like the man I knew in Mull that had a habit of swearing, and one day in a storm a thunderbolt hit his house and knocked half the chimney down; and he looked up the vent and started to curse, and at that a stone fell and broke his nose and four of his teeth. He did not speak a word for a week, and ever after that when he was minded to swear he used first of all look out of the door to see if there was a cloud anywhere in the sky."

"We will put a salve on that cut," said the surgeon, laughing, and drew Ranald Ban into the kirk.

"Oh, sad day!" cried Tadg Mor tauntingly after him. "The rest of the year now you will be telling us even on of all the men you killed at Auldearn—and most of them snug at home."

A deep long breath was drawn at my shoulder and I turned to look down into Iseabal Rose's dark eyes.

"It is terrible," she breathed. "How can you make fun of it?"

"I told you to run."

"I tried to, but my feet would not carry me. How can men be so terrible and so fierce—and still laugh and banter?"

"Do you know any better way of facing death day after day?"

"It is all wrong — wrong — wrong!" The colour was out of her face and her eyes were all black pupil. "I think that I am going to fall," she said quietly.

"You will be all right, girl dear," I whispered, my arm round her. "I should not have let you see."

She leant against me. "I did not know it would be like that—but it had to be—I did not know—and you went down into it."

"And kept well out of it too, as you saw."

I looked over her head at the field of battle. "It is time for us to go."

Hurry's centre had come out of the woods at last, three regiments in line. His left having failed its push he had to bring up his centre, and that fine disciplined column dressing its line along the margin of the wood looked massive enough to restore the balance of the day. And I knew that the swing of that balance would give me plenty to do. We hurried off the mound, the girl holding my arm, and Tadg Mor behind us. Black Rab Fraser had stayed behind in the gardens.

"If he gets the chance," said Tadg Mor, "he'll be off with the Frasers."

I did not see any more of that battle, but all the world knows about it. I am often sorry that I missed seeing the charge of the Huntly horse. When Montrose galloped back from the kirk-mound he knew that Alasdair was in a tight place, and that he himself had to strike home now or never. He drove in amongst his cavalry, shouting to young Lord Gordon: "It is a great shame on us that one man should always be winning the honours. There is great Alasdair beating the enemy before him. Let us charge at once and win our share of the glory!"

And the Huntly horse went yelling forward, knee to knee. Drummond's troopers shirked that charge, but some say that Drummond was a traitor to the Covenant. Whether he was or not, he was tried for it and shot at Inverness three days later. Young Lord Gordon wheeled his squadrons finely and drove sheer home on the flank of the Lothian regiment, crumpled it to pieces against the centre already suffering from the steady Irish fire, and at that opportune moment the Highland clans and the Irish regiments made the onset. The iron door had clanged and the fight was won. O'Cahan and Clan Vuirich, to relieve Alasdair, dressed their lines to strike the Campbell Lawers, who staggered and broke under the blow, rallied again, and died dourly on the field. The Covenanters' left wing, seeing the disaster to the centre, drew back from the village, slowly at first, and then at a run for the fords of Nairn; all but the MacRaes of Kintail, three hundred strong, who had a boast that they never ran from any field while the blue banner of Kintail floated. It was then that Alasdair gathered his remnant for vengeance, and the Strathbogie Gordons, lashed to fury by the terrible tongue of Nathaniel, sallied forth, no longer shy, no longer backward, only eager to kill or be killed killing. And once again the Gordons proved their title to "Cocks of the North." The banner of Kintail went down, rose again, and flew over the fight till the last circle of the MacRaes died about it. It is said that such a fury of fight possessed Nat Gordon that day that even Colkitto wondered. Young James of Rhynie, so ruthlessly slain by the Covenant, was well avenged.

The dour stand of the Lawers Campbells brought many wounded to my station, and I scarcely heard the noise of battle trailing away westward and dying down. In time there was only the groan of wounded men and the soothing voices of women, broken once and again by distant gun-peal. And soon the women-bearers had rest, for there were no more wounded. But I was busy until the sun went low.

Let me say here that I do not believe these old stories we are told of the numbers engaged and the enormity of the slaughter in the battles between Gael and Gael or between Gael and Sassenach. For example, it is written that at the great battle of Pinkie, that took place nearly a hundred years before Auldearn, the English killed twenty thousand Scots outright. To my mind, and judging by the number of clans and families engaged, there was not that number in the whole Scots army, and it is known that a goodly portion of the clans, fighting a strong rearguard action, got safely back over the Highland line. Most of the leaders and chiefs were slain, it is true, but some of them were too proud to run, and of the many that were not, some were too slow and not a few too fat.

The *seannachies* telling of the death of a chief added a few thousand of his clan to help the story.

The Gael is an impetuous rushing fighter, for that is his proven method, but he is no fanatic like the followers of Mahound. He knows that he has his women behind him, and that if he is badly broken his women and wounded will suffer. He fights his best for that reason, but seldom in the frenzied fashion that throws away his life recklessly. Two times out of three he breaks the enemy in that first fierce drive, but if the hedge of pikes is too strong for him he does not impale himself on it like a mad dog. He fights a delaying action as well as any man, sometimes gets the pikemen to break their line, and strikes in again to win the day; but if the day is lost he falls back, rallies, throws out a rearguard, while his fellows and women and wounded are streaming away in apparent dismay along planned lines of retreat. That is why we wonder how it is that the Gael, after suffering an apparently disastrous defeat, will come again the following fighting season gallant and strong as ever.

I will not say that the Gael is a much better fighting man than the men of other nations I have known, though on balance he might just be the greatest soldier of them all. My own race, the Sassenach, has its parts, and in the pitched field, calling for steadiness and resolution, is hard to beat. The Dutch I saw in Ireland with King William some years ago were even steadier than the Sassenach, but slower; the Frenchmen more virile, but not so lasting; but for a hard campaign my choice is the soldierly, rough, humoursome Gael, and, naturally enough, I lean toward the Irish branch of that breed.

The army of Montrose, for its size, was the best and

most deadly in fight in the whole world at that time. Having written that down I will leave it stand. A young meat-fed army, supremely tough and sinewy, inured to hardship, making incredible marches, and following and loving a great leader, no equal number of men—not even Cromwell's great army of the new model—could stand to them in the field, or be so deadly in fight. But even that deadly small army never slew its thousands. The reported slaying, it will be noticed, mostly took place in pursuit; but a man running for his life will nearly always run faster than the pursuer, who might beat him in the games field, and often as not is safe at home by the time the pursuer is back in camp boasting of the killing. We had many wounded at Auldearn but not more than a hundred killed, and half of these were on Colkitto's wing and not necessary. The Covenant losses were heaviest among the men of Kintail and the Lawers regiment that refused to retreat; three-fourth of the others made good their flight, and we met many of them again at Kilsyth. And at Kilsyth we slew them, for at Kilsyth we were filled with a cold and savage bitterness that no slaughter could assuage.

But I am leaping forward in my chronicle.

Iseabal Rose proved her mettle that afternoon of Auldearn amongst the wounded. She subdued her first whimsy against blood, and, despite my dissuasion, kirtled her wine-red dress, borrowed an apron, and bared her arms—creamy soft round arms that soon showed ugly red stains. Once only she went away by herself, and when she returned I saw by her colourless cheeks that she had been sick. She stood by Margaret and myself hour by hour, and her firm hands and cool quiet voice were soothing to hurt men.

When the work was done and all our men moved to the shelter of the village houses—having won the fight there was no need for our hidden place in the Hardmuir—we washed in the burn and moved down by the side of it to Margaret's bothy.

"*Roisin Dhuv*," said Tadg Mor—he insisted on calling her that pet name, the little dark rose, "if you will be staying in camp, I fear there is one I know will have to look to her post."

"One woman is enough in camp, I think, tall man," said she.

"Dinna be haverin', young leddy," Margaret said brusquely, "an' forty and mair o' them aboot ye a' the day."

"I—and your Martin Somers—saw only one."

"The battle of Auldearn is over long ago," I said angrily.

At that point Black Rab Fraser came trotting up the burnside, his mouth open like a spent hound's, and his black hair in wisps over his brow. His surliness had almost given way to a grin, and he was more nearly in good humour than I thought he could be. His claymore was gripped in his oxter, and the rust streaks had been rubbed away.

"Where were you, Black Rab? We needed you here," his mistress asked sternly.

"West a bittock," he panted.

"I thought you were making off with your rogues of Frasers," said Tadg Mor.

"Na, na! Them were the red Lovat Frasers, and no kin o' mine. When I lookit ower the dyke down below I saw two men of the Findlaters o' Easter Ross—a piper and his brother—that misused me once over the sale of a stot at Geddes market. 'Here's for ye!' says I, and ower the dyke with me in front of the Gordons. An' it was hot work, I'm tellin' ye. I got one on the haugh of Ardersier, but the piper lad won away in a cobble into deep water off the Chanonry. Ah weel! I'll have him for another day."

"If Hugheon Rose does not come up with you first," said his mistress, and at that name the man at once grew surly and cowed. That sudden change showed me clearer than anything she had said that her father was a wicked tyrant.

"He would show me no mercy, I ken," his voice growled.

"My poor Rab!" said she, relenting. "You and I are in one boat."

And that was the end of that bloody day.

CHAPTER VI

LOCHLOY AT LAST

I

It was the afternoon of the Monday following the battle that we took Iseabal Rose down to the port of Lochloy. We could not do it earlier because of our wounded, and we had to do it then because Montrose decided not to lay siege to Inverness that time, but to march back at once through Forres and Elgin and establish touch with the second Covenant army under Baillie.

We had a good many wounded, mostly with pike and sword, but the men of the Gael at that time thought little of clean wounds given by steel. We half-surgeons were used to wash the wound out with sour wine, or even triple-run spirit if the hurt went deep, bandage it with a dry dressing of peat-hag moss and trust to nature and clean blood. Bullet wounds our fighting men did not like, and that is why they were inclined to be a little unsteady facing powder and ball. The bullet bit deep and stayed in the festering wound. There it was that the MacBeth surgeons showed their skill. With pointed, hooked and pincered small instruments of their own forging they were enabled to probe the wound and extract the bullet; and their salves and simples saved many a good man in the after-fever.

These clean-blooded, hill-bred fighters had a wonderful power of healing and recovery. I have seen them on their feet the third day after a wound that would kill most townsmen and lay any other men on their backs for a fortnight. Thus on the third day after Auldearn the greater portion of our wounded could march with their share of help from the women, and this help they often enough decried unless the loss of blood made them stagger. The few men hard hit we carried on stretchers, sometimes between ponies.

The little company that convoyed Iseabal Rose to Lochloy consisted of Ranald Ban MacKinnon, Black Rab Fraser and myself. Margaret Anderson came too, but she made Tadg Mor stay behind to watch two of our men in a fever.

"I maun see Uncle Alick ae day or anither," said she carelessly.

"You will not stay with him?" I put to her, showing some anxiety.

She looked at me. "What for no?"

"The Kirk has already reached a long arm to Lochloy searching for you."

"Ay would they. But how did ye ken?"

"I ken. Is your uncle a Covenanter?"

"He mightna be, but the Kirk has the power. In his young days he was a wild ane, and neither to haud nor to bind."

"In that case," said I, "he will now be the devil's own Covenanter."

"I will see him onywey." She threw her proud head in the air. "An' he can take a keek at me to see how ill ye gangrels hae used me."

"He might recall," I warned her, "that a certain

woman was resplendent in scarlet and bedizened with jewels."

"Ye'll be twa fine Covenanters thegither," she taunted me.

Ranald Ban's pierced cheeks hardly incommoded him at all, but perhaps the little heat in his blood made him more light-headed than usual. He insisted on coming. His jaws were bandaged, and surgeon MacBeth, in order to keep them steady, made him clamp his teeth on a kippen of peeled hazel. But he would keep on chewing it and talking busily out at the side of it.

Lochloy was not more than two miles across country, and we went there on foot over a low drum of arable land that on the far side sloped slowly to a shallow sandy beach. All that low countryside was sand-blown, and away to the east a great dune shone yellow in the sun above a low dark wood of fir. The hamlet of Maviston of Lochloy consisted of two score or so of stone and thatched houses scattered at all angles above the shore of a brackish tidal loch opening to the sea through sand-banks. A long low promontory, grown with bent-grass, jutted across the mouth of the inlet to hold off the beat of the northern seas, and so made the deep water of the basin a safe anchorage in all states of weather and tide.

Some five or six half-decked boats were beached on the sloping shore of clean sand, and the tide, half made, was lapping about their heavy rudders. Here and there a jelly-fish was pulsing in the clear green water.

"He-oro!" cried Ranald Ban between his teeth, looking out across the sparkle of the sea at the high portals of Cromarty, "it makes me homesick for the green waters of Mull and the white beaches of Iona."

Anchored a couple of cable-lengths off shore was a good-sized black vessel of two masts. I was not sailor-man enough to notice that its spars were bare and no furled sails on its yards.

"There is your Edinburgh boat, Iseabal Rose," I told her. "We are in good time."

The only soul in sight was an old bearded fisherman staunching a cobble above high-water mark. After one sour look over his shoulder at us, as we approached, he went on working tow and a brown resinous sub-stance into a crack in the planking.

"There is a hope in him," whispered Ranald Ban, "that he is old enough not to be worth the prick of sgian."

"God bless the work, boatman," I addressed him in the English tongue. "Could you be telling us where one Alexander Anderson lives in this place?"

"There be mony o' that name in this place," he replied coldly, and went on poking with his pointed stick.

"This one is Alick Anderson the shipmaster."

"Hoo wid I ken?"

"You mean you will not tell?"

"I wad tell ye naething," said he stubbornly, "for I micht be blamed for it and yer work done."

I looked at Ranald Ban, and Ranald laughed softly. "He is a Covenanter, this young fellow," said he.

"I hae my ain religion," said the old fellow dourly.

"And it a stiff-necked one," added Ranald Ban, and went on speaking carefully in English, his hazel stick like an Indian pipe-stem in his teeth, and a sus-piciously silky tone to his voice. "But indeed and indeed you pay us the great compliment, old man of boats, for you knowingly take shelter behind your old years, and you knowing that my sgian will not itch your ribs and your memory in the eyes of the ladies. If you would be a young fellow now you would go trotting the road in front of us, and if you would not trot, it is myself would make you trot. We will be doing you no harm surely, but if your memory does not come back to you in two hops and a jump we will be kicking two or, maybe, three holes in this fine black boateen of yours. Are you listening, father?"

I looked down at Ranald Ban's feet. He was wearing the soft raw-hide Highland brogues, not made for kicking holes. But I stepped forward and placed my shod horseman's boot on the gunwale.

"Where does Alick Anderson the shipmaster live?" I questioned.

"Take your time to it, man of boats," Ranald Ban advised him.

The old fellow straightened up then. "Ye wad dae Aelick a hurt?"

"We will be hurting no one this day in this place, unless it be this bit of a boat of yours——"

"Ah weel!" said the old man resignedly. "I hae done a' I could. The man ye want bides in the muckle hoose at the end of the street—a thackit hoose that shouldna be thackit. Ye'll ken it."

We left him standing there glowering after us, and if his eye carried the evil a blight might well have fallen on us.

"You would not hurt the poor man's boat?" Iseabal Rose looked up at me.

"Yon auld fool kent fine he would," Margaret answered for me.

133

Word may have gone among the houses that the Montrose scourge and some of its loose women were down on the fisher town, for no one moved out of doors and only women's eyes keeked at us through the bottle-glass panes. Some of the men would be at the fishing doubtless, and some of the younger ones in Sir John Hurry's army, and now getting their wind back at the safe side of Inverness. Not many would be dead, for the men of Nairn had made a fine run for it early in the day.

At the far end of the hamlet we came on a good-sized stone house of two storeys standing by itself, with a walled garden behind it. It carried a thick coat of bent-grass thatch, and Ranald Ban laughed when he saw it.

"The old fellow was right," he said. "This is it. Never before have I seen a thatched house with two floors to it."

The shipmaster must have seen us coming, for as we faced in to the house the door opened and he stepped out on the broad white-chalked door-tread. A tall, upright figure of a man in seaman's blue, well on in years but not old, and at the first glance I knew that he was our Margaret's uncle. He had the same mould of face, the same strength of cheek-bone, the same grey eyes, but his hair and his spade beard were not lint-white but snow-white. He stood up straight and looked us over, his glance flashing past his niece to rest on Iseabal Rose.

"My duty to you, Mistress Rose," said he, bowing briefly.

"I am come to see you, Master Alick," said she.

"And in strange company, young lady." His voice had Margaret's very quirk, though the Doric *blas* and way of speech were not so noticeable. His eyes came back and rested on his niece, and a light came in them that I knew. "I ken you, my lass. You are in strange company too."

"It is the company of my ain choice, uncle," said Margaret, quietly for her.

"Prood of it then?"

"I am. It is the finest company in a' the world."

Her voice had a thrill to it that time; her head was thrown up, her eyes flashing into his, and there was a spot of bright colour in her cheeks.

"It hasna shamed you anyway——"

"Waur shamed would I be bedmate to Andra Cant," she stopped him.

"Let's no' talk o' bedmates, my girl." He lifted a shoulder. "I can see for myself they have taken good care o' you and happit you well—if that's ony sign o' virtue." There was a softening about his firm mouth that hinted a humoursome mind behind his stern front. That set him in a new light for me.

"Master Anderson," said I, "I would ask you to be very careful worded in the things you hint to this lady."

"She is my niece, young man."

"You will be worthy of her then, I do hope."

"My sirs!" said he in half-mock wonder. "Dinna tell me you are one o' the finest company in a' the world. Was it she gave you that bonny black e'e?"

"The ear is her favourite target," said I.

"Hoots, ye foolish men!" cried Margaret disdainfully. "Aye at the quirkin'. Uncle Alick, this is Surgeon Martin Somers of O'Cahan's Irish regiment, and this is Ranald Ban MacKinnon of Clan Ranald."

"Now we ken. I hae heard Brodie of Brodie speak

his mind of O'Cahan's Irish, and the three or four times they prostrated him house and lands." He smiled at Ranald Ban. "And as for Clan Ranald, all Scotland has heard Clan Ranald wonder at the greatness of that clan."

"Man, oh, man!" said Ranald Ban. "I feel at home with you already, and I listening to your niece the better part of a year."

"Mistress Rose has business wi' you, uncle," Margaret cut in. "If you would deal wi' that, ye micht then hae time to turn your fleerin' tongue on me and my frien's."

"Business, Mistress Iseabal! That's another thing." And he bowed to our dark lady. "Will you ladies—and gentlemen—come ben the house."

Iseabal Rose, who had listened silently to this joust of tongues, spoke up. "No need to trouble you that far, Master Alick."

But he was firm. "Na, na! I wouldna have it said I kept one o' my ain blood on the cauld side of the door. You will come ben to please me."

We went inside behind the ladies, but Black Rab Fraser turned away and moved down towards the beach, swinging his mistress's satchel. Ranald Ban whispered in my ear:

"I knew fine Meg came of sound stock. I often said it——"

"And other things as well."

"Eist! only fun between friends."

Our host led us into a wide room with a low-beamed ceiling, a carved mantelpiece, and dark carved oaken furniture that must have come by sea out of Edinburgh. He opened a press and placed two odd-shaped wicker-covered bottles, a brown jar and some big crystal

glasses on the table; and at his call a serving-woman
—he was widowed and childless—came with a dish of
cakes.

"Sit ye!" he invited. "This is of the dry grapes
of the Garonne, and the ladies need not fear it; and
in the joog ye have a triple brandy-wine of a neater
flavour than our Highland spirit."

He served the ladies and, before I might halt his
hand, filled my glass with a rich amber spirit. At
that time, probably due to the strange American blood
in me, strong liquor went to my head over quickly;
and so I was very cautious supping that powerful spirit
that had in it a flavour of grapes and sun and dry sand.
And as I sipped I noticed how the shipmaster's glance
could not keep away from his niece Margaret. The
lustre of her eyes and the linten of her hair lit up that
dark room. She would be at home in a house like this.
That was the thought in his mind and in mine.

Iseabal Rose came to her business without delay.

"Master Anderson," said she, "your friend John
Balfour, the minister of Ardclach, sent me down in
charge of these gentlemen to take passage with you
to Edinburgh."

"Then I know they are gentlemen," said he. "But
Edinbro, Mistress Iseabal?"

"Edinbro it is."

"But have ye no' heard? The plague has struck
Edinbro and the port o' Leith is shut to shipping—
these two months."

"Do you not sail then?" her voice remained quiet.

"Not to Edinbro. That canna be."

And that was that. Reports, indeed, had reached
us that the terrible plague was in the Lowlands as
far north as the links of Forth; and that was one of

the reasons that kept our army behind the Highland line.

"Edinbro is hard come by," added the shipmaster, "and the dead lyin' unburied in the narrow wynds o't."

Iseabal Rose turned to me, her eyes dark and wide, and her voice gathered that strange husky prophetic tone.

"I knew it in my bones, Martin Somers. I knew I was setting out on a strange adventure when I rode behind you over Lethen Bar."

But I turned to the shipmaster. "Where do you sail then?"

His hand was in his beard, his smile almost shame-faced.

"Just a fancy I had sin' I was a loon. All my days I hae been ploughin' back and forth to Leith, and two or three times to Kingston-upon-Hull, and once to London Port, but I aye had the notion to sail north-about on a voyage of my ain."

"To what port?"

"A long-off one." He was a trace eager now. "But there would be no loss in it that I can forecast. Drink up, gentlemen! Ye see, I could load a half-cargo of wool hereabouts, and pick up a puckle more down the west side, and a wheen o' hides and salt and ale out of Dublin, an' a bolt or two of broadcloth at mouth of Avon in Bristol, and then—and here's my fancy—face the seas of Biscay for the port of Bordeaux and a barter for a cargo of Garonne wine, same as that. I could make my money out o't in London, and in Edinbro too if the plague abates—as well it might by that time."

"When would you sail?"

"Ah weel! There's the rub. Facing yon seas the *Moray Quoine* calls for a new suit o' canvas and rigging. Not before the fall of the year at the earliest."

There was no more to be said. Iseabal Rose could not make Edinburgh by sea. She sat, eyes downcast and the middle finger of one hand thoughtfully tapping on the table. And as if in answer to that tapping came a loud knocking on the door. We were silent, listening to the serving-woman shuffling along the passage, and then came the depth of a voice that I knew.

"That is my foster-brother, Tadg Mor O'Kavanagh," I told them. "Will you pardon me?"

And I went out to find the serving-woman holding the door against Tadg Mor, with Black Rab Fraser behind him.

"A word in your ear, Maurteen," he said, short of breath after hurry, and drew me out into the roadway. Black Rab sat down on the white step and waited.

"Manus O'Cahan sent me," began Tadg Mor, "and here is his message. A man has come into camp looking for his daughter"—he set a thumb towards the house—"one Hugh Rose of Belivat, where we were two nights ago."

"That is she," I agreed. "He brought his courage with him."

"And ten men to join Montrose, and a friend with twenty as well. And there is the point, brother. Seumas Graham is not like to offend a man of Nairn friendly to his King's cause. He has been asking for you and Ranald Ban, and for me too; and Manus slipped me off to warn ye. We will have to attend at the house of Boath this evening."

"Things are getting worse as they go," I said.

139

"Mistress Rose was to sail in that boat for Edinburgh, but it is not sailing at all now."

"And the man Rose will get back his daughter?"

"I could not tell you that yet. Stay where you are."

And I went back into the house.

"Master Anderson," said I, "our thanks for your hospitality, the first offered us kindly under a Scots roof-tree."

"We'll no' be sayin' where the blame might lie," said he.

I looked at Margaret then, but her eyes for the first time avoided mine. "It is time for us to go," I said in a loud voice.

"Man, man!" protested our host, "your glass is full. Wasna the liquor to your taste?"

"A very great liquor," said I, having learnt some courtesy in Ireland—sometimes to my hurt, as now. "Good health with you and all under your roof." And I tossed off my drink, and it burned its way deeper than I thought I had stomach to hold it.

The uncle was looking at his niece now.

"Must you be going so soon, my lassie?" he put to her quietly.

"Would you bid me stay, uncle?" Quiet she was too.

"By the Lord, an' I would!" His voice and his eyes flared like her very own. "For it is mostly my blame that you are where you are. It was my thrawnness in single ways that held me from bringing you out o' Aberdeen when your mother married the second time. You are my ain blood, and I dinna mind anything that has befallen you."

"Nothing has befallen me," said she proudly.

"I will take your word for that." Then he struck his hands together and shook his massive head like a strong man helpless against something stronger. "It canna be, my quoine! The Kirk has a hand out for you already, and Brodie of Brodie would ken you were wi' me by the morn's morn. A kindly man in his heart, but hard thirled to the Kirk, and with him it would be Aberdeen for you—and you'll ken what that means. Na, na! my bairn. Guid kens I may be wrong, but you maun bide where you are till the times do alter—if alter they will."

"It is we will alter them," said Ranald Ban, remembering the song Tadg Mor was ever singing. "Listen you! Margaret Anderson will ride a white horse into Aberdeen, two thousand and three thousand and five thousand men of the Gael at her back—like Joan of France."

"Laddie, laddie!" said the old man. "This is cauld Scotland and north-about is sunny France. But we can aye hae our dreams." And then he faced Margaret and placed his hands gently on her shoulders. "Wha kens? If you are not too far away an' the will with you, mind that the *Moray Quoine* sails this year. Look you! I will make it the last week of October. Sunny France is south awa', and we hae naething to hold our bones in cold Lochloy. Will you mind?"

"I will mind weel, Uncle Alick." And the two looked into each other's eyes, not heeding us. And then the girl's eyes lowered.

He shook his head again. "Do I see another dream ahin' your e'en, lassie? Weel, weel! The Lord keep you!"

2

Alick Anderson stood at his door and watched us go up the sandy way, but not for long. Margaret went with downcast head and did not look back. I did, but the door was shut then, and it had been shut softly, as a sad man would shut it.

At the end of the houses where the made road split into two tracks, one Nairnwards and the other inland towards Auldearn, Iseabal Rose came to a halt.

"We part here, my friends," said she, low and even.

I looked at her, my mouth open. Like enough it was the strong spirit fresh-buzzing in my head that made me forget that this was the end of her road in our company.

"We part here?" I repeated.

"This is Lochloy, and your duty done. It is only for me now to thank you for your great courtesy."

"You stay in this place?"

"I am not sure where I shall stay, but that is my own poor concern."

"I would not agree with you as far as that," I protested, feeling full of clear reason, "for it might be held that our duty did not finish until you were safe aboard a boat for Edinburgh. This question, as I see it, has to be considered carefully."

"Ranald Ban MacKinnon!" roared Tadg Mor. "Did you let Martin Somers drink usgebaugh?"

"A whole mutchkin of the finest, warmest liquor this side of the Sound of Mull—brandy-wine of France— and he poured it down so quick that I heard it cry clink at the pit of his stomach."

Tadg Mor looked at me with a resentful eye. "'Stay there,' says you, and in with you to your drink, and me with my tongue stuck to my palate."

"Drink softens you, brother," I told him.

"I left you in charge of the wounded, Tadg Mor," Margaret reprimanded him coldly.

"I know—I know." And then he laughed resignedly and turned to Ranald Ban. "Let us give Maurteen his head for a small bit, Ranald boy."

"We must," the other agreed, "or here we will be and the rearguard crossing ford o' Spey."

"Ye talk too much," I stopped them, and put my hand on Iseabal Rose's arm. "This young woman, whose concern it is, has yet said nothing. She is in a narrow place this day, and that is the thing we have to consider. Let us sit yonder."

There was a small hollow in the sand by the side of the track with tussocks of bent-grass crowning the lip of it. There we sat in a circle, all but Black Rab, who knelt on one knee behind his mistress's shoulder. Our heels scooped a rest in the sand, and Ranald Ban winced as the sharp-edged grass pricked his brown legs below the kilt. Anyone seeing us from the hamlet might wonder what evil we were planning.

"Ranald Ban," I began, my head clear as well-water, "I and you and Tadg Mor will leave the ladies out of this, for they are not accustomed to use reason in difficult places. Tell me, is there any bright thought in your mind that might help to resolve this lady's difficulty?"

"I take it," said Ranald Ban, humouring me, "that this lady's difficulty is that she does not want to go back to her home or to that place you took her out of so nice and handy."

"That is my difficulty," she agreed in her equable way. "I will not go back unless I have to."

"Are you sure that that is your mind?" I put to her.

"It is the only thing that I am sure of in all the world at this minute."

Ranald Ban chewed at his hazel for a space and

looked sideways at her. "I do not know what the lady fears," said he.

"I will not hide my fears from you," she told him, meeting his eyes fairly. "I am afraid of my father, and I am afraid of the man he would force me to marry."

He looked at her thoughtfully and, suddenly, it was as if only now he was looking at her for the first time. Maybe the drink was buzzing in his head too, or, it could be, that a small fever was working in his blood from his wound, but all at once he had a new vision of this bonny dark young woman, the soft lovely duskiness of her face, and that strange quietness that hinted an inner force, a secret fire. Outside the white bandage that Margaret had put on fresh that morning the blood came flushing to his cheek-bones, and a vibrant note came into his voice.

"While you are in this company, dark rose," said he, "you need not fear any man."

She did not make any answer to that. She was watching her small clenched hand trying to hold its full of the dry fine sand, but the sand kept trickling from the heel of her fist—like youth, joy, life that will not be held.

"Well done, Ranald Ban!" I said. "You have brought us to the very heart of our difficulty." I turned to my foster-brother. "You will tell us what you know, Tadg Mor."

"It is soon told," said Tadg Mor. "*Roisin Dhuv*, your father is below in Auldearn looking for you, and he has the ear of Seumas Graham of Montrose."

She did not flinch, eye or voice, but there was a pause before she spoke. "Will Montrose listen?"

"Why not he, with your father and a friend bringing in thirty men to fight for his King?"

144

"A friend?" Her voice snapped for the first time.

"A man of the Dunbars," Tadg Mor told her. "A gallant tall devil, with hair like my own and hands on him to break a stag's back."

She turned to me. "That is the man. What will Montrose do?"

"What I would do in his place," I told her frankly. "Hand you over to your father for a vapourish young woman with foolish notions, and, like as not, get his own chaplain to marry you off out of hand to cure your whimsies."

"You are frank, indeed," said she.

"And the only way to be in this gap of danger. That man Dunbar wants you."

"This is the end of the road then," said Iseabal Rose, opening her hand out of which all the sand had drained, and her eyes went out over the serenity of the sea and of the mountains. "I am only a woman and I may not keep my soul and my body clean. I would that I were drowned deep in that green sea." Her voice struck like a slow bell.

Ranald Ban MacKinnon spoke up then. "There is a place I have in my mind, dark rose, where no fear would touch you."

"What place is that, fair man?"

He did not answer her directly nor did his eyes lift from the sand between his heels. "We brought you out of prison at your own word, and our safe conduct still holds. I am of Clan Ranald, and what Clan Ranald puts its hand to Clan Ranald likes to finish. A small escort through Badenoch and Lochaber, down Loch Linnhe by water, and in five days one would be under Ben More in Mull looking across at the white beaches of Iona. My father, Ailin, has a strong house in that place, and a hand of welcome, and there no fear would touch you."

He looked quickly at her and down again, and she looked for a time at his flaxen downbent head. And then she said, slowly moving her head:

"Alas! Fear I cannot escape. The fear I would have in that place is the fear of doing a gallant gentleman a hurt I could not salve."

"I do not know what the lady means," said Ranald Ban.

"I know," said Margaret Anderson. "Mistress Rose, is there no place at all where you could bide in safety till Edinbro opens its gates?"

"There is a place might serve for a month or two if I could get at it. I have an uncle who is a dominie in the King's schools at Aberdeen: my father's brother, a strong Covenanter and no friend to the wild Hugh Rose."

"The road to Aberdeen will be open," said Tadg Mor, "and we after settling with General Baillie next week."

"Meantime we have to face her father in camp," I reminded him.

"I have a dirk," growled Black Rab Fraser.

"That is a road too," I agreed.

Iseabal Rose opened her hands to us. "Friends, friends, why do I trouble ye? There is no road to safety. Let you and I go our own roads to death."

"I like you fine," I told her then. "There is in you the quality of a man, for your own integrity is dear to you. Holding by that, would you face the scandal of tongues?"

"I will face anything but the danger of falling weak and in love with baseness, for there is bad blood in me."

146

"That being so, there is one way you can be safe in camp until it is safe for you to leave it for Aberdeen or Edinburgh."

"Or Mull of the mountains," added Ranald Ban.

"Mull surely," I agreed.

"Is there that way?" Her eyes were considering me steadily.

"There is," I said, "and if you will come with me I will tell you what it is."

I was on my feet and my hand out to her. She put hers in mine, and it was dry and very cold; and I knew then that there was fear in the marrow of her bones, notwithstanding that she faced fate so steadfastly.

"Come you too, Margaret Anderson," I ordered.

"Go on, girl," urged Tadg Mor on the hesitating Margaret. "He has his finger on the snarl."

"He's neither to haud nor to bin', drink in him," she protested on her feet. "On with ye then."

I strode across the hillocks of bent-grass, and the two girls followed at my heels. My head was light, yet steady, and my feet were steady too, but that sudden big drink of brandy-wine was curling the devil in it through all my blood. I went on striding, care-less of how far I went till Margaret called out to me:

"Would you hae us swim for't?"

I halted then on a sand-bank crowning the shingle of the shore, and the wavelets broke in white and ran and soughed to themselves in front of me. The girls came at my back and I faced round on them, the tall, fair, lissome one, and the small dark one whose lines flowed just as subtly.

"Haver awa' now," said Margaret. "Are ye gone daft?"

"I am," said I, "and I will be sorry for myself to-morrow morning. But do not make me angry, Margaret Anderson, for you have been a great trouble on me since the day I saw you sit in your shift, and here is another one now with her trouble on my shoulders. God, but I do not like women!"

"I ken that fine," said Margaret. "But if I am a trouble to you I am nane sorry."

"You dislike us because you are afraid," said Iseabal Rose.

"That is true," I agreed, "however you found it out."

"How is it that my trouble is on your shoulders?"

"Because at this juncture I am the only man you can trust and keep your integrity in your own hands."

"Do you tell me that?" she said a little derisively. "And yet you dislike me?"

"I tell you that I dislike you so that my motives shall not be in doubt."

"Yet I may doubt them."

"You may, but if ever you do doubt them you will have cause to be sorry for yourself. Listen now! Your only safe place for the time is in O'Cahan's regiment."

"With my father and Walter Dunbar having the ear of Montrose?"

"Even so. If you are bold enough to go down and say, 'I am a woman of the regiment, here of my own will with Martin Somers,' not even Montrose himself dare put a finger on you. That is the law and the custom of the Gael. But, mark this, to win to that safety you will have to throw your good name to the winds—everything, everything but your own integrity. You will have to be my woman in the camp. That is what I have to tell you."

"Your woman in the camp?" Her voice was slow and her eyes steady on mine. "What does that mean?"

"Nothing that you do not want it to mean. Margaret Anderson will tell you what it means."

"Will Margaret Anderson tell me that?"

"Margaret Anderson has no need to tell anything," said that woman briskly.

"Whatever that means," said the other.

"Think well, Iseabal Rose," I warned her. "The price of safety is high. You can be your own woman —if you wish—and you can leave camp when you wish, but you will be of very ill repute amongst women that men call honest."

"You put things clearly," said she, and she turned her back to me, her head up and her shoulders braced. Margaret Anderson turned away too and looked along the shore towards her uncle's house. And I waited, looking over the dark one's head at the slow lift of the green uplands into the curving brown moors of Cawdor. But in a little while I grew impatient and spoke—with bitterness, I fear.

"It is hard for you, dark lady, *mo roisin dhuv*, my little dark rose. You are a lady of blood and, in the bit, your good name is more precious to you than any inner virtue. Go you home then to your father's house and your red man's bed."

"There you are wrong, surly Sassenach," she said, without turning her head. "My feet are on the road and I will walk it to the end. I am now a woman of the camp in O'Cahan's regiment—but my soul is my own."

And that fine small lady went away from us through the humplochs of sand, my Irish cloak trailing behind her across the leaning bent-grass noble as a queen's robe. Margaret Anderson, without looking at me, followed her, but Margaret's head was down, and her feet no longer sure amongst the tussocks. I stayed behind for a while staring out over the restless green of the sea, wondering why destiny, in its own obdurate way, was using me as a finger in the game. But, though my back was turned, I was watching Margaret Anderson's downcast head, and my heart was troubled.

I went back to the others then. "Come we down to Auldearn."

"All of us?" queried Ranald Ban.

"All of us. And look you, Ranald Ban! I will not ask you to keep your tongue quiet behind your hazel kippen, for that is beyond your power and mine, but I will ask you to follow my lead in any talk we have with Montrose."

"That is right, Ranald boy," urged Tadg Mor. "He has loosed the snarl, and we will be seeing it in our own time."

"Not a word at all will I let out of me," said Ranald Ban.

When we had gone a hundred paces or so Tadg Mor held my shoulder, and I looked behind to see that Margaret was not following us. She was facing the other way, her head still down, and one foot tapping the ground, a habit of hers in a mood of perplexity. Tadg Mor and I went back to her.

"What is it, girl?" Tadg Mor growled gently.

"Naething," said she, without looking up. "I was just thinking I was ower short in the temper with Uncle Alick."

"What else, and you in your health?"

"But I jaloused that he liked me."

"And don't I like you?"

150

"Hoots! He would like me fine to stay ae nicht under his roof."

"One night," said I. "That is reasonable. You will be safe enough for one night. We march to-morrow."

She looked up at me then, a warm flash in her grey eyes. "Ae nicht or twa nichts, or three nichts! What is that to you, my fine gentleman?"

"There is our wounded," said I soberly.

"And there is your Iseabal Rose wi' her bonny fine hands, and she a fine lady. I am only a puir lass o' Aberdeen."

And then she turned on her heel, swung her flaxen plaits at us, and marched off towards the hamlet.

"Let her go!" I stopped Tadg Mor, my hand against his breast. "You and I could not force her."

"I know that," he said heavily. "You hurt her, Maurteen. Some way you hurt her with your bitter tongue."

"She is gone now, brother," said I, "and I am sorry, but it might be a good thing if we never set eyes on each other again, for she has been a trouble in my thoughts day and night these many months."

"And in mine too," said Tadg Mor.

CHAPTER VII

WOMAN OF THE REGIMENT

I

Manus O'Cahan, our colonel, was waiting for us outside Auldearn, by the side of a belt of lindens in full leaf on the margin of the green park facing the house of Boath. He looked us over with a stern eye.

"Ye are back again then," said he, his eye resting meaningly on Iseabal Rose.

"A poor place to stay long in, yon Lochloy," said Ranald Ban.

"Ye may find Auldearn a poorer place in a short while," said Manus ironically and turned to me. "Martin, if you will be getting me into trouble with our Captain-General I will not like it, and you will not like it either. I am after learning that you took this young lady out of her father's prison, and already I knew that she was given a safe conduct to Lochloy. She is back again?"

"She is back again, colonel," said I, "and I would have you remember that she has been three nights in this camp, and helped with the wounded two whole days."

"For which my thanks. But now her father, Hugh Rose, is here to claim her back."

"We had better see him then."

"Is that all you have to say?"

"I would say less if I could, colonel."

"Less or more may not avail you with Seumas Graham." He swung on his heel. "Come then—all of you, for you are all in this."

And I whispered to Ranald Ban: "Mind what I told you, loose-tongue."

"You are as black a skillet as ever I saw," said Ranald Ban.

Behind my shoulder I heard Rab Fraser groan out a deep breath. "Red man," growled he to Tadg Mor, "if Hugheon Rose sets eye on me I am a dead man."

"Where is that dirk you boasted about?"

"A boast only! He would kill me like putting his heel on a rat."

"My hand! it would please me greatly to see him try it this day," said Tadg Mor, and there was a grate in his voice that I knew.

"You are in a bad temper, Tadg Mor," I cautioned him over my shoulder.

"I am, Maurteen, and I like it. I will be doing someone a hurt before the day is done—and Meg no longer here to put a thumb on me."

"Someone will put a thumb on you."

Seumas Graham of Montrose, for all his sheltered breeding, could never bide indoors, and that was one of the many reasons the men of the Gael had for admiring him. When he came to us first he had one evil bout of fever in the hills above Dee, but after that he took to the life like a duck to water. He could sleep sound as a bairn in the rain under a wet plaid, march or run with the hardiest of us, sit a horse as surely as Nat Gordon himself, put an arrow in the slot with any man of Clan Finlay; and he could laugh in the fork of hardship and crack a joke with an Irishman in the face of death. He sat now on the sandstone smooth steps of Boath under a Greek portico, his body-armour laid aside and his hair loose to the breeze that warmed his brown cheek. There was a lace collar to his neck and a brilliant rose sash at his waist.

His staff, about and behind him, were much more formal in dress and manner; all but Colkitto, his Major-General, who leant a careless shoulder against a pillar and held a long flagon in his hand. Alasdair nodded his head and grinned at me; any ploy concerning a woman did not trouble Alasdair.

I knew all of Montrose's staff by sight and name, but there were three men now present that did not belong to it. One of them I had met already—John Balfour, the minister of Ardclach. He stood behind all the others, his back to the wall, his rugged face white and stern, and his eyes, under heavy brows, fixed on Iseabal Rose. I could put a name to the others too, though I had not seen them before.

One was a short, thick-bodied man in a leather jerkin. A thick strong body like that should carry a massive head on a bull neck, but out of that man's heavy shoulders rose a long round neck and a long, lean, black-avised head carrying a hawk's nose and a slit of mouth slantingly asmile at one corner. There was something snakelike in that long neck and lean head. He was Hugh Rose.

The other was a man I could like, given the chance: a big, finely-shaped man in half-armour, a fresh-faced red man, handsome and gallant as any man there, with nothing weak or loose about him. He stood at ease, his arms folded, and his bold blue eyes half smiling at Iseabal Rose, not careless of her, yet not greedy for her. He seemed easily sure of himself, hinting in all his bearing that he liked a hard game with a woman for the sake of the salt of having his own way in the end. That was Walter Dunbar of Moyness, and there was a hard game and a salt ending before him.

Montrose rose to his feet as he saw us coming in a clump, Iseabal Rose between Ranald Ban and me; being courtier-bred he would not stay seated before any woman. He lifted finger and bowed a head to our salute, and then spoke over shoulder.

"Is this the lady, your daughter, Hugheon Rose?"

"So it is said, Lord Marquis." The man's voice was light for his great body. "She is the one I am looking for, anyway."

To Montrose's frown was added Colkitto's laughter. He lifted his flagon to the lady and drank, his red-brown eye roving from her to Ranald Ban. And Ranald Ban cursed him under his breath.

Montrose looked at Ranald Ban and nodded. "Glad your wound does not incommode you, MacKinnon," he said. "You got it gallantly."

"I could do fine wanting it, Montrose," said Ranald Ban.

"And I could wish that you would keep your gallantry for fight," said Montrose, and turned to O'Cahan. "Have these gentlemen explained the bad business, colonel?"

"There was nothing to explain, Captain-General," said I before O'Cahan could open his mouth.

Montrose looked at me carefully and gravely, and then his eyes crinkled in a way they had when he was astonished and close to the brink of half-amused irritation. He was not a blunt man. There was nothing he liked better than an undercurrent of meaning and a subtlety of thought and intent. That was another reason why he was at home with the Gael. Many a night I had seen him in a group round a campfire listening to and making talk worth the making.

"Nothing to explain!" said he. "Nothing to explain! So this is everyday work, and young ladies can be wrested out of their father's jurisdiction for a holiday to overlook a battle and visit the sea. I saw Mistress Rose with you on the kirk-mound three days ago."

I had been sure that his eye had never rested on her that morning of the battle. And at once I knew that I could not fool this man; but I had to try.

"We did not wrest this lady out of anywhere, Captain-General," I began. "The lady will tell you that——"

And there I stopped, for there came over me a sudden bleak shame of the irrevocable thing I was getting this young woman to do. The drink was dying in me, and I could no longer conjure up any fine vision of noble sacrifice, no longer thrill to the greatness of throwing one's good name after one's shoe to save one's soul.

But that young woman boldly took her own fate in her own two hands and did not give me time to act on my change of mind. She lifted up her round young chin, her darkling eyes met Montrose's grave grey ones, and her voice was clear and low and slow.

"I am here of my own free will, Lord Marquis, three days and three nights. I am a woman of the camp with Martin Somers in Colonel O'Cahan's regiment."

"*Chreesta Tigearna!* " That was Ranald MacKinnon taking the name of the Lord in vain.

It was done now. There was an abrupt silence, and

then feet shuffled, and all eyes looked at Iseabal Rose and looked away again—all but Montrose's that never flickered. His voice came coldly.

"Will Adjutant Somers confirm?"

"I have enlisted her," said I, "in the nursing corps under Margaret Anderson."

"That settles it," cried Colkitto, and oh! but I was glad to hear that impulsive voice.

Montrose looked up at him where he leant against the pillar, ankles crossed easily, and Colkitto nodded down at him.

"There is no more to be said, Seumas Graham."

Montrose was face to face with a law and custom that he dared not break. Breaking that law would gain him thirty good men to his King's cause but it might lose him a clan and a regiment. A leader has to move carefully with an army of Gaeldom. He knew that Colkitto was wise and cunning in a question like this, and that his seemingly impulsive decision was given to help his leader in a difficult place. And he also knew that there was more in this business than met the eye, and that the red man of the Dunbars had a finger in it somewhere—and he could guess where. Abruptly he shot the young woman a question.

"Your age, young lady?"

"Two-and-twenty past, Captain-General."

"Old enough for any choice," said Colkitto.

There was another gap stopped. If she had been under age Montrose could override the law.

And there Hugh Rose, her father, laughed a mad skirl of laughter. His long head was thrown forward like the head of a reptile ready to strike, his close-set black eyes unwinking on his daughter, and his twisted mouth open to pour out its venom. I shrank within myself. But before any word could come the big Dunbar slapped a big hand on Rose's shoulder.

"A word in your ear, Hugh," he said loudly, and drew the man aside. And the dark man, who seemed to have lost all control a minute agone, shut his mouth crookedly and allowed himself to be drawn away.

"There is my father for you," murmured Iseabal Rose.

"I do not mislike the other," I murmured back.

"But I do."

"And so we are here."

Montrose's eyes were studying us under his firm brows. He was exasperated with us, but would not show it. We were playing a game, and he knew it. But he could prick us still.

"We will not make or break a law, Sir Alasdair," he said, his eye still on us, "but within the law I can put Martin Somers and—the woman—out the bounds of the camp."

"It is your right, surely," agreed Alasdair weightily.

And Tadg Mor saluted. "I go too, Montrose."

And Ranald Ban MacKinnon bowed from the hips to the lady.

Montrose had difficulty not to smile. "Ye three will be loyal enough to one another—I know that," he said chagrinedly.

"And to you too, Montrose," said Ranald Ban. "We await your orders."

But at that juncture Rose and Dunbar resolved the difficulty. They came to the front together, and Hugh Rose's mouth was more twisted than ever.

"I have this only to say, Lord Marquis: this girl has chosen her bed—let her lie on it. She is no daughter of mine any longer."

And Walter Dunbar bent his strong shoulders and said:

"We can give you assurance, Captain-General, that this will make no difference to our loyalty."

It was done as easy as that.

We got our curt dismissal then, and Montrose turned and went up the steps into the house, his staff following; and Alasdair, going last, called out to me over his shoulder:

"Keep your two bonny ones well apart, Maurteen."

"A narrow thing for ye," said Manus O'Cahan, still stern. "I hope Montrose will not hold it in mind"

"Will you, Manus?" enquired Ranald Ban.

"I will if it spoils your duty," said Manus, and followed Alasdair.

2

We had not gone twenty paces down the avenue before a high-thrown voice stopped us:

"Black Rab—Black Rab Fraser!"

We turned, and there was Hugh Rose coming at us from the steps. Walter Dunbar came after, but some distance behind and slowly. Not that Rose came quickly. He seemed in no hurry. His head was thrust forward, his eyes, fixed as a snake's, on Rab Fraser, and his hand on the cross-hilted dagger at his hip.

"This man is mine at least," said he, "and him I will have."

Black Rab Fraser, half-turned towards him, stood dumb and helpless as an ox; and I wondered at the wicked force of this black Rose that could so dominate a man that, in another place, had shown such readiness to fight and die; and I wondered too at the force of a small dark lady that could gainsay such a father. I do believe that Black Rab would have stood dumbly there and dumbly taken dagger stroke if Iseabal Rose had not cried out:

"He will kill."

"He will kill no one," said Tadg Mor softly and stepped between. Tadg Mor was still in a bad temper; I knew that from the silkiness of his voice and the smoothness of his stride.

"Out of my way, red calf!" cried Hugh Rose, his dagger out of its sheath.

But no sooner had it taken the light than Tadg Mor had the wrist of the hand that held it, that wrist wrenched and the dagger in his own hand.

"Still! you black snake!" And the dagger point was firm against the front of the leather jerkin. "Whisper! That man is no longer yours. He is my man now."

Rose strained back a stride from the press of dagger, but Tadg Mor stepped smoothly after, and the point pinched. The man stilled.

"Whisper again!" said Tadg Mor. "He is my man, but I am urging you not to mind that. He is your man if you can take him, and you not minding your own black dirk over your own black heart."

And then, one of his feet moved like a lash in one of his wrestler's clips, his hand thrust, and Rose was flat on his back. Tadg Mor snapped the dagger blade between his fingers and threw the pieces on him.

"There is a small lesson to begin with," said he, and turned his back, grinning pleasantly, the temper cooled in him.

Walter Dunbar lifted Rose to his feet and held him,

and Rose rubbed his wrenched wrist, his eyes seeking his daughter sideways.

"That is a man of my regiment, Rose of Belivat," said she. "You will know where to find me."

He smiled his wicked crooked smile at her. "I will find you at the end of the string I have tied on you." And he shook himself free from his friend and went back towards the house of Boath.

"Are you over your temper now, Tadg Mor?" I put to him.

"I am so, Maurteen, and I hope *Roisin Dhuv* will forgive me."

"I would forgive you, fine man," said she evenly, "even if your point bit deeper."

"Girl, girl!" I cried. "How can you hate your father so?"

"I hate myself for being his daughter. Now you know the blood that is in me and the road it leads."

But now Ranald Ban MacKinnon, smiling too, was facing Dunbar, eye to eye.

"Dirk or claymore, which is your favourite weapon, tall man?"

"I will tell you that in my own time, highland-man," said Dunbar easily. "This time we are fellow-soldiers."

I was tired of this, and the brandy-wine sour in me.

"Enough, enough!" I cried. "This has ended well, and let it stay so. We will go now."

"Come on, Ranald *avic*!" said Tadg Mor, hooking that man's arm and swinging him round, and the two marched off shoulder to shoulder.

I, too, took Iseabal Rose's arm and turned her round, and we followed after. But Dunbar kept pace at my shoulder, and Iseabal Rose pressed my hand against her side.

"Are you not on the wrong road this time?" I said to him.

He chuckled pleasantly. "It is not a safe road, I will admit. But I would like to come to an understanding with you."

"We understand each other very well."

He looked aside at me. "You are the man that took Mistress Iseabal out of her father's prison—Captain Martin Somers is it not?"

"And you the man that helped put her there—Walter Dunbar of Moyness?"

"The lady told you so?"

"I told him that I would never marry you, Wat Dunbar," said the lady.

"He must have a quick way with ladies," said Wat Dunbar.

"And you a foolish one," I told him. "Could you not take this lady's dismissal?"

He chuckled again. "A lady's dismissal is never final. Did you not know?"

"It could be so. But to my mind a man is foolish that will not take the first one and thank the Lord. Did you think that thrusting a girl into prison would make her love you?"

"Girls can be made to change their minds, and the harder the change the deeper. Did you not know that also?"

"Let us leave girls out of this business then. If you are so knowledgeable about dismissals I wonder would you accept a man's one?"

"It would have to be strongly put."

"Very well so! If you in any way trouble Iseabal

Rose while she is in O'Cahan's regiment, Tadg Mor O'Kavanagh and Ranald Ban MacKinnon—there they are in front of us—will not like it."

"You will not like it yourself."

"Tadg Mor and Ranald Ban are much handier cutting windpipes."

He laughed at that, and heartily too. "That is putting it strongly indeed. I know where you stand now, and I will tell you where I stand. I know ye had some plan in mind that miscarried, and that ye are planning afresh. I know that this woman is not yours; she is not that kind. I know that she has twisted you round her finger for her own purposes, as she would twist me; but I know also that some day she will be my wife."

"You know enough and to spare," said I.

"I do. And now I will give you my promise. I will not trouble Iseabal Rose in any way while she is in your regiment, and I will only ask you to remember that I have some practice in cutting windpipes."

And at that he turned on his heel and strode off, a tall and gallant figure.

"There is Walter Dunbar for you," said Iseabal Rose.

"What is wrong with him?"

"He likes his own way and gets it."

"Not with a certain one."

"He is as sure of that one as of himself."

"He has a sound man's parts, and besides——"

She shook my arm. "Bairn! Is that what Margaret Anderson calls you? Do not pretend to be wise and bitter."

I dropped her arm. "You are as bad as Margaret any day," I cried.

"Was she bad?"

"No," I said, and went on head down.

But she put her hand within my arm. "Poor Martin Somers! You know that girl is not coming back."

"I was afraid. Tadg Mor will go down for her in the morning."

"If you yourself will go she might come."

"I will not go," said I; and she said no more.

We had come to the bothy below the kirk-mound. It was evening then and the sun was shining slantwise through the door. Tadg Mor and his new man were inside talking to Sorcha MacNeill, who was preparing supper, but Ranald Ban stayed outside, and when Iseabal went under the lintel he pulled me by the sleeve to the gable end. He was inclined to be angry and his hazel was chewed to the last inch.

"That was a terrible thing you did, Maurteen!"

"What was a terrible thing?"

"Getting her to say that in the face of men."

"It would not be said at all if you and Tadg Mor, seeing I had drink taken, had dipped my head under the breakers a couple of times; but, being said, how else, will you tell me, could we keep the girl safe in camp?"

"Yes, but safe?"

"Safe from everyone but you."

He pulled himself up and his eyes went dangerous.

"Better be careful, Martin."

"Very careful, Ranald Ban. If any harm comes to her I will blame you."

"Say that again."

"In another way, and so that you will follow. You may have dreams in your head of the Island of Mull, and you will have ten days or so, thanks to me, to smit another with your dreams. But listen! If your dreams come true, when you present the lady to your father above your white beaches of Iona, you will be able to look your father in the eye."

He glared at me half a minute and then he spat out the last of his hazel stick.

"You bloody Irish Sassenach!" said he, and, turning on his heel like Walter Dunbar, strode furiously up the lane. A lovable, hot-tempered man. I often wonder since how my neck escaped breaking at his hands or at Tadg Mor's.

3

We had a visitor before we sat to food. The sun was low in the west and I was admiring the golden red of a beam shining across the floor when a long black shadow was cast along it. The caster of that shadow was John Balfour the minister.

He had no more than bent under the lintel, with a salute off his tongue, before our Iseabal Rose made accusation against him.

"Did you repent of your good deed, then?"

But he only shook his head at her, hurt in his deep eyes.

"You came down with them?"

"To warn ye. I had word with Colonel O'Cahan." He turned to me. "Ye were at Lochloy?"

She answered for me. "There is no boat out of Lochloy. The plague is in Edinbro."

I saw many things moving in his mind, but all he said was: "I am to blame."

She read that in her own way. "Lost amongst the barbarous Irish?"

But she could not anger this man, and why she tried to I do not know. He smiled sadly at her.

"One could be sorry for your Irish gentlemen."

"Through her guard," I said. "Reverend sir, will you eat with us?"

He hesitated. "Let me not trouble——"

"Sit down, man," she shot at him. "My Irish gentlemen will not poison you."

"I will teach you a little discipline to-morrow, young lady," I warned her.

John Balfour dipped his fingers in the dish with us, saying a grace under his breath out of deference to Sorcha MacNeill and Tadg Mor. I do not remember any talk, because I was thinking things over in a mind that was no longer crystal but muddied. An explanation was due to this man but I did not know how to make it, and he would not help me out by asking questions. For some reason Iseabal Rose remained obdurate against him, and in the end put him a question half bitter.

"Have you no advice to give me now, John Balfour?"

He contemplated her dark calmness for a while.

"No!" he said then. "I will not advise you at all, Iseabal, though I came with that intent. There is something in you that of itself moves you to trust men that can be trusted. I will call it the finger of God, and it will hold you back from an end that is ignoble." He rose to his feet. "My thanks to ye all, friends. I must reach Ardclach before nightfall."

He went out of the house without again looking at Iseabal Rose. Tadg Mor and I went with him. We accompanied him out of the village and to the head of the first brae, not that he ran any risk in the camp, where we had some royalist ministers of his cloth. We were silent enough on the road, but when he reached me his hand in farewell I gripped it hard and forced myself to say:

"No harm will come to Iseabal Rose that we can help."

"I know that, my friend."

"You may think it an ill thing the thing she said to Montrose, but it was the only way I saw then of holding her safe from her father and the other. You will believe that."

"I believe it."

"We are still ready to give her a safe conduct to any place she thinks safe—Edinburgh or Aberdeen."

"Aberdeen?"

"She has an uncle there."

"I doubt if he is to be trusted." He looked at me consideringly and smiled. "I wonder why we—you and I—are so eager to help her?"

I wondered too. Was it just admiration for her cool courage, for the steadfastness of her purpose to keep her soul her own? Or had she some secret force in her to impel men any road she wanted? That last frightened me.

"Master Balfour," I implored him, "will you take her off our hands?"

He held out his lean big palms. "They are helpless."

"Here only," I urged. "Come with us to Aberdeen or Edinburgh. There are men of your faith in the army, and Montrose is a strong Kirk man. I think she is angry with you because you will not come. You are not against the King?"

He shook his head sadly.

"I have thought it all out long ago, Master Somers. Joining the King now would be no more than pandering to the blind urges of the human heart. No. There is a spark amongst my poor wild ones that may yet blow into a flame of goodness, and that spark I will stay here to nourish as best I can. God be with you, my brothers!"

He turned away and left us, and we stood looking after till the gloaming covered him between the dark trees.

"No one could make me believe it," said Tadg Mor, "but you get good men everywhere, even in the Kirk."

I liked that man, John Balfour. I liked him from the beginning. He was a minister of the Covenant, and we of the Irish army had no single small reason to love or respect that body. I have said many hard and bitter things against the Solemn League and Covenant, but let no one hold that I am against the Scottish Kirk when I say that that Solemn League and Covenant was the most bowelless, Christianless institution that ever shackled Scotland in the name of religion, and Scotland has been sorely shackled three or four times. I am myself Episcopalian though not a Roman, but I do believe that the National Covenant, renewed and proclaimed seven years before the time of which I am writing, was a very necessary weapon to save the religion and freedom of Scotland from the episcopal follies of the first Charles. And I maintain that the rebirth of that Covenant twenty years later in the persecuting time of the second Charles was a noble one, and gave the blood of the martyrs for the rights of reason and tolerance. But I also hold that the body of ministers and lairds that ruled Scotland in the name of the

Solemn League and Covenant during the wars of the Parliament was the most tyrannical body in all Christendom before or since—and there have been many tyrannies in Christendom. It was a theocracy whose real aim was Power; the god it fulminated was a Jehovah more terrible than any mad Jahveh ever conjured up in the mad dreams of the maddest prophet of Israel. It humiliated noble men, set its heel on the helpless, butchered women, tortured prisoners, slew honest fighting men surrendered under quarter, broke its bond, sold its king, sold its country, bartered its conscience; and Cromwell, whom it helped to make supreme, crushed it into fragments under his own firmer heel as something too abominably intolerant for that most intolerant age.

Even now, an old man, my gorge rises when I think of the way the Covenanters behaved towards our three Irish regiments fighting for a Scots king. It treated us as wolves, and created a tradition against Irishmen that still holds. And sometimes, when passion darkens in me, I have a dream that, risking the plague, we stormed the high Castle of Edinburgh, where the Kirk Estates sheltered in their tigers' den, and used the northern guarding cliff as a Tarpeian rock for the death of traitors—traitors to great Scotland and the fine tolerant traditions of the race. And then my mood changes, and, though I am of English blood, I grow proud as Lucifer of our three Irish regiments and the Highland clans, rough soldierly men, terrible in war, with a fine, reckless, salty humour in good days and in bad, and knowing how to die no matter how ignominiously death was dealt them. Some day history will do them justice.

John Balfour of Ardclach was a forerunner of the

great ones that died martyrs in the cold Lowland moors beneath the spears of Claverhouse, who was a Graham too, and of the blood of Montrose—and his avenger some do say. And these martyrs need not have died had the first Covenant done its duty by God and Nation. . . . I withhold my pen from writing more. . . .

Tadg Mor was talking to me, a frown between his eyes.

"Maurteen, I am troubled in my mind."

"I know you are."

He rubbed the angle of his strong jaw and his voice was gloomy.

"Maybe it would be better for you and me to have nothing at all to do with women—and here we are with two of them on our hands."

"We have fifty on our hands."

"And two that count, and two that do not like each other."

"Without reason."

"You hurt our Margaret to-day—some way you hurt her with your bitter drunken tongue."

"I was bitter enough."

"Could it be that she saw you had a liking for the little dark rose?"

"That she could not see."

"Mind you, the little one is a girl that a man like you could grow to like." His eyes shifted away from mine. "I see no reason in the world why you would not grow to like her."

"And be rival to Ranald Ban?"

"Why not you——?"

"Wait, brother! If we are talking about liking there is no girl I like better than Margaret Anderson, and I will tell her so to-morrow—and I will tell her other things as well, and they will be bitter things."

And after a while he said, as if warning and assuring himself: "Nothing will come between you and me, my brother."

4

But I did not see Margaret Anderson on the morrow. Tuesday morning before we marched, Tadg Mor went down to Lochloy to convoy her into camp, but he came back without her.

"She came to the door herself," he told us perplexedly, "and there was a coldness on her face, and her hand did not reach for my ear. 'Are you ready, Meg girl?' says I. 'No,' says she, 'I will stay a while longer with Uncle Alick, and when I want ye I will send for ye.' That is the very way she said it—distant kind. 'Martin Somers has something to say to you,' says I then, and she stopped me. 'If Martin Somers has anything to say,' says she, 'let him come and say it.' And she shut the door in my face. She was in no temper at all, mind you, my ear handy and all, but she shut the door so fast she near caught my nose in it."

"That would be the fault of the nose," said Ranald Ban. "Why did you not drive in the door with your bull shoulder and bring her in on your back?"

"The thought was in my mind," agreed Tadg Mor, "and it is not too late——"

"I think," said Iseabal Rose, "that she will come in on her own feet if Martin Somers will go down and ask her—if he is man enough."

Indeed it was in my mind to go down and reason with her, but I put the thought aside.

"She is safe enough with Moray under our hands,"

was what I said. "Let her bide a few days with her uncle. He is a lonely man."

"If it is of him you are thinking," said our dark rose.

But the few days lengthened out to seven weeks before I again set eyes on Margaret Anderson; and when that time came she and Tadg Mor and I were in the very jaws of death.

CHAPTER VIII

"I WANT YE NOW"

I

WALTER DUNBAR of Moyness and myself walked together through a wood of Scots pine somewhere behind the hamlet of Alford in the shire of Aberdeen. That was on Tuesday, the first day of July, seven weeks after Auldearn, and we were expecting another warm fight the following morning.

I had given a final inspection to my wounded station behind the lines, and now, with time on my hands, was strolling forward to the camping place that Tadg Mor had established for our party in the foreground of the Gallows Hill overlooking the river and the valley of the Don. Wat Dunbar had joined me in the main camp, and we walked along side by side talking amicably enough. It was a warm summer evening and I was in my shirt sleeves.

Walter Dunbar had not broken his word with Montrose or with us, though we had half expected, half hoped that he would desert the army after his failure to secure Iseabal Rose at Auldearn. Hugh Rose, pleading his age for a hard campaign, had gone home from Elgin, but he left his ten men with Dunbar's twenty, and thirty good men they were under able leadership, and faithful too, though all their kin—

Dunbars, Baillies, and the great Kilravock Roses—were out with the Covenant. Moray-bred on the border of the Highlands, they had the hardy qualities of both breeds, and a dourness all their own. Once in a rearguard action at the ford of Avon, near Ballindalloch, they held the left bank against the whole weight of Balcarres' horse, and Dunbar himself in a fair broadsword fight killed the field cornet and brought in his pennant.

I could find nothing at all wrong with Walter Dunbar, and in another situation might have grown to easy friendship with him. Even as things stood we were not unfriendly. He was gallant and good company, and amongst men he had fine soldierly ways; it was no business of ours if he had ways of his own with women so long as he left ours alone, and I will say for him in this place that his conduct was of the highest. He kept his word and never once pestered Iseabal Rose. Neither did he avoid her, nor did we deny him our company or hers. He was often in our lines in friendly ease, sat with us round the camp-fire and made his share of talk and fun, broke bread with us when we had any, dipped a finger in the pot, and behaved all the time as a soldier should. Tadg Mor actually liked him, and more than once Ranald Ban told him a story and was pleased with his laughter. But, on occasion, I saw Ranald Ban sizing him up with the swordsman's cold eye.

We came now to where the wood thinned, and could see open country in front of us. Tadg Mor with his squad of women had thrown up a wattled shelter within the margin of the pines, and some of our little company were taking their ease in front of it. I could see my foster-brother's red head and wide shoulders hunched over something gripped between his knees; and there was Ranald Ban's flaxen pow leaning over towards a raven one that nodded sometimes to the flow of his tongue.

Walter Dunbar stopped walking, and I heard the deep draw of his breath.

"I am thinking," said he, "that only one of us will be welcome in yon company—and not too welcome at that."

I looked up at him. "A great pity," said I, "you took the crooked road with *Roisin Dhuv*."

"It was the road that led straight to the thing I wanted."

"And it has landed you here. How could you hope to improve your cause with the daughter by letting the father impound her?"

"By teaching her sense—other ways failing."

"You did not know the lady very well."

"I know women, and they are all much alike."

"And you would force her to wed you?"

"For her own good in the end, as well as mine. Do you know the luck of tocherless lasses in our country?"

"I can guess."

"Do not guess high. Mistress of Moyness and my wife, she would be a lady of Moray, and not a lowly one. And she would learn contentment, I know."

"Do you know? Where is your experience? You are not a young man, I agree, but what do you know of wedded life?"

"I was a married man, a foolish lad of eighteen, and a widower at twenty. That taught me something."

"Not continence?"

"A man cannot help his nature, and I will do the right thing by Iseabal Rose."

175

"Are you as sure of her as that?"

"I am." He looked at me keenly. "I am—unless you yourself—you know what I mean?"

"I do not."

"Let it be. There is a man amongst you that does not hide his thoughts as well as you do."

"Did you ever see that man swing a broadsword?"

"I swing one myself, and never asked more than fair play."

"You are getting that."

"I am. I would not want better company than the company I am in." He struck his hands together and there was a desperate note in his voice. "I am a fool —I know I am a fool. All the wicked looseness in my life is coming home to me. But God, Somers! that dark one is twisted into my very marrow. I must win her or die."

He turned on his heel and strode off through the wood. It was the first time that his self-control had given way, and, somehow, I was sorry for him—and afraid too. Death only could beat that man. Death only.

2

I walked round to the front of the shelter, and the group sitting there looked at me with careless friendly eyes, and went on easy-talking. It was a sunny evening in the heart of summer, and the brown turfy soil under the trees was dry as bone. I sat down a little apart near-by an ant-heap of pine needles and small sticks as big as a haycock. I mind that small fact very well, because I was foolish enough to sit in the path of the busy little soldier beasts, and, presently, swearing to myself, had to shift ground in a hurry over to where Iseabal Rose sat on my cloak in the crouch of a root.

She was busy sewing on a bone button on the breast of the coat I had taken off the Aberdeen minister—a shabby old coat now but still serviceable. One small foot was thrust out below the hem of her wine-red skirt and showed its silver buckle, but the other foot was hidden, and the shoe off that foot was gripped between Tadg Mor's knees, where he sat handily stitching on a new half-sole. Black Rab Fraser, that faithful man, crouched as ever on one knee behind his mistress's shoulder. Ranald Ban MacKinnon, drawn as by a magnet close as he dared, was turned on his elbow at her side, leaning towards her; and as I pulled out a corner of the cloak to sit on he frowned at me. He had no cause to frown that I knew, but I also knew the thought behind the frown.

I looked from Iseabal to Ranald Ban, and in my own mind decided that if love lay between these two it would be a very fitting thing: and I had a queer small pang thinking that so love might lie. Tall and lithely built, with a high eagle face and hair of golden flax and with the strong whip of a spear in him, he might have been one of the famous Red Branch Knights that had gone out to war behind Cuchulain. The small white scar of his arrow wound marked one brown cheek, but the other had healed without leaving mark.

The first time I had seen Iseabal Rose in the bell-tower of Ardclach there was a soft feminine dusky loveliness about her, and her quietness and her strength came on one as a surprise. She was still quiet and still strong, but seven weeks of the hardest campaigning had kneaded the softness of soft living out of her. Now she was a shapely slip of a girl, as Tadg Mor would say, with a brown and lovely face and a brown and lovely neck above her square-cut collar: and her eyes looked bigger and darker, and the whites of them were touched with blue. On her black hair she wore the blue knitted cap she had taken from Tadg Mor, and the red toorie of it hung to one shoulder.

As I looked at her I had an eerie feeling that she and Margaret Anderson were moving on parallel roads. We had taken Margaret out of the stocks, and promised that she would be with her uncle in Lochloy in ten days, but she had not reached that place for eight months. We had taken Iseabal out of her father's prison, and she was to be with her uncle in Aberdeen in ten days also, but already she had been with us for seven weeks. How long more?

The truth is that we found the road to Aberdeen a hard one to open. William Baillie, the second Covenant general, was a prudent man and a better strategist than John Hurry. He refused to stand and fight till all the chances were in his favour, and as the weeks went by the chances leaned more and more to his side. For not even Seumas Graham, the darling of the clans, could hold a Highland army in the field for months on end. It was shieling time in the glens, and, moreover, the clansmen, loaded down with the fine fat pickings of Moray, were anxious to dispose them in a safe place against a lean season. So by the time we reached Balvenie and the Spey, on our back drive to clear Gordon territory, the Highlandmen had trickled away from the army in twos and threes and twenties and thirties, leaving the Irish, the Gordon cavalry, and a skeleton force of Clan Vuirich, Clan Finlay, Clan Duncan, and Clan Ranald under Angus of Glengarry to deal with Baillie. That force was ready and willing to onset Baillie, if he would only stand for us; but that canny man, though he had four first-line regiments, seven squadrons of horse, and levies from Aberdeen and Stanehive, still refused to face us on the stark field, and made himself a campaign of march and countermarch, hoping to manœuvre us between his forces and the sea. Moreover, the Kirk Estates drummed up a second army under one Lord Lindsay of Byres, and there was Montrose once again in danger of being caught between two fires.

I might say here, if I have not said it before, that Montrose's final aim was to march his army over the Border to help his King. But even if he had succeeded at that time I doubt if he would have been in time, though, if he were in time, the battle of Naseby might and would have had a different ending. Naseby was fought in the middle of June, and patient Cromwell proved, at the first time of real trial, that his army of the New Model was a weapon truly forged to his strong hand. After that battle there was only one army that could face Cromwell in the field, and that was a joint one of Owen Roe O'Neill's in Ulster and Montrose's in Scotland. But King Charles could never be persuaded by Strafford or Ormonde or Antrim to loose an Irish army on England. And in due time that foolish reluctance lost him his head.

Montrose could not make his drive for the Lowlands and the Border while two covenanting forces held the field. And so, for six weeks, he was compelled to play a game of hide-and-seek, with sallies and rearguard actions, over and through and round and in and out the rugged Grampian Mountains, from Strathbogie of Huntly to the South Esk of Angus, and back again.

No one, no history, can fully trace the new roads we nosed out, the savage glens we threaded, the high passes we crossed, the torrents we forded. Montrose could, but he is dead. Montrose's mind had the eagle eye, and that eagle eye grasped and read that upheaved, far-flung, tortured land as surely as the common eye might grasp and trace the lines in the hand's palm. And glory of God! had he not a supremely hardy army to lead that tortuous road?

His strategy was masterful. By a series of mighty marches, retreats and advances he patiently spread the two armies of the Covenant far apart, Baillie north on the Dee, Lindsay south in Atholl; and that done he faced about and went northwards, forced march after forced march, to deal adequately with Baillie, who was harrying the Gordon lands.

We found the Covenanters posted in a strong place behind a ravine on the Deveron River near Keith, and behind that ravine they stayed. Montrose sent in a challenge, Nat Gordon skirmished the Huntly horse down their front as a bait for their squadrons, O'Cahan deployed his regiment with a flank nicely exposed for turning; but Baillie would not be drawn just yet. And then Montrose turned tail and marched away in a hurry. And just at that time word reached the Covenanters—Montrose made sure it would— that the mighty Alasdair and his Ulstermen were away on a recruiting campaign. That drew them. The Lowland foot at that time had such a fear of Alasdair that Baillie would not trust even his first-line regiments to stand against him. But, with Alasdair away, Montrose was beatable. So the Kirk Estates thought, whatever Baillie thought, and they forced Baillie's hand.

We streamed away south, in full retreat as it were, and the Covenanters came hot-foot after us. We beat them to the River Don, crossed by an easy ford called the Boat of Forbes, and took up position a mile back from the river above the hamlet of Alford. Montrose hid our centre—Highlandmen under Angus of Glengarry—behind a rough, heathy, wooded ridge called Gallows Hill, deployed his horse and the Irish musketeers on his flanks, held a few clansmen and Irish in reserve, and waited. To the Covenant army hasting from the north our force looked no more than a strong rearguard holding the hill; but if Baillie crossed at the Boat of Forbes, as he would have to, he must needs outflank us on our right with treacherous ground and the river in his rear. And that would be the end of Baillie and his army—and of the Committee of the Kirk Estates we hoped.

3

Iseabal Rose, then, had taken Margaret Anderson's place and filled it in her own way. She came of a different tradition and a different race—not a finer race but a prouder race—lairds and fighters, saints and devils, men and women of toughness and courage, and intolerance too. Nor did she belie her breed. In mind and body she was finely wrought, and she went through that campaign as hardily as the most war-hardened camp-woman in Colkitto's tail. It was as if she had taken hold of herself with her two small strong hands and said: "You are in this place to keep your faith in yourself, and you dare not falter." Nor did she stand aloof from the life of the camp. She made her own little corps of women about her, ruled them, laughed with them, worked their troubles out for them, made them her very own. She would ride a pony or march on her feet, clamber a corrie handy as a hillman, and come leading her company singing into camp; and with hurt men she had the lovely healing touch and a firm gentleness that served me many an hour. But in that she was no better than Margaret Anderson. She was no better and no finer in any way. I insisted that to myself as I looked at her brown loveliness against the pale trunk of the pine tree that soughed softly to itself above her in a strange lonely contentment with its own hushed sorrow.

But that lonely sough made me lonely for Margaret, and I wondered why she had forsaken us. Tadg Mor and I had taken her out of the stocks to a new full-flowing life, and there was a tie of comradeship or more that bound the three of us. In my mind's eye I could see the tall lissome slenderness of her, her straight back, her blown linten hair above her clear brow, and the lustre of her grey eye that went deep below the surface. I sighed and turned away to look over the wide scene before us.

The River Don, a deep strong-flowing river even in this dry midsummer, made a fine sweeping double loop below us, and at the arch of the nearer one the water ran in broken silver where the only easy ford was. Beyond it were the few thatched bothies that made the township of Forbes, and I caught the flash and glint of steel amongst the houses. We had an outpost planted there to ensure that the Covenant outriders did not get across to disclose our position. Behind the township the land swept slowly upwards in great curves—a rich country of woods and pasture and bright corn—into smooth moorland hills that, still slowly, lifted into one tall mountain that tilted a bald head over to the west towards the sun coming down yellow on its shoulder. A peaceful scene indeed, and, but for that glint of steel amongst the bothies, no sign of war anywhere. But I knew that the Covenanters were advancing behind one of the nearer folds.

"A great pity," I mused aloud, "that men should go to war at all. I see no need for it."

"Why are you in it then, my sober fellow?" Ranald Ban wanted to know.

And Iseabal Rose, a thread in her white teeth, turned her head sideways and contemplated me with dark and thoughtful eyes.

"Indeed I often do wonder, Martin, how you are here amongst the reckless fighting Irish."

"Ask Tadg Mor there. It was he made me."

"Why did you do that, Tadg Mor?"

"Why not I, *Roisin Dhuv*?" said Tadg Mor, grunting over the awl that he had "borrowed" from the village souter. "If I got in a tight corner I wanted him handy. Do not you be fooled by the buttermilk mouth of him. There he was in Callan growing an old fellow before his time, and blinding the sight of his eyes over writings about drenches and herbs and broken collar-blades — and I well knowing he was young inside him, and we like two young colts on the flanks of Mount Leinster. We had an aunt, an old single girl, and she used leather the two of us, as a matter of duty, night and morning, and that was a grand salve for us before and after. A good woman and quick in the hand—Meg Anderson often reminded me of her."

His hands went lax over the buckled shoe, his chin sank on his breast, and his eyes looked out under his red brows at the tilted cowl of Benachie. But he did not see Benachie, as I knew by his fixed look. He was seeing Margaret Anderson as I had seen her a minute agone.

"But you brought him soldiering?" Iseabal insisted.

He resumed his stitching.

"That is true enough, and I often wonder at it, for he was the devil and all to go his own road. When the war started, Colonel John Preston raised one of his regiments along the Nore and Slaney, and says I to the lad here: 'Look at the two of us—you blinding your eyes and me wasting my time at locks and bolts and other things not so good for me. Let us go soldiering for a piece and see life.' 'We will not,' says he. 'Very well so,' says I. 'All the same,' says he, 'we might as well and you with your mind set on it.' Just like that."

Ranald Ban laughed.

"Just like that surely! He reminds me of a man I knew one time at Misnaish in the Isle of Mull. A man of the MacLeans he was, Coll by name, and a right peaceable honest fellow, unlike most of his clan. People took advantage of him often; and a certain Lachy Stuart came over the Sound one dark of night at low water and went back again with two of Coll's stirks in front of him. And Coll did nothing, nothing at all, and kept his friends from doing anything as well. 'For,' said he, 'the Stuarts are robbers by nature, and no man can change a man's nature except with a dirk, and that I will not put my hand to, for I am a man of peace.' And so it lay. We used be making sly fun of him for weeks, and maybe he grew tired of that in the end. One day he called on my father, and I was there, and we drawing off the third run of a still. 'Try a horn of it, Coll,' my father invited him. 'I will not, Ailin, and thank you,' said he. 'Just two drops then,' my father coaxed him. 'No, nor one drop. I took a gill of it one time three years ago, and the remains of the head it gave me is still with me.' 'Cover the bottom of the horn,' said I, sly kind, 'and it might give you courage the next time Lachy Stuart calls on you.' 'I do not need courage against that robber,' said he, 'but since you are so pressing I will take one thimbleful.' And that thimbleful he took, and it a tailor's one without a bottom, and two more on top of it, and one to finish off. And that night, all by his lone, he swam the Sound, and burned Lachy Stuart's house, and chased Lachy and his grown son up a hill with a claymore, and swam back to Mull with five cows, two stots, and a yearling bull. He was an honest man after that as well."

"And will you tell me, fine-talker," demanded Tadg Mor, "how Martin Somers going soldiering reminded you of that night-robber of Mull?"

"Because Martin had the urge in him all the time and let a big red sheep's head think it was doing all the planning."

"We will say nothing about a sheep's head till another occasion," said Tadg Mor meaningly, "but by my hand, when I come to think of it there is something in what you say. Look you! we did not see much life in Preston's regiment, for beyond taking a few strong houses we kept to the safe side of Kilkenny and left the fighting to Owen Roe O'Neill and Roger O'Moore. So when Randal of Antrim sent down Colkitto and his Ulstermen to make an expedition to this Scotland out of Wexford, I put it to the lad here.

185

'That is a place I have in mind this many a day. I am told they run usgebaugh three times in the still and store it in a peat bank three years, and as for the girls—— and besides,' said I, 'some of them are said to be handy with a broadsword they call Andrew Ferrara. What do you think, Maurteen?' 'I am thinking,' says he, 'I will stay where I am, and you with me.' And, 'Have it your own way,' says I, mild as milk. And after a while he said, 'There are famous surgeons in Scotland, and there is a school of the MacBeths I would like to visit.' And without another word we up and joined Manus O'Cahan's regiment, where the men were mostly true-bred Irishmen and none of your b—— none of your half-bred Scots. He was leading me on all the time, it could be."

"But he is not a fighting man despite that," insisted Iseabal.

"He was a fair good imitation of one at Tippermuir," said Tadg Mor dryly.

"If ye are talking about me," I broke in, "I was frightened into a corner that time, and how could Manus O'Cahan stand up for me before the Judgment——?"

"But he could not do that for you, Maurteen," Tadg Mor stopped me. "You are a Black Protestant, and I would have to go to hell with you."

Iseabal Rose had her head turned sideways, and there was a pleasant crinkle about her dark eyes.

"True enough," she said, "the first time I saw you in the doorway of Ardclach tower you put me in mind of Auld Clootie, and frightened me to the marrow."

"You hid it well then."

"But my heart was stopped with fear. 'Here is one will show me no mercy,' was my thought. But you did—a little. It is, perhaps, the honest Sassenach in you."

"Do not be hard on the Sassenach," mocked Ranald Ban. "Though I say it against my will, the Sassenach is honest in the main and a doughty fighter, as he has proved often on the Irish and the French—and on the Scots once or twice, maybe. But it might be the Indian blood that he talks about that put the fear on you."

"That could be," I agreed. "I heard my father tell that the Indians of Virginia were the most bloody-minded, feelingless race of men in the known world, smiling at wounds and death, and singing under torture. And once he saw a young chief of the Mona-cans, naked to the breech clout, kill a fully-armed bully man of the English with his bare hands."

"And that blood runs in you?" wondered she.

"I could not tell you. I hate pain and do my killing by proxy. My mother I never saw and my father was taciturn, but my brother, two years older, is as fair as Ranald Ban—and near as foolish. Still, a serving-man that came out of Virginia with my father—that was the time King James sold him a small estate in Ireland—that man used say that my grandmother was a full-blooded princess of the tribe of Pipeshaw on the James River. That is all I know."

Iseabal smoothed my threadbare old coat with gentle fingers and put me a quiet question:

"When this war is over, what will you do, Martin?"

"If we win out of Scotland, Tadg Mor and I have a house and lands below the Walsh Mountains in Leinster, and the first time he opens his mouth to plan a new campaign I will open a blood-vessel for him."

"And there is the black Indian blood for you!" said Tadg Mor.

But picturing our own peace in the future I was minded of our dark lady's future, and a trouble that was not new came to me. I touched a finger on her brown wrist.

"Iseabal, it might be near the end of your road with us?"

"But not the end of the road," she said, without looking up.

"If we win to-morrow or the next day——"

"Ye will win. Before Auldearn I spoke foolishly of what the men of Moray would deal you, but now I know ye will not be beaten but by mischance. Ye will win indeed."

"And the road to Aberdeen will be open?"

"Where else can I go?"

"There is Edinburgh."

"And there is Mull of the Mountains," said Ranald quietly.

"I can see it through your eyes, white Ranald: the high head of Ben More above the purpling of the heather, and the grey royal tombs of Iona across the green water."

"And is it not bonny as you say and see it?" said Ranald.

She shook her head slowly.

"Nothing would be asked that you would not give," whispered Ranald.

"Nor would I take what I could not give. My time is nearly done in this camp where I have been happy and the care of men about me."

"And you doing a noble share of the caring, *Roisin Dhuv*," said Tadg Mor softly.

"It has been good, and I shall not forget. It has restored my faith. But now I know that there is

nothing more for me here, and I must go—I must go."
She placed my old coat across my knees and gave me
a sudden hot flash of her eyes. "And when I am gone
you will send for your Margaret Anderson."

And as she spoke that girl's name a rotten stick
crunched under a heel in the wood behind. I looked
over my shoulder to see two men coming towards us
between the trees. One of the two was Walter Dunbar.

4

The man who came through the wood with Walter
Dunbar I did not recognise at first, and when I did
I sprang to my feet, trampling my coat. Alick
Anderson, shipmaster of Lochloy, Margaret's uncle!
He was in his seaman's blue cloth, with a tricorne
hat and horse-boots, and it was plain that he was
spent with travel, his eyes without light, his cheeks
above the white beard hollowed with weariness.

"Alick Anderson of Lochloy would like a word with
you, Martin Somers," said Walter Dunbar.

My heart was strangely hollow and I could think of
nothing to say, but I kicked my tunic out of the way
and made to go aside.

"It is no' private," Alick Anderson stopped me,
lifting his hand. He looked about at us, smiling but
unsure, almost shy, and bowed to the lady. "Ye are
aye in the one company and keep well together. It
is good to see you so bonny, Mistress Iseabal, and I
am thinking the company does not mislike you."

"I chose it carefully, Master Alick. Are you well?"

"I am well." He hesitated then, and his hand
came up to his beard. He did not know how to begin,
and I was afraid to put him the blunt question. I

looked at Tadg Mor to see if he had more courage, but Tadg Mor was swallowing his words with a gulp and twisting Iseabal's shoe in his hand.

"My, oh my!" said the shipmaster, making a fresh start. "The trouble I had to get at ye, and I no' used to the saddle-horse. I rade down the Spey to Abernethy and ower the shoulder to Tomintoul, and by the Licht to Corgarff—and just missed you there. Ye had been in that place a twa days and were off again east and by north. So I came tackin' down by the headwaters o' Don, and more by good luck than good steering ran into a foraging party of Clan Chattan —MacPhersons of Badenoch they were—and it was near bad luck at that, for they were in twa minds whether to hale me into camp or cut my throat for a blue-coat Covenanter. Here I am, anyway, and my windpipe nane the waur. Four days it took me."

"Sit down here by me, Alick," Iseabal Rose invited him, patting my cloak.

"Thank you, Mistress Iseabal. It will be easier for me."

He unjointed himself stiffly to the ground, took off his tricorne hat and looked into the crown of it, wondering what to say next. But there Tadg Mor helped him by blurting out in a voice strangely loud and unnaturally careless:

"But how is Meg—how is our Margaret?"

"She is grippit," said Alick Anderson, with a little hopeless upward jerk of his head.

"Grippit?" Tadg Mor was on his feet.

"Ay! The Kirk has her." He said it tonelessly.

My legs went pithless and I sank down cross-legged in front of him. Tadg Mor leant a firm knee against my shoulder.

190

"In Aberdeen?"

"No' yet. But Aberdeen it will be, early or late. Brodie of Brodie is holding her in the palace of Spynie. Ye ken it—three miles out of Elgin?"

"We marched three times round it after Auldearn," said Ranald Ban, "but it did not fall to us."

"That's the place, and there she is."

"Brodie will not deal with her himself?" asked Iseabal Rose, the coolest head there.

"Better if he did, for if he is hard in the rind he has a kind core. Na! To Aberdeen she maun be sent when word comes, and ye will ken what that means to a poor lass that has been in the Irish army."

"It means death."

"That is what it means."

I felt Tadg Mor's knee stiffen against my shoulder.

"When did it happen?—tell us all you know, Alick." Iseabal urged him.

"Ay will I. Eight days ago. I was aye feart and tried to keep her hidden. Ye can blame me fairly for holding her, e'en that she was my ain blood. Still, I did tell her it was no safe place for her, but she was someways thrawn and wouldna be moved. And then I hurried the work on the *Moray Quoine*, and cursed myself for having the cordage down, or we would have slippit out to sea in ballast and north-about for France. But it was not to be. The word got to Brodie, new back from Stirling, and he rade down with Kinnaird of Culbin and whippit her away. He could have jooged me as well for harbouring her, but he kent it was against nature to give up one's niece. That's the kind of him. All he gave me was a tongue-lashin'—and I gave it to him back."

"She is in Spynie Tower?"

"That is where he took her, for he was afraid of Lewie Gordon. She was in it four days ago."

He looked round at us one after another, and then he looked again into the crown of his hat, and went on, as it were reading out of it, with a steady dourness, determined to get his mind rid of what was in it.

"There was nothing I could do, and no appeal against the Kirk; and then I minded the way she spoke of her officer Martin Somers and of a big red man she called Tadg Mor"—he gestured a hand towards that man without lifting his eyes—"and I was minded the day ye called on me at Lochloy and the way she was proud of her ain gentlemen. Ye were far away, and only here and there a rumour of yer whereabouts, but there was no chance I wouldna grasp at; so without weighing chances I saddled horse and off my twisty road. But indeed and indeed I weighed many a chance as I rade and rade; and when I came down through this wood a whilie agone and saw ye sitting here at ease in the quiet sunny evening I knew myself for a vain gowk. For ye are strange and foreign sojering men facing battle, and I couldna hope that ye would make the business of a poor Aberdeen lassie yer business—and a darksome business at the doors of death. And e'en if ye did, what chance is there to break down the strong walls o' David's Tower in Spynie? An auld fool! But I've said my say, an' if ye tell me it is no business to embark on I will understand fine."

"It is my business," said Tadg Mor, slow and heavy.

"It is your business?" The shipmaster looked at him, and his eyes were the very eyes of Margaret now that the light of hope was breaking in them.

"I have no other business on top of earth till

Margaret Anderson is free, or till I am dead. Look at me!" I heard him strike his breast above me. "I will tear down Spynie Tower stone by stone to get at her."

"And I at your shoulder," cried Ranald Ban.

"And Black Rab Fraser as well," growled that man.

"I have thirty men," said Dunbar from where he leant against a trunk.

I had nothing to say, but I watched the old man's head bent to his knees and his shoulders shaking as he murmured, "I might hae kent—I might hae kent, an' she so prood o' her ain men."

But Iseabal Rose brought us back to reality, making herself one with us.

"We cannot take David's Tower, thirty men or ten times thirty, and we ought to know that first thing."

We did know it. Spynie Palace, as it was named, was a jumble of ruins and one mighty rectangular tower four or five storeys high on the shore of a wide sedgy loch opening to the Moray Firth. It had been the palace and stronghold of the old fighting bishops of Moray, and the strongest place between Spey and Ness. The last of King Charles's bishops had been driven out of it five years before by the Covenant, and it was now used as a shelter-hole by the covenanting lords and burghers of Moray. Brodie of Brodie used it, and Kinnaird of Culbin and others. After Auldearn fight Montrose circled it for three days, but found it too strong to be taken without breaching, and as he had no heavy pieces he marched us away without attacking it; for he would not waste a good soldier to smoke out broken lairds, and he had no fear of strong places in his rear. Our Margaret was in it now, and we had to face what Montrose had drawn back from.

"As I see it," said Iseabal, "this thing must be done with cunning—if it is to be done at all."

"Ay, surely!" agreed Ranald Ban. "And in that game two are enough and three often too many. Tadg Mor and myself——"

"Is Margaret in dungeon?" I asked the shipmaster.

"Na, na! Brodie is human. I went across to Spynie the day after she was taken, but Brodie wouldna let me see her. He said it could only be a hurt to baith of us. That's the kind he is. But when I was coming away she heard my voice lifted, and my brave one waved a clout out of a barred window—the topmost turret window in the nor'-west corner of David's Tower."

"You know the inside of the tower?"

"As well's my hand. Many the barrel of French wine I landed there for auld Bishop Guthrie."

"We will talk of this again," said I. "The tower is garrisoned?"

"Thirty or more, with Brodie and Kinnaird."

I went deep into thought then, but I drew nothing out of the deeps. We had to do something, but I could not see how any force of cunning could avail against dumb walls and barred doors. But still something had to be done. My body stirred to the travail in my mind, and Iseabal Rose leaned forward and touched my long chin with light fingers. I looked at her. Her cheeks had gone bloodless below the brown of the sun, and her eyes glowed at me dark and deep.

"You will get her, Martin," she promised me, the husky prophetic note in her voice. "You will take your Margaret out of the midst of her enemies. I know it. I can see it. I can see you riding into camp on your tall horse and she riding pillion behind you. When do you go?"

I threw a hand behind me and my heart lifted. "There is our road, west and north, but the Covenant are on it to-night."

"But not to-morrow."

"Not to-morrow, I pray God."

She reached a hand towards Tadg Mor. "Give me my shoe, Tadg Mor, before you twist it in two."

She rose to her feet then. "We will go back to camp now and refresh our guest. We have the night before us for planning."

She made herself one with us, and when the time came, that was not forgotten for her.

CHAPTER IX

THE TOWER OF SPYNIE

I

I AM in a hurry now, and the battle of Alford is soon told. It was the maddest, most formless tulzie in all that war. Montrose weaved his tactics ably as ever, and Baillie planned his attack as well as he was able, but the Gordons broke every rule of war and settled the issue in the first hour. They were no longer gun-shy, and, moreover, they were powerful angry that morning. Baillie had been wasting their lands of the Brae-of-the-Plain and the Bog-of-the-Winds for a fort-night, and their one desire was to get close enough to hack. Even young Lord Gordon, usually a prudent leader after Montrose's own heart, was recklessly angry and swore to wrest Baillie by the neck out of the midst of his army.

Baillie crossed by the Boat of Forbes on Wednesday morning, and swung his line to outflank the Gallows Hill, but when he saw the full strength of our position he changed front and halted. He was wisely minded to fall back across the river—if he had time—but Argyll and Balcarres were set against that, and before he could make up his mind the fight was down on him. A picked body of MacPhersons trotted forward as a challenge, and the half‑Gaelic hardy regiment of

Cassillis of Lower Ayr pushed forward to meet them. Balcarres galloped forward on the left. And then the Gordons, horse and foot, charged home, every man yelling "Strathbogie." O'Cahan drove in on the flank, Clan Ranald and the Atholl reserve came leaping down the Gallows Hill into the midst of it, and in less than five minutes the fight became one wide welter of horse and foot hacking and plunging and grappling in an old-time hand-to-hand tulzie.

Ranald Ban MacKinnon, who was in the midst of it, told me later that for minutes he had his targe up and his point down, for he could not make out friend from enemy; until Nat Gordon, driving in behind Balcarres, began to hough the horses. That broke them and gave the foot room to fall apart and kill.

There could be only one ending to that fight, for in hand-to-hand encounters the Highlandmen and Irish had no equals. The pitched fight was over in an hour, and the tide of flight and pursuit poured down the valley of the Don. The Gordons showed no mercy that day, and pressed the broken Covenanters so fast and so furiously that even Argyll, usually the first man off a lost field, was very nearly caught by a Clan Ranald horseman.

We had not many killed, though a good number of wounded amongst the horse. In our regiment we had only a few flesh wounds, and Iseabal Rose and I had little to do after noon. But the army and Montrose suffered one very grievous loss. Lord Gordon, with his hand out to grasp Baillie, was shot from behind, and died under the horse's hooves. He was a noble and generous youth, and some say that his death changed history; for he loved and was loved by Montrose, was steadfastly loyal, and maintained the fine Gordon horse constantly in the field. His brothers, Lord Aboyne and Lord Lewis, were loyal enough, but suffered from the strange perverse nature of so many of the Gordon chiefs, and might at any moment withdraw their forces for a ploy of their own, or for a mere whimsy of temper. It was their defection and Alasdair's that lost us Philiphaugh.

That is enough of the battle of Alford.

2

We crossed the dark-flowing stern Spey at the wide ford of Gight, the stiff press of the water up to our saddle-girths. That was on Thursday evening; and there were three of us on horseback and a guide of the Gordons on foot: Alick Anderson, Tadg Mor O'Kavanagh, and myself. Ranald Ban MacKinnon had wanted to come in my place, but when I pointed out to him that someone had to stay behind to stand by Iseabal Rose, he soon agreed with me that he was the best man to do that. We had exchanged the ship-master's tired beast for a broad-backed shelt; Tadg Mor had borrowed a tall horse from Nat Gordon, and I rode my Moray saddle-horse. We might need strength and speed in our horses before all was done, and Tadg Mor had to yield his liking for a pony.

The three of us had left Alford on the Wednesday evening after the battle and ridden most of the night, a distance of some forty miles, through safe and easy Gordon country to Huntly's stronghold at Bog of Gight, a mile back from Spey. We were then only a matter of ten miles from Spynie Tower. The headstrong old earl was holed up at Strathbogie, but his retainers had received us in kindly fashion. We brought them the

198

first news of the victory and of the exploits of the Gordons, but their exultation was sadly dampened by the death of their beloved young chief.

We had rested all that day and slept when we could; a mile or two beyond the river began Covenant territory, and we dare not venture close to Spynie until the half-dark of the summer night was at hand. In the evening we had stored our saddle-bags with enough provisions to last us for three days, and so plunged across the ford on our very doubtful and dangerous venture. A tall young Gordonach, answering to the name of Dod Myron, with the sandy Gordon pow and the limber legs of the bog-trotter, offered to guide us a safe way to the vicinity of Spynie Loch, and his offer we accepted. He splashed across the ford up to his waist holding Tadg Mor's stirrup-leather, an old targe slapping on his back, and an unfleshed basket-hilt sword under his oxter. "For," said he, "I wouldna mind cutting a couple o' bluidy Covenant throats to help the young laird rest easy."

At the other side of the ford we sent Alick Anderson homewards. He did not want to go, but we told him bluntly that a man of his years would be more of a hindrance than a help.

"Can you run?" Tadg Mor asked him.

"No sailor could ever I knew."

"Then we will be better wanting you, for ourselves will be running like hares."

He made no more demur. Between us we decided that he must make Lochloy the long road round, avoiding Elgin and Forres, for it might be well for him, in any later enquiry, not to be remembered coming the Huntly road. I rode with him some short distance up the river bank and, before we said farewell, got him again to go over every detail he could remember of the interior of Spynie Tower, checking him on a plan I had made on a sheet of paper I had borrowed off the chaplain. But though I had made that plan most painstakingly I had no dimmest notion of any way of putting it to use. Still, it was as well to be prepared. We had to get inside. We had to.

"Listen now!" I said at the end. "In two days' time, not sooner, you will come boldly to Spynie and ask for Margaret. If she is not there you will hear about it. But if she is, you will go home and come again later. In that way you will know if luck is with us or against us. And listen! if we are lucky, Margaret must come with us—to her old life—whether she likes to or not."

"I see that," he agreed sadly.

"When do you sail?"

"I should be ready the last week of October."

"Then, by that time, if God is good, we will find a road to Lochloy for her. You will wait as long as you can."

"I will wait." He looked me in the eye and then at his saddle-bow. "I'm by way of being a fair judge o' women, old or young," said he, "and I am thinking there is a man in your army my lassie is over-fond of." He looked up quickly then.

"That could be," I agreed, "and the man might not be far from here." I gestured head downstream.

His eyebrows lifted in some surprise. "She is safe in his hands?"

"He is the finest man in all the world," I told him.

"Goad!" he exclaimed deeply. "Is it not grand when men trust each other!"

We gripped hands then and parted, not for the last time.

West of Spey and north of low hills the land rises in a slow ridge of woodland, and then drops by small lochans to a desperately flat and cultivated country all the way to Elgin and Spynie. We had marched that way more than once. But our Gordonach did not strike over the ridge; at the reiver's jog-trot he led away northwards on the edge of it inside the trees, and so down into a rushy hollow and up again, and along the margin of other wooded slopes. After an hour's steady going we crossed a cart-road that led, he told us, to a fishing port at mouth of Spey; and from that point we mounted a long sandy hill and came round the shoulder of it to look out on the northern sea; the same northern firth that we had looked on from Auldearn and Lochloy, and the same strung blue wall of mountains beyond it. All the water sparkled to the sun leaning down to the breast of a tall mountain that lifted a nipple into the mouth of the sky.

It was a clear evening in the heart of summer, shortly after the longest day, and in that northern clime dawn and day and gloaming spaced twenty hours of the twenty-four. An hour before midnight one might read ordinary print. Tadg Mor, I mind, cursed the summer and the sun and the cloudless sky, for, as he said, anything we might do must be done in the few brief hours of the half-darkness.

All that coast westwards to the Loch of Spynie is a mile-wide unpeopled belt of sand-dunes and shingle-banks, interspersed with patches of close-growing wiry grass scattered with the stars of the sea-pink. On the inland margin was a fringe of old whins that had not yet shed their golden bloom, and as we pushed through them they crackled softly in the evening warmth and gave out their dry and pleasant odour. There were rabbit holes everywhere and we had to ride carefully.

"We are safe enough this side of the loch," Dod Myron told us, "but at the other side the Elgin fat-bellies go down to the sea links summer evenings to play a dom foolish game they call gowf—hitting a bit ball of feathers with an iron bossed shinty stick."

"Shinty! That is no foolish game," denied Tadg Mor. "I have seen the Gordons play it."

"Na, na! Nae shinty. There is no one playing the ball against them. They just clout the ball along the ground and clout it again and into a wee bit hole in the grass, and they swear by their Maker when they miss their putt—and count a hundred or twa."

"Any game that makes a man swear is not a bad game," said Tadg Mor weightily.

"It is a good game then," said the Gordonach, "for they swear most awful."

Another hour's riding between the dunes brought us to the sedgy margin of the Loch of Spynie. Once it had been a sea loch with ships sailing into it, but the blowing sands of all that shifting coast had gradually silted up the sea channel, and it was now only a wide brackish expanse of shallow water into which the sea flowed at the very top of spring tides. Along our side of the loch, a matter of three miles, was a marshy desolation, but the marsh had a sandy foundation and the horses did not bog down in it. Dod Myron went splashing ahead of us through shallow pools without heeding where he put his feet, and we followed securely.

Great beds of swaying reed and whispering sedge grew far out into the loch, and the water beyond them was a lovely soft blue. A desolate scene, one might hold, but there was a quietude about its desolation and a brooding about its stillness that makes it live in my mind. And then a water-fowl bobbed its head among the sedges and two noble swans came sailing down outside the reeds, six grey cygnets in a flotilla behind them, and the ripple that flowed and slid across the water had the rhythm of a song.

"A great place for swans, the Loch of Spynie," said our guide. The faded matted reed mounds of their nesting places stood out of the water all along the shore.

"How near do you want to get to Davy's Tower?" he asked us after a while.

"To put a hand on it in the dark," Tadg Mor told him, "but now we'll be doing with a look at it as near as we can get without getting a hand put on us. We must not be seen."

The Gordonach thought for a while. "I know the place," he said then.

He led along the eastern shore where the reeds were so tall that even from horseback we could not be seen over them, and in time came to a good-sized stream flowing into a corner of the loch. There the horses drank of the fresh water. We splashed across, knee-deep, and at the other side our guide warned us to dismount and move canny. We had circled to the south side of the loch now, and slipped along westwards until we came to a sand-beached small curve of bay; and there, a cable-length off shore, a bluff of islet stood tall out of the water. It had a grassy knowe above crumbling sandstone, and a hazel copse clad the sides of it.

"There it is for you," pointed Dod Myron. "No one comes anigh it except flintlock fowlers in the harvest-time and winter for a shot at the ducks and wild swans."

Without hesitating he waded into the loch, and, leading our horses, we followed. The water was limpid clear, still with that soft blue tint, and we could see the yellow sand at the bottom shimmering with sun ripples. It was nowhere more than thigh-deep. On the outer side of the islet facing the loch was a small wedge of grass cutting into the sandstone bluff, and, at the head of the wedge, an ancient ruined anchorite cell with a sloping door having one great slab for lintel.

"Made for us, my darling lad," commended Tadg Mor.

"Ay, but come away up and let me show you," urged our guide.

We tied our unwilling horses to a hazel; they kept straining to mouth the grass.

"Your fill in a minute, my *buachal*!" said Tadg Mor, slapping his big brown cavalry horse.

We clambered up through the hazels. Our great lad of the Gordons was already at the summit, lying flat on the grass, his head carefully lifted between two bosses of stone. We followed his example.

"There is Davy's Tower for you now," he whispered. "The walls of it are nine feet thick, and if ye are for cracking them ye'll be wondering."

3

There was David's Tower, indeed, not more than half a mile distant, plain in view over the reeds fringing the shore: a tall rectangular tower of masonry on a slight elevation above the water, with the ruins of the old palace buildings below and above it. A little farther away a few bothies stood back from a wooden jetty, and nearer at hand, but some distance inland, were the half-burned buildings of a farm steading. Colkitto had done that burning after Auldearn. In front of the tower, facing south, was a walled kitchen garden, with tall trees beyond, and, still southwards, farm land and scattered steadings all the way towards Elgin. We could not see Elgin for a low ridge between, but the castle of it stood up on Lady Hill, and to the left we could see the ruined roof and main tower of the great cathedral, that lovely lanthorn of the north so foolishly ill-used by the Reformers.

We were looking direct at the eastern face of David's Tower, in which was the main entrance with its portcullis pent, and were near enough to make out the narrow defensive slits at each side of the gate. I counted four windows, one above the other, up to the battlemented roof. No one moved about the tower or in its vicinity; but there were masons at work among the farm buildings, repairing the damage we had done seven weeks before: idle work at that, for Lewis Gordon was to come raiding in October and burn the steading once again.

We studied all that wide view slowly to hold it in memory: the smooth swell of the rich farm lands lifting to brown moors far in the south, the heavily wooded ridges tilting and flowing away westwards to the horizon over which lifted one purple bald mountain, and the wide serene blue floor of the loch where swans sailed and gulls' wings shone and flashed, and one ferry-boat was pulling out towards a fishing port at the mouth of the sea.

"It is strong surely and hard to come at," murmured Tadg Mor, more to himself than to me.

"Along by the reed beds and below that ruined wall," I pointed out.

"With whatever night is in it to cover us," he agreed.

We slid down then to the grassy hollow, unsaddled our horses, and pegged them out to graze; and thereafter the three of us sat against the ruined wall of the cell and shared food: bannocks and oatcakes and cold meat, with a mouthful out of a flask of usgebaugh laced with honey.

"We owe you our thanks," I told Dod Myron, munching away companionably, "and if we get the chance we will not forget your fine guiding. We know our road now, and it might be well for you to make your way back to Gight."

"There is no hurry on me," said he.

"And too much hurry in a small while, maybe," hinted Tadg Mor.

"I dinna ken what ploy ye have in mind," said the Gordonach, "but if it is against a Brodie or a Grant I'm with ye."

"It is against Brodie of Brodie his own self," Tadg Mor enlightened him. "He holds a friend of ours yonder that we must deliver by hook or by crook."

"It canna be done," said the other firmly, "and the tower held."

"We will be making a sort of middling good wallop at it whatever," said Tadg Mor cheerfully.

"Ye will do that, I ken, for the warld knows Coll's men and the chances they take. But man, man! the portcullis is aye down in dangerous times and only one bit of a postern door at the far side."

"Men walk in and out of that bit of a door?"

"Ay do they."

"And could not we be taking a daunder in ourselves in a friendly way?"

The Gordonach laughed. "Myself would like to see how ye do it. If ye dinna mind I will hang round a whilie. I could keep an eye on the horses and hold them ready in case of a sudden push; there would be no fear for myself with the bulrushes handy; and look at the story I might be having to tell in after days."

"If there is a story in it—or an after day."

He was a sound youth and so very keen to stay that we did not gainsay him. And when the time came in the gap of danger he did his part like a man, though for a time then I thought we had brought him to his death.

It was as dark as it would be any time that night when Tadg Mor and I slipped along the shore towards the tower, but, indeed, there was no depth of darkness to hide us. The sky was clear and full of stars that paled towards the north where a white glow suffused upwards from the horizon behind the sand-hills of the coast; and the floor of the loch was a wan, dimly luminous floor of silver. Our hope was that no pickets were night-posted outside the tower. We moved very slowly and circumspectly on the margin of the reeds, crouching along head down, and lying flat every minute to listen. We had seen shepherd dogs among the farm buildings, and one of them, on a night hunt, might easily raise an alarm, more especially if the news of Alford had reached Spynie. But the night remained still. We could hear our hearts beat, and ever and again, as a breath of air shivered in the reeds, they whispered a small lonely aware whisper to themselves only.

So we came safely to the northern face of the tower, and lay flat on a dark patch of grass above the beach that was here sandy and clear of sedge. We looked at the tall bulk of the wall on the head of the slope above us. There were eight windows in pairs of four on this side, and the bottom one on the left, ten feet off the ground, showed a dim red glow. I knew from my plan of the building that behind that window was the main guard, and I visioned it as the shipmaster had described it to me: a big room with a stone floor, a wide hearth for burning peats, and an arched roof; there was a double stair leading to a gallery and the upper floors; and in the far corner near the main door was the well of the spiral stairs leading to the portcullis pent and the turret room. From that turret room Margaret had waved to her uncle, and we had to get at it somehow.

Our eyes went up the wall to that topmost turret window on the north-west corner, and my heart gave a stir when I saw that it was lit—dimly lit as by a taper, but still lit.

"She is there," whispered Tadg Mor.

"Someone is there," I whispered back.

But I knew it was Margaret. I felt her near me. I could call out her name, and her clear high voice would answer me. But instead of doing that folly I crawled up the slope and came to my feet by the wall. Tadg Mor was at my heels.

Close under the heavily barred windows we stealthily made the full circle of the tower. As we knew, there was only the main entrance on the east side and a narrow postern door on the west. On that west side, some distance from the tower, were the ruined or half-ruined buildings of the old palace, mostly low structures

208

full of small chambers. We slipped across there, into a broken doorway where nettles grew, and out of the dark took a long look at the postern door directly across from us. There was the black square of a shuttered grill high up on the face of it.

"If we walked across and knocked," whispered Tadg Mor hopefully, "who knows but they might open to us, and if they did, could we put enough sudden fright in them to give us time to make the turret and back again?"

"They would not open without looking through the grill, and it is not they would be frightened then."

"We will not disturb them so. What are we to do now?"

"Nothing more to-night. To-morrow we may be able to find out how strongly the tower is held."

"The three of us——"

"Three?"

"The Myron lad has the clear fighting eye. We could manage a good few—ten maybe—surprise against them. I could pistol two and dagger one and cut down a couple more." He paused, and then, "Do you want to go on with it, Maurteen?"

"Fear or no fear, I will be inside that door to-morrow night."

"Man! is that strange sure feeling on you again?" He patted my shoulder softly. "The thing is as good as done then. Let us away back to our den and be taking a sleep to ourselves, in the name o' God."

And we went back to our little island as carefully as we had come.

In spite of damp trews as well as mind travail I slept well that night, and had no dreams under Iseabal Rose's plaid. I awoke before early dawn, and a little breeze ruffled the wan surface of the loch, and made the water lap-lap on the sandy beach; and all the reeds swayed softly and whispered, "Hush—hush! sleep you now." And sleep I did.

It was cold feet wakened me for good in full daylight. Iseabal Rose's plaid was on the short side, and I often cursed it for that. I am an old man now and have slept softly lapped in down these many years, but never have I slept so soundly as in those far-off days of my youth in Scotland, in rain or shine, dark or day, frost or heat, with the peril of ugly death round every corner.

Friday was a long, long day, but it passed. While one or the other of us kept a steady watch on the tower the other two had nothing to do but lie about on the grass and talk. Once I found Tadg Mor and Dod Myron at long jumps, with the Gordonach having the better of it, and I tried a jump myself and beat them both, thereby rising in the lad's estimation; up to that I suspected he did not think much of my qualities for the dangerous business in hand. I think I have said before now that, a young man, I had no great bodily strength, but I should say also that I was reasonably fast and of good endurance. It might be the Indian strain in me, but I do not remember any time that I was leg weary—not at Inverlochy, nor at Dundee in that terrible night retreat, nor in any of the stupendous marches in the welter of the Grampians. I was just built that way for toughness.

Another time I found Tadg Mor trying out the Gordonach at sword-play. The lad knew some of the cuts and guards and was immensely eager to learn of the Irishman's skill and experience.

"Now, in an onset," said the master, "the one and

only way is to keep your targe up and go in with the point. A man's bowels girn facing the stap, and he is apt to yield a step and break line; but if you come in slashing he is inclined to lean his targe and himself against the blow, and so is hard to break. Go back there a piece and I will show you."

After the midday meal we risked sending Dod round about into Elgin to pick up any news that might be. I hesitated to do it, for I was afraid that his half-Gaelic Gordon twang might get him into trouble, but he eagerly insisted that a plain country lad without arms was in no danger whatever. He brought back word that Brodie of Brodie and Kinnaird of Culbin were holding Spynie with about two score men, and that there was dismay in the town at the news of Alford. There was talk of an early meeting of all the Moray lairds at Darnaway Castle near Forres to prepare a defence of the Laich against the Gordons, who would be sure to make a fresh raid now that Baillie was out of the way. At that time the local Covenant was used to hold a sort of half-parliament in the Earl of Moray's castle at Darnaway, though the earl himself avoided politics and war.

"Two score men!" said Tadg Mor, looking at me. "Are you sure of yourself now, Maurteen?"

"I was sure last night, and to-night I may be, but now I am sure of nothing."

Some time in the afternoon Tadg Mor was above on watch, and I was idly questioning Dod Myron on the manner of life that the Gordons followed in Gight and Strathbogie—and finding it the same in work and play and way of thinking as in our own Leinster—when Tadg Mor whistled down to us. We scrambled up to his side.

211

"There is a stir on," he whispered in some excitement.

There surely was. Saddled horses, two or more to each horseboy, were being brought round to the front of the tower; the portcullis was up and the big door open; and men in half-armour moved in and about the arch. We had not long to wait to find out what was toward. In less than ten minutes a strong body of horse moved away from the tower on the Elgin road. We were too far away to make sure, but we agreed that there were not less than thirty men in that company, and we were near enough to be sure that there was no woman amongst them.

"To-night!" said Tadg Mor, a gleam in the eyes that met mine.

And I nodded my head for I could not trust my voice to hide the tell-tale beating of my craven heart.

The horsemen did not go up to Elgin. Where the road forked they swung away westwards at the round trot.

"The Forres road," Dod told us. "They are off to their meeting—and well guarded."

"To return when—to-night?" Doubt was all alive in me.

"Darnaway and back is thirty miles. They will be late whatever."

"And too late," said Tadg Mor, sanguine now beyond reason. "Tell me, Dod *avic*, did you ever blood that fine sword?"

"Give me the chance," said Dod eagerly. "I'll no' be a man till I do."

"A lad in his first fight," hinted Tadg Mor soberly, "is sometimes not as bloody-minded as the day before it. I saw the Gordons at Auldearn."

"Ay! that is held against them, but, mind you, they came again."

"There will be no coming again to-night."

"Try me then," said the lad vehemently.

"This is wrong, Tadg Mor," I protested.

"Maybe it is, but for this night I would take the devil himself bearing a sword. Why did you not let Ranald Ban come?"

"I will be the devil for you," said our gay Gordon lad.

4

That night, at the first dark, the three of us crouched inside the ruined doorway and looked across at the postern door. We were fully armed for the venture, except that Tadg Mor, for ease of movement in narrow places, carried no targe. The leather coat, purchased for a stolen keg of beer at Aberdeen, had long ago been cut short at the hips and would turn a sword-cut. I had loaned Dod Myron one of my pistols.

Our plan was a simple one but very desperate. Dod Myron, the plain country lad, was to walk across to the postern, lay down sword and targe by the wall and knock boldly. The warder would, without doubt, come to that knocking and look through the grill; and Dod, a man from Rothes on the edge of the Covenant country, would have an important message for my lord Brodie. Anything might happen then: the door open, the warder, suspicious of the caught Gordon twang, might insist that the message be given through the grill, or he might even call up the guard before opening the door. It was a dicer's throw. But if the door did open, Dod was to put his foot in it and we were to drive across. And then? Then our swords and luck.

But at the very last minute something happened that made us change our plan. Dod was in the act of getting sword and targe loose before slipping across the yard when we heard the snick of the grill being lifted, and then, after a pause, the door opened and a man took the single step to the ground. The door clanged on his very heels, and the grill jerked back into place. Even if we had been straining on the leash we could not have made the door before it shut.

The man came directly across the yard, and took one stride to pass our door. He did not take a second. For Tadg Mor's long arm, like the circling lash of a whip, had him inside; and a hand, struck hard over his mouth, strangled the squeal of terror and surprise. His feet kicked amongst the nettles, his hands clawed, and suddenly he stilled. The whole thing happened more quickly than the telling.

"There is a dirk at your heart." That hissed whisper would still any man.

Tadg Mor held his prisoner from behind, one hand over his mouth and the other under his oxter with the dagger point below the breast-bone. The hand over mouth slipped to throat, and the man, looking down, saw in the dimness the gleam of the steel. He was very still.

"Question him, Maurteen," whispered Tadg Mor, "and if he lifts his voice his soul will lepp out after it between his jaws."

"Goad! The Irishers!" the man whispered.

I leant close, my mind at stretch.

"How many hold the tower to-night?"

He was silent gathering his wits.

"The truth! How many? Quick!"

"Six—eight—no more—seven maybe."

"Where are they?"

"In the muckle room—a meenit ago."

"Is Brodie there?"

"Him and Kinnaird are away to Darnaway."

"Are they coming back to-night?"

"Hoo would I ken? Sometimes they stay."

"Are there any prisoners in the tower?"

"Ae woman in the turret room."

"Who opened the door to let you out?"

"The warder."

"He keeps all the keys?"

"A bunch at his girdle."

"Good man yourself, Maurteen!" whispered Tadg Mor.

"H-s-sh! Who are you?"

"Tam Murdoch, the builder."

"Why were you in the tower?"

"Having a drink to himself—I can smell it," said Tadg Mor, and Dod Myron chuckled to himself softly.

"Na! I was complaining to the steward aboot two trowels stolen on me to-day."

"The Moray robbers!" whispered the Gordonach, only a plain reiver by inclination.

"You can get in again?" I suggested.

"I have no business."

"You will have." My mind was working smooth and fast. "Listen! You will go back to the door and you will knock at it, and when the warder comes you will tell him that you have an important thing to say to the steward about the roofing timbers. Do you hear me?"

"I canna——"

"You will go back."

"They would hang me the morn."

"The man that opens to you will hang no one."
That was Tadg Mor's meaning whisper.

"How many are ye?" I could read what was behind
that question, so abnormally was I strung then.

"Three."

"Only three?"

"No more."

He was very badly frightened, but I will not say that
he was a coward, for he hated to be the betrayer, and
wanted something—anything—to prop his self-esteem.
If there were even a company of us he might need a
shrewd prick, but three men, he would tell himself,
though he took me to be lying, could do little against
six or eight soldiers—except die.

"I'll do it," he said, and drew in his breath.

It came about that easy. But we had to move fast
now, and the mood was on us for fast moving.

"You take him, Tadg Mor," I began, but Tadg
stopped me impatiently. In action he needed no
lesson.

"I know, I know! Come, mason! You need fear
no one but me."

It touched some mad sense of laughter in me to see
Tadg Mor crouch across the yard behind his victim.
The man was short and slender, and Tadg Mor could
never hope to hide his great shoulders. Dod Myron
and I crouched inside the doorway like men set for
a race, our swords drawn.

"We did that well," he whispered to me, making
himself one of a trinity.

Tadg Mor set his man on the step of the door, and,
himself, straightened up flat by the side of it, his head
back and turned sideways, a pointed pistol in one hand

and his dirk in the other. There was enough light to see the steel dim-gleaming.

The man Murdoch knocked on the door, at first timidly, and then despairingly loud as Tadg Mor gestured at him.

And the door opened. It opened after what seemed a startlingly short time. It looked a miracle to me. First the grill lifted and a growl came through; and then before Murdoch could raise his voice a chain clanged and the door was flung wide.

"You dom ninny, Tam! What did you forget this time——?"

That half-angry warder got no further. The builder got back a spark of spirit.

"The Irishers, Will!" he cried, and made the essay to bolt like a rabbit head down between the warder's legs.

But Tadg Mor was quicker than the hound Bran, for he pivoted himself round the jamb, hurled the builder aside with a thrust of the hip and struck and grappled the warder, all in one shattering motion.

The Gordon lad and I leaped across the yard and reached the door shoulder to shoulder. What happened the mason I do not know, for we neither saw him nor heeded him. Tadg Mor was already easing the warder's body to the floor. It was a dead body, I fear, though Tadg Mor, changing his mind at the last, had given him the hilt instead of the point; but the head would need to be thick to withstand that dunt.

The whole thing had taken place with very little noise—the yelp of the mason and the thud of a blow— no more—and the only noise now was the clinking of keys at the fallen man's belt as Tadg Mor fumbled at them. The main guard was at the other side of the tower at the end of a long passage, and a good shout would be needed to rouse the soldiers there. I forced my body into the passage beyond Tadg Mor—that is, with my mind I forced it, for there was room enough—and he straightened up behind me, the keys clinking as he thrust the bunch inside his belt.

"Quick now, brother!" he whispered.

I looked into blackness down that long passage, and, far away, close to the floor, saw a chink of light. There was the door of the main guard. I put my sword under my targe oxter, put a hand out before me, fixed my eyes on that chink of light, and went forward on tiptoe over an uneven flagged floor. Tadg Mor's grasp was in my belt, and Dod Myron came linked behind. In time my fingers touched the wood of that final door, and groped softly over it until they found the latch. They found it on the wrong side, I thought. I levered up the latch noiselessly and pressed, but the door held firm as a rock.

"Locked!"

But Tadg Mor's hand came over my shoulder, found my wrist and tugged gently; and the door came with his tug.

"Well now!" I whispered, and took three long soft strides out into the main guard.

I tried to take everything in at one glance. I stood half-way up the long room, and it was much as I had visualised it: a great stone hall with a table running down the middle, a huge fireplace at the top end, and the double stairs going up at either side of it. A fire of peats flamed on the hearth, for in that stone room, with walls nine feet thick, even July nights would hold a chill. A crusie iron lamp stood lighting on the table end, but the hall was so big and high that the smoky flames of fire and lamp no more than made a ruddy gloom in which shadows lurked and leaped.

A group of men—six or eight, I do not remember—sat about the fire on benches or hassocks. They were not in armour or armed, were bareheaded, and their hoseless feet were set comfortably in the warm ashes.

We stood there and looked at them, and there was a strange tight unreal feeling all about us. We could have strode ten paces and cut down three men like sheep. And then a guard turned his head. He might have felt our eyes on him, or even such a small thing as the draught from the door. He stared at us a moment, and then started to his feet.

"The Hielands!" he cried.

Then we were down on them. They were no trouble to us at all. They would see three men in line, could imagine other men crowding at the door; they would see the terrible points withdrawn for the thrust, the brown targes with bosses and studs gleaming, and eyes white with the lust of death. They bleated and scattered like sheep, a bench fell, and one man in the scurry fell backwards into the red coals. As that man roared and rolled and leaped to his feet the Gordonach blooded his sword, yelling with all his might: "For the young Laird!"

Tadg Mor and I did not draw any blood. We were not bloody-minded men. The guards, all of one instinct, bundled towards a door at the side of the fireplace below the stair, and thrust themselves through in one mad press. Tadg Mor leaped behind and brought the flat of his sword on their crouched shoulders; I thrust one man through with the boss of my targe; and then the door crashed shut in our faces. But they were in such a hurry that a hand of one of them was caught and crushed in the jamb; and Tadg Mor, with a sudden mighty thrust of shoulder, drove the door an inch, and the hand disappeared.

"Obliging fellows!" he shouted, his fingers feeling round the keyhole. He was a locksmith by trade and got the right key at the second trial.

"If there's another way out," said he, "who will be looking for it?"

The man that the Gordonach had pierced was kicking his heels on the flags, and I knew what that kicking meant.

We wasted no time. I picked up the crusie light, and ran down the length of the hall, shading the flame behind my targe. The door to the turret stairs was in the right corner by the side of the main entrance. It was shut but not locked.

"Let me first, Maurteen," said Tadg Mor at my shoulder. "I have the keys."

He took the lamp from me and we started upwards. There were four, or it could be five, storeys in David's Tower, and the stone spiral was a long one, but I had plenty wind left at the top. There were narrow light slits in the outer curve, but no door above the portcullis pent until we came to one in an alcove below the last spiral. Tadg Mor bent down and shone the smoky flare of the lamp about the keyhole. There was no light from within, nor was there the least sound. My heart sank a little.

"Is this the place?" Tadg Mor whispered up over his shoulder.

"I think—it should be."

He found the right key very quickly, turned it with the faintest click, and his lamp shone across a room that had been dark a second ago. There was an open barred window in the far wall and a pallet couch along one side. The silence held for still a moment, and then the coverings stirred on the couch and a quick loved voice came out of the stir.

"Wha is't?"

That was our own Margaret, and she had been asleep. It was only natural that she should be asleep, and the hour near midnight, but all the same I was mightily surprised at her. So was Tadg Mor. He stepped inside the room and held the crusie above his head.

"She would sleep through God's thunder," said he.

At that she sat bolt upright and her eyes stared wildly at us. Her face was paler than its wont, but the good bones below it were firm as ever; her linten hair was in two plaits over her breast as I had so often seen it; the lovely curve of her throat and the smooth of her shoulders were whiter than curd; and as she looked at us the old soft lustre deepened and deepened in her grey eyes.

"My ain loons!" said she softly. "My very ain loons! Ye would come—ye aye came."

And there her face crinkled as a child's will, and her head turned from us and sank to her knees. It was the first time I had seen her weep. It was the last too.

Tadg Mor strode across the narrow floor and, of instinct, her shoulder swerved from his hand. She always hated to be touched.

"Girl!" he whispered urgently. "On with your clothes, quick!"

She shook her head to clear her eyes.

"Ye've the tower ta'en?"

"Or it us."

I was at her side now and with a firm hold of her wrist. And she looked up at me with swimming eyes.

"There are only the three of us."

"Three! Did ye kill them all?"

"No. The others may be back any minute. Come on, my dear!" And I tugged at her wrist.

She smiled up at me cooler than I was, and brought her other hand down on mine. "Easy, laddie, easy! Would ye shame me? Turn your backs a meenit and I'll no' keep ye."

We turned and Tadg Mor put down the crusie on a small table that already held a black-wicked tallow dip in a sconce. Dod Myron stood inside the door, his stained sword lax in his grip, and his astounded eyes on Margaret.

"Your manners, hero!" said Tadg Mor, and swung him round by the shoulder.

And the Gordonach looked back at him, blinking. "A woman! Did we do all that for a woman—and she out of Aberdeen, by her tongue?"

"You missed your schoolin', Dod boy," reproved Tadg Mor. "Did you never hear of Grecian Helen, or Deirdre of Glendaruel, or Izod of Dublin?"

"And Mary of Scotland as well—but Aberdeen—at our ain doors?"

"Far-away cows have long horns. Hurry, Meg darling!"

She did hurry. I had known her to spend an hour at her preening, but this time her toilet did not take three minutes.

She might have taken twenty for all the good her hurry did.

5

Indeed and indeed, things had been happening too easily for us all this day and night. Fate, as it were, had stood off and watched us into a trap; and now she pulled the sneck, and there we were close caught, and any way out was by the way of death. For, as Margaret straightened up from the silver-buckled shoon we had got her out of Dundee, and said, "I am ready," a sound came through the window bars that struck us to the marrow. It was the clack of horses' shod hooves on the paved causeway about the tower. Not the clink of one or two but the rumble of a whole squadron. There was no mistaking what that meant. The garrison was back from Darnaway. And as we stood stricken, there came through the window the murmur of men's voices, a murmur that carried yet no note of alarm.

Tadg Mor swore hard and leaped for the crusie.

"Come!" his voice grated. "They will be round by the front and I have the keys. We can make the postern before them."

But he was no more than on the top tread of the spiral before a cry and a clangour broke out far below. He checked abruptly at that, and slowly backed into the room, pushing us behind him.

"The door was wide to the wall," said he, his voice even, "and a dead man on the threshold. They have found him."

"The men inside would have called a warning," I added.

He shut and locked the door, and the sounds dimmed. We looked at each other. There was nothing I had to say, but Tadg Mor would not let us yield to panic.

"The game is not played out yet," said he firmly. "We are safe here."

"We can hold the stair against them all," cried Dod

Myron, a lad after Tadg Mor's own heart. "We can hold it for ever."

"An hour or two shorter will do us as well," said Tadg Mor. "Maybe you should not be here, my fine young lad."

"I hae a bite to me yet—and a man afore me," cried the lad.

But Margaret Anderson took hold of my arm with her two hands.

"How near is help?"

"Fifty miles."

"Oh, Martin! Am I to be the doom of you at last?"

But I shook her hands off. "Give me time to think, will ye?" I cried irritably.

I am not, I never was, a brave man, but I do not think that I can fairly call myself coward. I have full share of cowardice in me, but most times—not all times—all my life I have been able sufficiently to subdue that cowardice to do a thing calling for some boldness and resolution. In our present case cowardice—or call it prudence—would not serve at all. Neither, indeed, might anything bold to desperation. Those below would kill us as soon as they could get at us, and courage or cowardice would not avail. And so one might as well face death on one's feet, and biting. I wonder is that a rat's courage? That is how I felt in that corner: a little desperate and in a hurry to get the thing finished. I would bring about that finish.

The locked door I would not stand. The room was so small that it reminded me of a coney's burrow, and we the conies at the end of it waiting head down for the stoat.

"Open the door, Tadg Mor," I said, and he looked at me quickly.

But Margaret stopped him. "They mightna ken ye are wi' me."

"That would not serve us in the long run. Open the door for me, brother."

"I will do that," said Tadg Mor quietly, "for I see that you have the bit in your teeth."

He unlocked the door. "Leave the key in the lock," I told him, "and open the door wide. Ye will do what I ask ye now—and say nothing. Tadg Mor, stand here." I placed him back to the wall by the side of the opening. "Do not be seen, and wait on me." Dod Myron I placed at the other side, but behind the door. "Be ready to slap it shut when I tell you." His eyes glared at me as if he saw a stranger. Finally I took Margaret's hand and led her to the corner behind Tadg Mor. "Stay you there, girl!"

Her fingers closed on mine firmly. "I dinna mind if I die now, Martin."

"You will not die now, my dear." I was sure of it as I said it, and I softly tugged the plait of her hair.

I lit the tallow dip from the crusie and pushed the table close to the wall so that the light shone through the open door to the head of the spiral. "Make no sound," I warned finally, took up the lamp and went out into the shallow alcove. I put the lamp on the second step of the stairs on the widest part of the tread, and its light shone down into the first curve. Then I took the stand that I meant to keep, at the brink of the alcove, my shoulder inside the rim of my targe resting against the pillar of the spiral. I held my sword in the hand that went through the loop of the targe, and my primed pistol was in my right hand. I leant there, my eyes above the studded rim, and I listened with all my might. I was cool enough now, and the blood was no longer surging in my ears, but my mind was busy and intent.

I was, in fact, putting myself in the place of the men in the main guard, and particularly of the leaders, Brodie and Kinnaird. Whatever they did meantime, they must come to the head of the stairs in the end. They would not know how many had seized the tower. Two men were dead, and the guards had been driven like sheep—three men could not do that. They would be fearful of an onset at any moment, and in fear they would face the double stairs and the search of the other rooms. The turret would come last, though it might be in their thoughts first. That would check the boldest of them, for to get at it they would have to climb the long spiral that, like all old spirals, gave the defender his right hand against the attacker's left. But they would have to come to it in the end.

I could see them in my mind's eye peering in through the open door at the curve going up into blackness, will and flesh shrinking back from that long climb, with the chance of desperate men lurking above. The man who would lead that climb would be the best and boldest. He would be Brodie or Kinnaird. And on one or the other I had set my desire. Give me one of the two leaders: on that I set my will. But I have since been told that the most likely man to come first would be some plain soldier of brute courage. That could be, indeed, if all the plain men of proved courage were not away in the Covenant army.

That narrow well drew sound like a pipe, but for a long time there was no sound at all. And then a shod foot clinked softly far below, and then another, and my ear against the pillar that ran straight down heard or felt the clap of hands or scrape of fingers against stone. They were coming.

I expected that coming to be a very slow and cautious one, but it was not. Whoever was leading mounted steadily, not in a hasty scramble, reckless of the blows in the dark, but steadily, one foot after another. A man of great hardihood of mind—and no common soldier. The first thing I noticed was a wavering glow of light on the underside of the spiral as far down as I could see. They were lighting the road with a torch. I drew myself stiffly against the pillar and waited. The leading footsteps sounded firm on the stone below me. Then they stopped. Whoever was there could see the crusie lamp on the outer tread. If I swung out from the pillar he would see me too, but I remained behind my shield. The footsteps came again—one, two, three. I waited no longer. I leant from the pillar outside the rim of my targe, my pistol hand forward.

"Stand, dead man!"

The man stood against the curve of the wall and looked up at me. His head was level with my feet, and I could have shot him dead in that instant. He was full in the light from the crusie, and another light shone from below. A helmeted head darted round the pillar and jerked back again. Though I stood above him I saw that the man against the wall was not tall and that he was slenderly built. A youngish man, but bearded. His head was bare, he wore no armour, and carried no weapon. There was a white collar at his neck above dark cloth. There was no sound or movement anywhere, on the stair or within the room.

"If you move," I said, "if anyone moves, *you* die."

"Am I not still enough for a mark?" said the man in a calm deep voice.

227

"Tell your men to go down four steps."

He gestured downwards with his hand, and I heard a receding shuffle on the stairs. His men did not want him to die. That was good.

"You are Brodie?" I questioned.

"I am Alexander Brodie."

"Brodie of Brodie?"

"Men call me so."

"You are very welcome, Brodie of Brodie. I will talk with you."

"Who are you that kill my men in a strange house?"

"You flatter me; but I am Adjutant Martin Somers of O'Cahan's Regiment."

"I am not surprised. The Irish have had dealings with me. Why do you wait?"

And indeed I must have looked deadly enough with my black eyes and devil-slit chin beyond the rim of the targe.

"I will not kill you or anyone if I can help," I said.

"If you kill him," a deep voice boomed from below, "you will take a long time to die."

"Silence, fool!" my voice, too, boomed against the wall. "We are dying all our days. Come on up, Brodie, and talk to me."

"I will talk here."

"You will talk inside this room or you will die— and you can please yourself."

His eyes were just above the level of the alcove floor, and he looked past me into the room. All he would see was the barred window and the candle lighting on the table against the wall. He smiled then at some thought of his own.

"I am in no haste to die," said he, "though death is all about us. I will come and talk to you."

"God, Sandy!" said the strong voice below him.

"Hush, Kinnaird! It is but a poor foolish den of lions."

And he slowly mounted the steps towards me. I backed to the door and stepped aside outside it, but he strode straight in and across the room without turning his head. And that was the bravest thing done that night, for he must know that desperate men lurked within.

I leaped into the room behind him.

"Shut!" I cried. The door clanged, and I jarred the lock of the bolt home.

"A darling bit of work, Maurteen!" said Tadg Mor.

But the Gordon youth leant against the door and wiped his face downwards, and the eyes that looked at me had fear in them for the first time that night.

"His voice was colder than the frosts o' death," he muttered.

"There is no fear, brother," I told him. "The game is ours."

But he would not believe that. He shivered.

Brodie turned round below the window and looked us over; and a little surprise came into his voice.

"Only three? Ye are brave."

"So are you, Brodie."

"Bravery! A virtue of scoundrels, Irish and the rest."

He was a young man and soft-bearded, but his nose had the straightness of strength, his eyes the blue clearness of vision, his brow was domed for thought. I knew that we could not persuade this man to do anything that he did not want to do. He ignored us and turned to Margaret Anderson, straight in her corner, not afraid of him.

229

"Margaret Anderson, do you know these men?"

"My ain men, Laird Brodie."

"Have you lost all shame then?"

And Tadg Mor said smoothly. "Softly, my bonny man, softly!"

"Brodie," I cried. "Listen to me for a while."

"I listen," said he. "Your speech has not been idle."

"There are four of us here who wish to leave this room and this tower in safety."

"Four?"

"Five, counting yourself, but I speak for four. Listen! We have no reason to trust the Covenant, but we will accept your word. You will give us a safe conduct out of here and one hour's grace."

"You take the woman with you?"

"That is why we are here."

"Then you do not leave here." He turned to Margaret again and spoke her urgently. "Margaret Anderson, you will not go back to that shameful life."

"Shamefu' life! You blind fool!"

Tadg Mor strode across the room and brought his hand down firmly on a shoulder that did not flinch.

"I warned you once, man little, and I will warn you now for the last time. If you speak the bad word of that girl you will mouth her shoon."

Brodie looked at him fearlessly. "I do not speak ill to beseech her not to go with terrible men."

"There is no fault in that," agreed Tadg Mor. "Talk away."

"I will talk then. I saw your trick and played one of my own, though it may cost me my life. I knew that ye were up here and could not be many, or ye would have attacked us. I knew that ye would not want to die, and that ye would kill many of my men before ye died—if we attacked. That is why, risking my life, I walked into your midst. Ye are in a trap. Open that door and ye will face the blast of arquebuses."

"You will be dead."

"And the only life lost in killing you." He smiled half wistfully. "I do not want to die, and I do not want any more dead men in this tower. That is why I will give you your safe conduct and an hour's grace. But you leave the woman here."

"Your proposal is a reasonable one," I admitted. "But what will you do with the woman?"

He thought for a moment. "I will yield all I can to meet you. I will be lenient with her. To-morrow I will send her back to her uncle at Lochloy."

"And will you guarantee her safety with him for three months? Think well. Only three months."

He considered for a space and then shook his head.

"I cannot do that. I have not the power."

"Your Kirk is stronger than you are. Will the Kirk have mercy? Tell me that. Will your Kirk have mercy?"

"Our bodies and souls are in the hands of the Kirk for our good."

"And for the Kirk's power. Margaret Anderson's body is forfeit to the Kirk, but her soul never."

But here Margaret Anderson stepped from her corner, her hands out to Brodie.

"Laird Brodie," she cried, "let my men free. I will go back to my uncle."

"A wise choice, my girl," said he.

And Tadg Mor lifted up his great red head and laughed.

"Brother, is she not our own Meg, as we knew her?"

But she obstinately and hopelessly repeated: "I will go back—I will go back—I will go back to my uncle."

"You will go back," said I, "when we take you, a regiment at your back, and all the pipes playing *Farewell my Fair One.*"

"And she riding on a white horse," roared Tadg Mor, "a Spanish comb in her plaited hair and a silver belt on the span of her waist, like Maeve the queen."

And, his blue eyes blazing into mine, and his sword keeping time, he lifted up his great voice in his old song, so that the bars of the window vibrated:

> " And she shall swing a silken gown,
> A milk-white steed to ride upon,
> With silver buckles on her shoon,
> And in her hair a Spanish comb."

I often wonder what the men waiting outside thought of that mad singing.

"Oh God—oh God!" cried Margaret. "The madness of drink is on them again."

"Not so," I protested. "But the fear of death is headier than wine." And I faced Brodie, whose eyes had wonder in them. "Your game is played, Brodie, but ours is only at its beginning. You are a brave man, as so many rascals be, but you have other qualities as well, and one of them, I think, is likeableness—the power of drawing men to love you. On that quality —if you have it—I am now going to stake your life and ours. If there is an unfriend of yours outside that door you are a dead man and we dead with you. First I will tie your hands behind your back."

"Ye are strange men," said he, "and steadfast, but though ye will do your worst on me ye will never leave this tower alive with that woman. Why waste lives then?"

"We will leave without a life wasted. Tadg Mor, here is my belt—you do the tying."

"Whatever you say, brother," said Tadg Mor, sheathing his sword. "I do not see farther than my nose, but I will put a knot on him for you, and ask his pardon."

He deftly strapped Brodie's wrists behind his back to his body sash. Our prisoner made no effort to resist or hinder him, and I minded the minister we had mishandled at Aberdeen in our first rescue of Margaret. The Kirk endowed the same stoical quality on all its worshippers.

"Hold him so with your left hand," I directed Tadg Mor, "and put your pistol against him there. That way. Come now."

"Thunder o' God!" cried Tadg Mor. "I see your plan at last."

"See that your finger does not twitch then and sound the death of us."

"It will not twitch till I ask it," said Tadg Mor. "Open the door for me."

I pushed Dod Myron aside from the door. He had been leaning against the jamb, and his first fine hardihood had ebbed low. In the rush of onset and plain cut-and-thrust he was as ready as any man of his breed, but, after all, he was only a youth, and this mad parleying with words in the face of death in a den must unman him. He would again find his spirit out in the open.

I took the bunch of keys from the lock and leant an ear to the keyhole, but there was no sound that I could catch. Then I put my lips close and shouted:

"Kinnaird—Kinnaird!"

There was no answer, but this time I heard a shuffle at the head of the stairs. Again I called aloud:

"Kinnaird, be careful! Brodie is coming out."

I clenched teeth then, unlocked the door and pulled it wide; and Tadg Mor, holding Brodie, stiff-armed by wrist and sash, thrust him into the opening. I stepped to Tadg Mor's side, and looked over Brodie's shoulder.

The mouth of the alcove was a press of men. Three lay flat on the floor, three knelt behind them, two more on the second step of the stairs; and eight flintlocks were trained on the door. Behind, where the stairs curved into darkness, stood a tall heavy-shouldered man with a black beard above polished corselet, holding the crusie lamp above his head. The muzzles of the levelled pieces wavered and sank.

"Who is Kinnaird?" I asked.

"I am Kinnaird," said the dark man holding the crusie.

"Listen then, Kinnaird! We are going down the stairs now, and if you value Brodie's life you will send your men down ahead of us. You can see why."

Kinnaird looked at Brodie, looked at the grim, hook-nosed, fighting face of Tadg Mor, saw the hilt of the pistol that was held so firmly against his friend's back. He was a prompt man.

"I can see," said he. "They will go down."

"Kinnaird!" cried Brodie, and he tried to jerk and prostrate himself free of Tadg Mor's grip; but Tadg Mor's arm was as rigid as a steel bar. "Kinnaird, you will do your duty."

"I am doing that, Sandy. I warned you that your plan would fail against Colkitto's men."

"Let it not fail. These men are slayers, and they would take a prisoner of the Kirk—a woman—into their libidinous army. They must not leave here alive. Do your duty and do not heed my poor body. If you fire now you will kill two terrible men, and there is only one poor fool left in the room."

"And a bigger fool outside it in Kinnaird of Culbin," said that ready man.

"I am your commanding officer," Brodie lifted up his strong voice. "Arquebusiers, Attention! Look to me. Point arms! Fire!"

Only one man of the eight wavered towards obedience. But Kinnaird saw the lift of the long barrel, and, hesitating not an instant, brought his gauntleted hand terribly down on the obedient man's neck. Then he caught him by the collar, swung him upright and hurled him behind into the darkness of the spiral. Man and weapon went crashing and checking and checking and crashing downwards, and then came stillness. There was no need for a second lesson.

Kinnaird trampled over and through his men and faced round on them. "Down, down!" he roared. "Down to the guard with ye!" He pushed them with his knees, threw muzzles aside, and did not desist forcing them until they were out of sight round the second curve. Then he came back, still swearing. Strangely enough the crusie was still alight in his left hand. He glared at Brodie, and Brodie had nothing to say.

"There is my answer for you, foolish man. Do you think we can waste the only man we can trust in Moray for two wild Irishers and their woman?" His eyes met mine over his friend's shoulder. "What do you want, black devil?"

"A safe conduct out of here and an hour's grace."

"And Brodie?"

"We will take him and loose him unhurt at the end of that hour."

"An Irisher's word!"

"And you a good judge of a broken one! We would not take your word either. That is why we take Brodie."

"If I had you in another place——"

"Then ride with us and we will deliver Brodie into your hands."

He looked at me shrewdly. "How many have ye lurking?"

"They would be here now, and your soul in hell minutes agone."

"You are not wise to be so bold." He considered me a while. "There is no other way," he said then, and shook his head at Brodie. "No need to talk, Sandy friend. I will take every chance to keep you alive. I will ride with you, and if we die we die together."

Brodie said never a word. He had lost his game and won his life.

And that is how we took Margaret Anderson out of the midst of her enemies in Spynie Tower, to our honour.

CHAPTER X

THE LITTLE BLACK ROSE TAKES
HER OWN ROAD

I

THE short summer night was giving way to the pearl-cold tones of dawn when we came to the crown of the sloping bank running down to the Ford of Gight. Below us the Spey River ran wide and wan between its dark woods, and one long streamer of white mist unfolded itself on the edge of the trees. The sky had no cloud, no colour, no depths, and a round-topped hill far up the river was chill in purple. And the flame in me had died down into grey ashes, and I was no longer in the humour to give tongue in the face of death.

Two days before, we had taken two hours to get to Spynie the safe way round by the coast, but to-night we had ridden back straight and hard in something less than an hour. Margaret rode behind me, her arms round my waist, for I had no belt to afford her grip. My belt still bound the hands of Brodie, who rode in front of Tadg Mor, and Tadg Mor had slipped back off his saddle so that his prisoner might ride easily. My foster-brother's long legs were thrust out stiffly for a balance as we galloped, and he cursed pleasantly once or twice as the going jarred his spine. Kinnaird of Culbin rode ahead on his own horse, and Dod Myron rode in the rear on the horse that was to take Brodie back. I think it strange now that we did not trust these two gentlemen of Moray, but the old times had gone so mad, and the Solemn League and Covenant had grown so intolerant and ruthless, that we could trust no adherents of it to keep their word to the enemies of their Jehovah.

We had ridden holding no discourse, and now I was in no mood to begin any. In silence we grouped and halted where the track turned down the slope; and Tadg Mor unstrapped Brodie's wrists, and swung him to the ground. Dod Myron, already on his feet, held his horse ready. But before Brodie mounted he chafed his wrists briskly and looked up at me, but not sourly.

"I seem to know that beast you ride," said he. It was a saddle-horse of his own that Tadg Mor and I had taken out of his stable before Auldearn.

"One of the times the wild Irish had dealings with you," I hinted.

"Yes. Five times ye have prostrated me."

"You count this one?"

"And the worst because of what I lose." His glance went behind me to the girl. "I am grieved, Margaret Anderson, that I could not ensure your safety with your uncle."

"There is no fear o' me, Laird Brodie," Margaret told him, gently for her.

He shook his head and his eyes were pained. He was so sincere in his regret that suddenly I felt a desire to assure him—and to prick him too. I bent down.

"Look at this girl behind me!"

"I am looking."

"But you do not see. Look at her eyes, look at her

brow, look at her mouth—look at her mouth carefully. What do you see?"

"A young and bonny woman." He looked at me keenly. "And that is what you see too, at the back of all."

"You are a wedded man?"

"I am."

"You are lucky if your wife be like her."

At that his shoulders stiffened and I had a spurt of anger.

"You are a proud fool, and your bloody Covenant has clouded your mind. Listen! If the Irish were the Covenant and you Irish, you would need a fifth life for me to take this chill dawning. You had better go now, for one is often in a sour temper before breakfast."

Tadg Mor was watching Kinnaird with half-humorous, fierce eyes, and Kinnaird, his hand on his hilt, was peering amongst the trees suspiciously. This was Gordon country and no safe place for any man of the Laich.

"Let no fear be on you, man black," soothed Tadg Mor derisively. "The Gordons are late sleepers."

Kinnaird swung his horse round on him, his hand still on his hilt, and Tadg Mor laughed. I knew that laugh.

"Maybe you are not afraid after all," he half taunted, "and indeed you have cause to be angry. A small blood-letting would do you no harm!"

Kinnaird must have been nursing his resentment this past hour. Now it boiled over.

"By the Lord!" he cried, "I will blood one of you, whatever. Draw!"

His sword was out of sheath, his horse leaped to

the spur, and the blade went shearing at Tadg Mor's head.

Tadg Mor was ready for it. Kinnaird was a big and powerful man, and the blow was delivered with all his might, but Tadg Mor put such a terrific disdainful vigour into his parry, that the sword flew twenty paces out of Kinnaird's hand. And then Tadg Mor, recovering his blade, gave the Covenanter a steady easy point full in the centre of the polished corselet, and the stricken man swayed in the saddle and came upright again. Just as surely could the thrust have been through the throat. Tadg Mor swerved his horse away.

"Next time you have a poor Irishman under your sword," said he, "remember the dent in your breastplate. Dod, boy, give him his sword again."

"What for waste time?" cried Dod. "Gie't to him in the thrapple."

But here Brodie, already on his horse, spurred between.

"Enough killings this night," said he. "Let us part without blood this time."

And that was how we parted.

We sat in saddle and watched them go. But when Brodie had ridden a little way he reined his horse round and rode back to us.

"If I have misjudged ye, gentlemen," said he, "I ask pardon." He saluted Margaret like a courtier. "Your uncle, lady, will not suffer by me." And he swung his horse and drove it at the gallop.

"My hand!" cried Tadg Mor, "you get good men everywhere, even in Moray, and that is a strange thing."

Brodie of Brodie was, indeed, a man of parts, and

may have a name in history. Later on, I have learned, he went over to the royalist side, but he was too late then to save Scotland. King Charles was dead, Montrose was dead, and Cromwell was preparing to set his heel on the stiff neck of the Kirk. He did so set it, and stiff as that neck was, it broke under that firm heel.

2

We forded the river, mounted the other slope, and rode, quietly at last, across the level mile or two to the Gordon Castle. And Margaret Anderson had time to draw her breath and review her situation. The first thing she said was:

"Ye were like two wild men. Ye made me shamed the things ye said o' me—and prood too, Martin."

"You will need your pride."

"What way?"

"Because as soon as we get a quiet place I am going to skelp you proper for all the trouble you were to us."

"And weel I deserve it—but no' ower hard, Martin. Where are ye takin' me?"

"Back to your duty."

"I suppose I maun gang." And after a pause: "You are still carrying Mistress Rose's plaid?"

"You are sitting on it and should be grateful."

"She is no' in the camp?"

"She was, when we left."

"But she was for Aberdeen?"

"As soon as the road opened, and it is open now."

And there I wondered if Iseabal Rose was still with us. Somehow I could not see her go. She had made a secure place for herself, with her calmness and her force and a quiet ironic kindness—and her brown

241

healing hands. I knew then that if she went I would miss her, that a secret part of my life would be lonely.

"Was she her use to ye?" Margaret resumed her probing.

"No worse than yourself."

"She and I will no' get on weel thegither."

"That will be your fault."

"You would say that."

"You will be in charge of the women, under me——"

"She will not take that either—a lady born——"

"I wish that quiet place was at hand. If I have done anything to make you think that I do not look on you as a lady you can—you can complain to Tadg Mor."

"Tadg Mor is a better man and a trustier, anyway."

"I know that—the best man in the world."

"Ye mak' a pair. Och, Martin! only jealous I am."

"Jealous of what?"

"Let it be! You wouldna understand, lad."

"Tadg Mor," I called. "She has her hand on the reins already."

"And my ear already dingin'," said Tadg Mor, his hand up in the old familiar gesture.

He was riding close ahead, Dod Myron holding his stirrup-leather, and Dod was walking head down as if in a despondency about something. Tadg Mor noticed that, and bent down to slap the lad on the shoulder.

"Wake up, Dod boy! You are still alive this fine morning, and a man in your own right as well."

"And a cowardly one," growled Dod.

"You could stand at Finn MacCool's right hand."

"No me! I was feart as a rabbit in yon bit o' a room at the head of the stairs." Strange that he and I had been reminded of a coney burrow in that trap.

"You were not half as feart as I was," Tadg Mor comforted him.

"You werena feart, big man."

"The only man more feart was one Martin Somers."

"The devil out o' hell wouldna put dread on him."

"Whisper, *avic*! and I will give you a secret. We are so well acquaint of fear that now it no more than steadies us in the gap of danger. There it is for you. But what am I saying? You have the secret yourself. When I saw you at your ease leaning against the door-post, your sword ready, I was jealous of you. 'There,' says I to myself, 'is the coolest young one ever I met.' And were you not the first to blood your sword?"

"I did that, anyway," said Dod, and his shoulders began to lift. "If you would be saying a word to Nat Gordon for me he might pick me in the next levy."

"I will say a word to all the world," Tadg Mor promised him, "and, what is more, I will get Ranald Ban MacKinnon to put you in the verse of a song."

And in a little while Dod Myron walked proudly erect, one hand in his basket-hilt, and the other seeking the grip of my pistol in his belt. Then he remembered the owner of the pistol, and turned to me holding it in his hand.

"Before I forget, Master," said he.

"Dod Myron of Gordon," said I formally, "you will do me a high favour by keeping that pistol as a small token of all we owe you."

"Man!" His eyes flashed. "But ye might have a need of it."

"Put it away. It will be in a better man's keeping."

"Goad!" he cried. "Ye are twa bonny men, and I would follow you to Ireland and the dens of cannibals."

"Ireland has the bad name surely," said Tadg Mor.

But Margaret Anderson whispered in my ear: "A great shame for the twa o' ye, putting' foolish dreams in a laddie's head."

3

We took three days to come up with the army. And in these three days, camping and foraging and talking, our Margaret recovered all her old state and friendly hectorship. No doubt she had learned her lesson, knew that her only congenial place was in the regiment, and made up her mind to grasp that life close to her. They were three fine free days, and we were half sorry when we rejoined the regiment.

Montrose, after the burial of Lord Gordon in St Machar's Kirk of Aberdeen, had marched south for the final swoop on the Lowlands and the Border, and we overtook him in camp on a wide haugh near Fordoun of the Mearns. That was a great day for the army and for us. I do not mean that our arrival was the great thing. The very great thing was the return that day of Major-General Alasdair Colkitto MacDonald with his host of Highlandmen: three thousand of them, the finest fighting men in all Scotland—or the world, themselves would say: Clan Ranald under Eoin of Moidart and Donald Oge, Glengarry under Angus, Clan MacLean under Lachlan of Duart, Clan Vuirich of Badenoch, Clan Finlay of Braemar, Clan Stuart of Appin, Clan Cameron of Lochaber, MacNabs, Mac-Gregors, others as well; and Clan Duncan up from Atholl under Black Pate Graham of Inchbrakie.

We rode into camp early in the afternoon while the clans were parading before the Captain-General and his staff, each chief being introduced to Montrose by

Alasdair and fittingly welcomed. We came in quietly, ourselves, over the breast of a hill, with no wish to make any parade. We looked down over that grand array of fighting tartaned men, all their colours flying—we carried plenty of colours now—and all the pipers blowing shrill mad marches.

"There will be a couple of good hurley teams in that lot," said Tadg Mor carelessly.

And Margaret flung back her lovely linten hair and sniffed the breeze.

"It is like being hame again," she cried. "Already I can smell O'Cahan's Irish."

And whether she could or not, the Irish seemed to smell her. A company of O'Cahan's and its women were sitting about on the grass near the foot of the brae, idly but critically—like veterans—watching the parade of Highlandmen; and before we knew we were close above them. It was Sorcha MacNeill saw us first, and she scrambled to her feet skirling and pointing. They all saw us then, and they were all on their feet and all yelling. I have heard many slogans in my time, but the high-pitched shrill Irish yell always put a strange terror on me, as, indeed, it did on the regiments that had to face it. Now it brought the parade to a halt.

"*Iosa Chreesta!*" blasphemed Tadg Mor, and fell off his horse.

Before we might do anything a torrent of men and women poured about us. Margaret and I were pulled to the ground, whirled about and winded with hand-claps; and then, before we could even struggle, the three of us were lifted on high on stalwart shoulders, and the mixed company, falling roughly into formation, marched down and out and across the parade ground straight for the Royal Standard. There was nothing we could do there in the face of the whole army. An army could not stop us.

I do believe that there were half a thousand Irishmen and women in our tail as we swept round in front of Montrose and halted. Tadg Mor and I, gripping a tousled mop of hair with one hand, saluted with the other, but Margaret kept her head down, a flame of embarrassment and pride in her cheeks. Colkitto, towering at Montrose's side, his mouth open in laughter, beckoned us on, and our bearers eased us to the ground and shoved us forward, Margaret in the middle.

She lifted her head then and Montrose doffed his bonnet to her, giving her his pleasant, half-wistful smile.

"You are welcome back, Mistress Margaret," said he. "We need you and shall need you more."

She gave him her little abrupt curtsey and drew back. She had no tongue for Montrose. He smiled at us too, but a little teasingly.

"So you are haled before me again. Well! I knew ye would not fail, since ye are practised in the art of taking ladies out of strait places." He turned to Alasdair. "She was a prisoner in Spynie Tower and these two men of yours bring her out of it."

"Why not they?" cried Alasdair. "Had ye any fun, Maurteen?"

"Not what you would call fun, Major-General."

"No trouble at all, Alasdair," said Tadg Mor. "We just stepped in through a bit of a door and strolled out again, and away with her and us."

"If that was the way, red man," said Alasdair, laughing, "you would already be boasting sky-high of the men you killed."

"There is a camp-fire tale in this, Martin Somers?" queried Montrose, who loved a good story.

"Tadg Mor will have it, Captain-General," I told him.

"Be not in a hurry telling it, O'Kavanagh," Montrose hinted, and gave us a wave of his hand for dismissal.

We found our way to our regiment's quarters then, in a chosen hollow over a brae, near wood and running water, and there our other friends came round and complimented us: Father MacBreck the chaplain, my fellow-adjutant Angus Stuart, O'Lachlan our quartermaster, and finally, Colonel Manus O'Cahan himself, who took the hands of our girl in his own and kissed one of them.

"Our *Roisin Ban*, our fair rose, is just in time," said he, looking at me, "for our *Roisin Dhuv* is out of camp, I fear."

I knew that. She had not come to welcome us, nor was she amongst her women. She might not like our fair rose, but she would not hide herself away surlily; for though she might be a small bit obstinate on occasion, Iseabal Rose was never sullen. Another friend, and our closest, I missed too: Ranald Ban MacKinnon. His absence gave me to think.

"Is Dunbar of Moyness in camp?" I asked our colonel.

"He is—just below us." Dunbar and his thirty always camped near our regiment.

I said no more then, but went about my own business.

An hour before sunset, in the warm evening, I went down through the wood by the burnside below the camp and found a small pool deep enough to take me to the waist, and in it I had a plunge and a fine wash. It was brisk water and chill, for it came off the flanks of the Forfar Hills. My head was in a clean shirt, when a voice spoke to me.

"You are back? Good work yon at Spynie."

I thrust my head through the band of the shirt. The speaker was Walter Dunbar, tall and handsome, the low sun shining on his fine red hair. He looked at me keenly, and put me a quick question before I might collect my thoughts:

"Where is Iseabal Rose?"

But I was busy getting my arms in the sleeves, and then I felt the smoothness of my new-shaven slit chin. He watched me relentlessly. "Is she not hereabout?" I said at last.

"Have you seen her?"

"I am not long in camp."

"You know that she is not in camp. Where is she?"

"I do not know, but if I did know I would not tell you."

"I will accept that. Do you know that MacKinnon is not in camp either?"

"That is news to me," said I. I kept on belting my trews, but for some reason the blood drained emptily away from my heart.

"He was to come with me to Lord Gordon's funeral in Aberdeen," went on Dunbar, "but he did not appear."

"You went?"

"I did. I have not seen Iseabal or MacKinnon since."

"Are you saying that they are gone away together?"

"That is what I say." He picked my old cloth coat off the ground and reached it to me. "I have kept my word with you, Somers?"

"Like a man."

"If Iseabal Rose is out of camp there is no word to be kept."

"You would desert the army then?"

"If that is necessary."

"Walter Dunbar," I said, convincingly as I could, "if they are gone away together the game is played and you have lost. Can you not see that?"

"My game finishes with death."

"And your death it will surely be, if you pursue Ranald Ban MacKinnon where he may have gone. Why are you so stubborn? Leave the woman alone."

"God, Somers!" he cried, striking his hands together as once before, "I cannot help myself." He stared at me curiously. "It was you began this, and I should kill you, but, somehow I have no feeling against you at all."

He turned on his heel and strode away up the burn-side while I stayed behind to belt on my coat. I often think since that men of that hair and temper, when they finally set their heart on a woman, cannot see any other. There is Tadg Mor. I know that he has not looked at a woman since one terrible day in Methven Wood.

4

Ranald Ban MacKinnon had not left the army. He came to me that evening.

We were round our camp-fire that time, a fine circle of us. Donald Oge of Moidart had brought in a good *creach* of cattle from the borders of Marechal Keith, and we were after a good meal of fresh-killed beef— new beef is tender enough if cooked before it stiffens —and Tadg Mor, as a sort of after-feast, was picking a rib daintily. Colkitto and Nat Gordon sat at the fire with us, and Colkitto was clamouring for our tale, but Tadg Mor gnawed his bone and kept an eye lifting towards the little brae above us. He was a good story-teller, Tadg Mor—if not quite as good as Ranald Ban—and wanted his full audience.

"There is a lad at Gight, Nat," said he to Nathaniel Gordon, "by the name of Dod Myron——"

"I know him," said Nat. "When do you want him hanged? I near did that for him last year."

"Maybe that is why the Gordons are not so good," said Tadg Mor smoothly. "You hang all your best men. Dod is one of the best."

"You proved him?"

"We did so, as you will see." And then he laughed. "A funny thing! The morning of the second day he says to me, 'Can we be trusting that black lad there? I think his courage is failing him already.'"

In the following laughter Montrose, Rollo, and Maormor Ogilvie strolled down the brae. Room was made for them, and Rollo set his Indian pipe asmoke. He was one of the few men amongst us that had the habit, though I have fallen to it myself since then. That was only one of scores and scores of summer and autumn camp-fires that I remember of that year. Montrose loved to sit in the gloaming, bare-headed, his feet towards the fire, and talk from him and all round him. And if the midges got too wicked, he used borrow Rollo's pipe and make a puff or two of smoke about his hair.

Tadg Mor had his full audience now and cleared his throat for action. And it was then that a hand touched my shoulder from behind. I looked up to see Ranald Ban MacKinnon, his eyes shining in the red light of the fire. He beckoned with his head and

250

stepped back. I did not want to go, but he frowned at me, and gestured urgently. I slipped back then from the fire, no one noticing me, and followed him into the half-dark. He took my arm and drew me farther away.

"Tadg Mor will damn his soul with lies," I protested, "if I am not there to check him."

"Never mind! He will give you your full share of credit."

"You should have stayed to hear of the one time he wished you were with us."

"He will be telling me all about it for the next half-year. Come up this way."

He still held my arm, and now I noticed that his feet were not too steady.

"You are right," said he. "I have been drinking hornfuls all the day with the MacLeans out of Mull, but I have slept most of it off."

The clans usually brought a few pannier-kegs of usgebaugh to the hosting, but as Montrose would not permit our baggage-horses to carry liquor on campaign, most of it had to be consumed at the first gathering feast. The result was a noisome gay night, and ragged marching next day.

We went up to the head of the brae, and Ranald Ban, pulling me round, bent to look into my face.

"I will be cursed, Martin Somers," said he, "if I can see what women see behind your devil's mask."

"Women see nothing in me, loose-mouth. Mostly they dislike me."

He looked close into my eyes. "Do you believe that? By the Lord! but maybe you do." He patted my shoulder. "Your pardon, Sassenach! Let us sit down here for a bit."

We sat down side by side in the dry long grass and said nothing for a long time. All around us was the balmy summer night, and high overhead the pale summer sky lit thinly with stars that fainted before the white glow of the north. All the wide haugh below us was also starred with lines and lines of camp-fires, and it was pleasant to hear again the sounds of a cheerful and sanguine army—all the fires soft flickering along the curves of the braes, laughter and voices lifted in song, the drone of the pipes coming to tune, and, far away, a solitary piper playing a lonely long pibroch. And in the hills a curlew cried vainly for rain.

When at last Ranald Ban spoke he did not beat about the bush.

"I took *Roisin Dhuv* to Aberdeen," he said.

"Not to Mull?"

"Do not taunt me. I asked her to come to Mull to my father's house, but all she said was, 'I will go to Aberdeen now.' And when I said to her, 'Will you not wait till Martin Somers comes back?' she shook her head and said, 'You will take me a quiet way to Aberdeen if you are my friend.' And that is what I did."

"No one saw you go?"

"No unfriend. I took good care of that. I made a pretence to go with Dunbar as a bearer of Lord Gordon's coffin, but I let the funeral get well ahead, and then the dumb Rab Fraser and myself took her round about and in by Balgownie Brig where her uncle has a house."

"You saw him—the uncle?"

"From the corner near-by, but he did not see me. She did not want her uncle to know more than could be helped. A dominie he is, and the looks of him reminded me of one I knew in Dunvegan who leathered me every time I gave the right answer to make sure it would stick in my memory—and so it did. A lean man, with a lean head like her father's. He came himself to the door and was slow welcoming her inside, but, though I waited an hour, she or the man or Rab did not come out again."

"Where have you been since?"

"Out of the way." He gestured behind him towards the hills. "Only one hooded crow saw me for two days and admired my hair for a lining to its nest. I was in no humour to meet anyone, and Seumas Graham might not like me to cut Dunbar's windpipe."

"If you were able."

"I could be taking a slash at it whatever, as Finn Coll said to the Irish giant as he cut off his third head."

"A Scots giant as I heard it."

"I have something here for you," said Ranald Ban, his fingers in his kilt purse. In the half-dark I could see that the something was a folded sheet of paper tied with a dark thread. "She borrowed quill and paper off old Forrett the Secretary, and she gave me this for you."

I took it in my hand, but I could not feel her presence in it.

"There may be a message in it for you," I said.

"There will be no message in it for me. Put it away and read it in your own time." He got slowly to his feet for so swack a man. "I will go back to the MacLeans. Murdoch of Lochbuie has a piggin of triple-run I would like to taste again. Will you come?"

"I have no head—you know that."

"I do not. Man, Maurteen! is not the camp lonely without her? Ach! but you have your Margaret——"

"She is not my Margaret—you know that, anyway."

"Maybe I do. I know a lot I want to forget and some things I will not forget." He kept a fine restraint on himself.

I was on my feet and I touched Ranald Ban on the breast. "She will be lonely in Aberdeen, and she will remember your Mull and your mountains and the beach of Iona. Who knows, Ranald Ban——?"

But he pushed me away roughly. "Do not set my dreams running again. I know better. Tadg Mor will have finished his story by now. Send him out to me; I will wait here for him."

It was in the dawn of morning that I read Iseabal Rose's note. It was brief and, though simple, it had in it some hidden meanings and a queer brooding finality. The writing was small and firm like the writer herself. This is it:

"DEAR HALF-INDIAN AND BELOVED SASSENACH,—I am going to my uncle in Aberdeen and I will not see you again, and for that I have my own sorrow. I will not see any of you again, I think, but you I will not see ever. To that I am resigned as I write this, but how long I may be resigned I do not know, knowing what I am. This writing is to thank you. It is a writing that is trying to thank you, but there is a bitter wonder on me whether I owe you or any man thanks. But indeed you have done all you could—all—and I do thank you for showing me for a short time a life that I would hold if I could with all the small might in me. Fare-you-well now. But first I will give you my advice, because you need it and are very blind.

Give up soldiering and following armies, and send your foster-brother home. You will not send him away, but you must for his own sake, for he is a soft-hearted man and easily hurt. After that take to merchanting with Alick Anderson. I will not say any thing about any other. But tell Ranald Ban MacKinnon that if I am ever come to the point of marrying a man I do not love—no, do not tell him anything for he is too proud. That is all I will say of all I would say. Take my advice for it is given of my blood for one minute running clean.

"ISEABAL ROSE."

I near cried reading it. I read it again and did cry.

Before I come to the difficult part of my story I will clear the ground behind me.

While we were in camp at Dunkeld, north of Perth, Walter Dunbar deserted from the army with his thirty men. We could not waste any force to pursue them if we wanted to, for the Covenant army was threatening us, and we were short of cavalry at the time. We were only waiting for the Gordon horse before striking a smashing blow at the Lowlands.

CHAPTER XI

"JESUS AND NO QUARTER"

I

I COME now to the bitter part of my story, and it will not take me long.

Montrose marched his infantry round the base of the Forfar Hills to the town of Dunkeld, and there pitched camp. It was the grandest, strongest body of foot he had ever gathered on the field, but he had scarcely any horse, and horse were essential for the Lowland campaign. The Gordons had taken a turn home after Alford, but with a promise to return, and Montrose had perforce to wait for them. Ogilvie of Airlie brought in a squadron late in July, and early in August Aboyne and Lord Lewis Gordon rejoined with four hundred of the famous Huntly horse. Then we were ready for our great drive southwards.

But before the Gordons arrived Montrose was not idle. The Covenant Parliament, forced out of Edinburgh and Stirling by fear of the plague, was in session at Perth only fifteen miles out of our camp, and Montrose, half in fun half in earnest, essayed to put the fear of death in the lairds and ministers behind their stone walls. These stone walls were guarded by a strong force of infantry, and full five squadrons of horse outposted the northern and western marches;

but Montrose, nothing daunted, trotted ten companies of Highland and Irish down to Methven and made a display of all the men he could mount within sight of Perth walls. The prayings and fulminations inside clanged against Heaven's walls that time, for even the plague was not more terrible than the threat of Ulster. If Montrose had had the Gordon horse at that juncture, before the Covenant army had gathered its final strength, he would have made an end of the Parliament, and saved Cromwell that trouble many years later.

But men mounted on baggage-horses could do little against squadrons of regular horse, and, having made his display, to the terror of the Kirk, Montrose fell back on Dunkeld, fighting a canny rearguard action against Hurry and Balcarres.

It was then that the terrible disaster befell our women.

Tadg Mor and I were not in that drive to Methven. We knew it for a sally not meant to be driven home, and we made a sally of our own westwards towards the Loch of Tay with Ranald Ban MacKinnon and a couple of Clan Finlay bowmen after a herd of the great red deer of the hills. Two companies of O'Cahan's had gone with Montrose, however, their women with them to see what might be picked up on the road; and Margaret, with ten of her nursing women, had gone too in the event of any hurt men in the skirmishing. I told her there was no need, but at that time she was all for duty. Since her return to camp nothing could hold her zest for life; she was flowing with vigour and spirit and white happiness. As she herself said, she felt fey. I remembered that afterwards. She was fey.

We spent two nights in the hills very pleasantly, and I saw one of the Farquharsons marvellously bring

down a running stag at fifty paces with a single arrow.
On the third day, about noon, we came jog-trotting into
camp, haunches and quarters of venison slung on our
shoulders. The easy jog-trot was our usual pace, and
I have seen the army hold it for a day.

"Our Meg," said Tadg Mor, "is dainty in her diet,
and will be tired of hill mutton. She will cook this
that way she has, and give us our share."

But Margaret was not in quarters when we got there,
though the force from Methven had almost finished
streaming in in fast-marching scattered squads.

"She and the women will be an hour yet," O'Cahan
informed us. "I told her to circle westwards with
them to avoid the horse. They have no wounded, but
the women may have a load or two."

We thought little of that delay. The Irish women
were hopeless stragglers in foraging, and I had often
seen Margaret in a white heat trying to herd them
safely to camp. But they were old campaigners too,
and knew exactly how near they could skirt danger,
as they had proved in the terrible night retreat from
Dundee. Still, we grew anxious when the hour passed;
and when another passed, and no Margaret came,
Tadg Mor and I hesitated no longer. We took horse
and galloped the road to meet her.

We circled westwards and south through a rugged
wild valley that, unfittingly, was called the Small Glen.
We met no one until half-roads, and then round a
corner we came on four women helping along two
wounded ones. They wailed wild-eyed when they
saw us.

"Oh God! Oh God!" That was Tadg Mor, his
voice tearing him.

I quieted the women with an urgent hand.

"Where is Margaret Anderson?"

The tall big-bosomed Ulster woman, Sorcha Mac-Neill, holding a comrade in her strong arms, looked at me and shook her head, the tears streaming down her face.

"Where is she, you weeping *onshuch*?" I shouted, and she got her voice.

"She was behind us coming out of Methven Wood, and then the bloody horsemen came amongst us slashing. The last I saw of her."

Tadg Mor let one woeful cry out of him and drove furious heels into his leaping horse. And I, forgetting my duty to the wounded, beat and beat my beast into a gallop behind him.

What had happened was plain enough. This is it. The women, herded by Margaret, had worked westward through Methven Wood, and on the margin of it had been sighted by an outriding body of Hurry's and Balcarres' ruthless horse. What followed makes the telling too evil for me. I cannot tell it. By our roll there were exactly two-and-forty women in that party, and only six escaped death. Count the butchered. Covenant preachers have extolled that and other butcheries of women as the vengeance of their Lord God on the sinful bodies of the concubines of savages. But, as I have already written once or twice, they were not loose women, but the mothers, wives, sisters, sweethearts that always followed the male of Gaeldom to war, and were a necessary part of an army on campaign. I am angry as I write, and I could extol the vengeance of God too. Two thousand men left Ireland on that expedition, and only four hundred returned. But for each Irish man and woman slain in fight or butchered after it six Covenanters died in battle—and no woman died. Any man who reads history can make the count. And maybe it is not right for me to extol my God over theirs.

Tadg Mor and I did not give up hope. If any wounded women were behind, Margaret would surely be with them. We strained eyes for her at every turn of that twisting glen. But hale or wounded, we met no more women. In time we came out into open swelling country, and saw speared horsemen riding on the horizon eastwards towards Perth. We were desperate now, but as long as there was any hope we would not yield to folly. We threw ourselves off our horses and led them up the course of a stream, the bank hiding us. So we came to a cup in the hills and, remounting, rode up to the rim of it and so over an easy slope. The country was clear before us now, and across a wide and shallow valley a dark wood of pine flowed over the swell of a low ridge. We made for that wood at a gallop.

We came on one of our women pitifully dead at the edge of that dark wood, her face to the ground and her arms out towards us. Then we came on another, and then two more. But I will tell no more of that. . . .

2

We found Margaret deep in the wood, but she was not dead. She sat with her back to a tree, her head leaning against the trunk. It was as if she had settled herself down neatly for a rest, her lovely linten hair back off her brow, and her skirts down to the silver buckles that Tadg Mor used to polish every morning. There was no colour at all in her face or in her eyes, and her two arms were clasped tightly over her breast

260

as if she were holding something there. Something very precious indeed, for it was her very life she was holding for a little while—until we came. She smiled up at us as we bent over her, and her voice was a whisper.

"My loons! My very ain loons! I was waiting—I knew you'd be."

I put my hand gently on her elbow to unclasp her arms, but, "Dinna, Martin," said she. Her life-blood was welling against her sleeve, a frothy, bright red blood —I knew what that meant. She had been pierced through the body in two places and should have been dead long ago. But she had held her life against death with her two strong hands till we came. Now she yielded to that new strong lover.

"Hold me, Martin dear," she whispered, and her head slipped sideways off the trunk. I put my arms gently about her.

She let her arms go loose then, and one hand went out towards Tadg Mor. He took it in his, brought his face down to it, and softly clumped it three times against his ear. And he held his face to a gallant smiling with the strength of iron.

"My poor Tadg Mor!" And she smoothed his cheek with her palm.

"I was waiting for you," she whispered. "I kent ye'd come—ye aye come when I am in trouble. Am I no' the proud one?"

Her brow was cold against me, and she said nothing more for a long time, and then she used the Irish way she had learnt from us.

"But I will be troubling you no more now, Maurteen."

"Hush—hush, girleen!"

"Hush—hush! Ay, put your bairn to sleep."

"Sleep, then, and I will take you back in my arms."

"In your arms—on your saddle-bow. That will be the way. But will you be missing me a wee small bittie?"

"I will not, for you will be always at my side."

"I will sleep so. Tell Uncle Alick my happiness." And after a while she said: "A' my rough Irish laddies —a' my bonny Irish laddies!" Her lips were close to my ear. "But you were aye my ain hert's darlin'."

She turned her face in to me and I whispered softly in her ear, and like a child going to sleep she sighed deeply. And was dead.

I looked over her linten hair at Tadg Mor.

"She is gone from us, brother."

"She is gone," said he deeply. And he rose to his feet and turned away from us; and his voice lifted in a strange, little, lamentable tune that one would sing to oneself remembering beauty.

I took her body on my saddle-bow back to Dunkeld.

We overtook the six women on the road; and Tadg Mor rode behind me, a wounded woman in his arms and one behind him strapped to his belt. When we came to the margin of the camp the four women with us lifted their voices in the woeful Irish *caoine*, and Ireland and the Highlands, men and women, swept about us like the waves of the sea. Then did that woeful lament swell and roll against the walls of the hills, and in it pealed a savage note from the throats of the men. It shook all Dunkeld.

Colkitto, bareheaded, came running. Montrose himself galloped on horseback from the manse where he was lodging, his long hair flying behind him. The Irish and Highlandmen stormed round him, and

Colkitto, hearing the news, grasped him by the thigh.

"Lead us out now!" Alasdair roared in his great voice. "Lead us out now, Seumas Graham!"

But Montrose struck his hand away, lifted himself in the stirrups, and raised a clenched fist in the air. His face had lost all its fresh colour, and his eyes blackened under his black brows.

"The hurt is mine," he cried, and his voice carried across the valley. "The hurt is mine, for Scotsmen did this. I will lead you out and our vengeance shall be full."

And the high maddening Gaelic slogan resounded from all the hills.

That night O'Cahan and fifty horsemen brought in our dead from Methven Wood, and the whole army waked them till the dawn. . . . But why do I go on rending my heart? I am crying now as I write. . . .

We buried our dead in the clear pale dawn, and all the pipers marched behind playing the heart-aching *Soiridh : Farewell my Fair One.* In Spynie Tower I had promised Margaret that parting tune, and she had it now, though her ears were deaf. And three Irish regiments and ten Highland clans marched behind her; she was wearing her silken gown but it did not swing, and her silver-buckled shoon were on her feet; but she rode on no white horse, and she had no silver girdle on the span of her waist.

3

Kilsyth was the vengeance Montrose led us to. And in that battle, for the first time since Tippermuir, I carried a sword in the line and fought like all the Irish, stripped to the trews; and in me was not fear but a dark despairing anger.

Montrose had the greatest difficulty in restraining the army on the strategic march that led up to the battle. He swung us round the south side of the Ochil Hills through Mar and Kellie country, not unfriendly to his cause, but it was Lowland country too, and Highland swords were eager to be at all Lowland throats. The people in the hillfoot villages strung below the bold volcanic ramparts of the Ochils—Dollar, Tillicoultry, Alva, Menstrie—were warned to stay indoors, and did so very carefully; and only one brief explosion of temper in the small town of Alloa evinced the deadliness of our mood.

Montrose made full use of that mood when the time came. In a final forced march, outstripping his old antagonist General Baillie, who was advancing parallel on the north side of the Ochils, he thrust us at a Covenant force coming across from Lanark. The Lanark men, never too loyal to Parliament, did not stand to fight, but fell back as fast and as far as they were able. And then we faced round, established ourselves in the hollow of Kilsyth back off the main road, and gave Baillie three choices.

He could fall back on Perth, where we would exterminate him at our ease; he could risk marching across our front to join Lanark; or he could fight us then and there.

He had an army of seven thousand, but he was a prudent man when he was let. He wanted to fall back, but the advising Committee of the Estates insisted on fight. Argyll, the ancient and inveterate foe of Montrose, was sure that, at last, he had his enemy in his hands, now that he had him lured over the Highland line; and Baillie, when he saw that Montrose had failed to take advantage of ground on the slopes, decided that victory was at least possible.

The disadvantage of our ground was only apparent, and it was no more than Montrose's usual lure. Our position was on a level carse with a stream in front and hills on three sides. On the north side the hills narrowed to a ravine down which the stream flowed. Montrose permitted Baillie to occupy the hill in our front. But the brae so steepened at the foot that no cavalry dare charge down it. That is what Montrose saw. Also he knew that his own foot, trained tough as iron in mountain warfare, could charge up that brae fleet as deer, and, unharried by horse, could drive the enemy into marshland behind the hill. He would attend to the horse himself.

It was Lady Day in August, one of the hottest days in that hot year of the plague, and we stripped for the fight. We wanted no weight of armour to slow our movements or our sword arms. We wanted only targe and sword and the enemy within reach. The Irish were in trews, and many of them had cast their raw-hide brogans; the Highlandmen had shed kilt and plaid, and knotted their long bandle-cloth shirts between their legs; the horsemen, to avoid the confusion of friend and foe as at Alford, wore their shirts over their jerkins. Each company or clan carried its colours, and these were the only unnecessary weight carried that day. We must have looked a strange rabble to the orderly fully-accoutred army on the hill above us, and our appearance must have given that army confidence of victory. No one might guess our falcon readiness and fierceness.

Argyll was so sure that he had his enemy in his grasp

in the heart of the Lowlands, that, in order to cut off all retreat to the hills across the line, he insisted that Baillie deploy his foot-men northwards round and over the ravine. They made a quarter-circle close above us on the hills, and Alasdair leisurely swung his line to conform with theirs as they moved. Montrose, knowing that Alasdair was the leader for men in our mood, was with the cavalry on the right wing. I was in the front line of O'Cahan's regiment at the side of Tadg Mor, with the men who had lost their women at Methven about us. Sometimes I shivered, but not with fear. Manus walked between his lines as ever, but he had not need to clap any man's shoulder. Great Colkitto stood on wide-planted shapely legs, his back to us, head forward and his broadsword softly tapping the ground. His bodyguard had been distributed down the line, and Ranald Ban MacKinnon, leaning forward, caught my eye, and his nostrils flared in a marble-white face.

Half an hour before, Nat Gordon had ridden down the line on his black stallion, and the healed gash on his cheek had stood out red on his rigid face.

"O'Cahan," he had said, "I will do what I can to drive Balcarres' horse into the marsh behind that hill."

"We will be there," said O'Cahan, and a low vibrant growl went down the line.

Eager as we were, the battle was slow to begin. The enemy slowly circled above us, and, more slowly, we circled to face him. But, as ever, our fixed eyes on the foe, we kept slipping forward and slipping forward, until only a stony slope with a broken-down drystone fence separated the lines. And then a man in our second line, torn with rage and grief and the chance of slaking them, cried out: "Give me room, give me room!" and pushed against us.

And Colkitto chose that time well. Up went his blade and forward in his famous gesture, and he leaped forward roaring wordless. Then the torrent broke in one shrill slogan. The brae and the stone wall were submerged as by a mountain flood, and there was the enemy line in front of us.

O'Cahan's regiment was in the centre, Clan Ranald and Clan MacLean on either hand, and these three shocked the enemy in line. It was like a torrent striking a bridge of hurdles. It paused at the shock of meeting, heaped for a moment, and then drove straight through. And after that it was slaughter and no quarter. Tippermuir over again, and Inverlochy with it.

Tadg Mor and I charged in the front line of O'Cahan's regiment and we kept our places. More than that I will not say. I know nothing about the cavalry fight, but, I believe, it was hot give-and-take for an hour, until Nat Gordon turned a flank and drove Balcarres' horse slantwise off the field.

Tadg Mor and I got separated some time, and met again four miles from the battlefield on the edge of the mire of Dullatur. Our fierce company had driven the last of Balcarres' horsemen in there and killed them one by one. When we met we were both naked to the waist, and if we were bloody the blood was not ours. Ranald Ban MacKinnon was with Tadg Mor, and he was stark naked but for a wisp of cloth on his loins; and his eyes were glazed and a froth dry on his lips. Tadg Mor's matted chest heaved, his eyes were sunken in his head, and his sword lax. No one will know the killing these two men did that day. Tadg Mor looked at me out of his sunken eyes and shook his great head.

"Glutted—glutted! And to what end, Maurteen? . . . I will kill no more."

At that something broke inside me and came chokingly to my throat, so that I had to throw up my head and fight for air. Tadg Mor and Ranald Ban pressed close, their arms about me and their targes hiding me, for they did not want any man to see the way I was being torn with dry sobs.

After a time I quieted down and, shoulder to shoulder and very silent, we went back towards the field. But behind us we heard two men weeping terribly.

Montrose, riding ahead of his officers, met us at the back of the last hill. He drew rein in front of us and looked us over, a glow in his darkling grey eyes; and we looked up at him quietly, all emotion drained out of us.

"Ye have killed." That is what he said.

"We have killed," said Tadg Mor slowly, "and victory is dust in our mouths."

And Montrose had nothing to say.

That was the vengeance of Kilsyth.

CHAPTER XII
THE ROAD TURNS

I

THE three of us—Tadg Mor, Ranald Ban and myself—said adieu to Montrose in a moorland valley somewhere beyond Struan in Clan Duncan country. That was in October, two months after Kilsyth, and one month after the disaster of Philiphaugh.

Philiphaugh was not a battle, though the Covenant proclaimed it a great victory. It was a surprise by six thousand on a thousand or less. Montrose had only that small force with him at that time. Aboyne and Lord Lewis Gordon, in a perverse humour, had ridden off their four hundred horse for a campaign of their own in Moray; Colkitto had a notion of winning back some of his ancient patrimony from MacCailien Mhor of Argyll, and had marched away for Cantyre with eight hundred Ulstermen; the clans had no time for a winter campaign across the Border, and had hastened, booty-laden, back to their glens for a harvest already late; and Montrose was left with O'Cahan's faithful regiment and four hundred staunch Highlandmen—Robertsons, MacPhersons, and MacDonalds.

There was no covenanting army in Scotland to face that hardy small force, but General David Leslie, a

They were on horseback—there were many riderless horses on the field of Philiphaugh.

"Where are ye going?" shouted Ranald Ban, barring the road with his horse.

"A bit of a daunder—where you have turned your back," Tadg Mor told him with savage irony, and made to go by.

But Ranald Ban caught him fiercely by the leather collar.

"O'Cahan is down. It is all over."

"Let me go, MacKinnon."

"I will not let you go. You would be no great loss, but you are taking your brother to his death."

That quieted Tadg Mor. "But what can we do?" he cried.

"You can put your foot on mine and get up behind me."

That is how we rode in the end, Tadg Mor behind Ranald Ban and I behind the Ulsterman. Five of Leslie's troopers pursued us out of the glen and were overtaking us, but we tumbled off our horses and pelted their half-tired ones with stones. I have often noticed that not even a wicked stallion in the season will stand up to a good pelting. Their horses shied off close in, and stalwart Cornet O'Neill with a young rock brought a trooper out of the saddle. That man died there under Ranald Ban's sword. Another flung himself off his horse to come to his comrade's rescue, and Tadg Mor made sure of him. The others galloped. Tadg Mor took on a little cheer.

"If they would come at us by fours and fives," said he, "we could win this fight yet." But no more came. We had a horse apiece now and made better speed.

We rode all that day and most of the night through

a country of shallow pleasant valleys about the sources of the Tweed, and on the afternoon of the second day came up with Montrose at the waters of Clyde in Dalziel. He had gathered some fifty men and a few officers—young Napier, Crawford and the great old Maormor Ogilvie—and these were all that were left of his force. Lame Rollo was a prisoner; so was Nat Gordon, who had staunchly held by Montrose though his kinsmen had forsaken him.

Montrose was not necessarily finished by the surprise at Philiphaugh. Atholl and Struan would rally to him; Clan Ranald and the Highlands would come in for a spring campaign; Alasdair might be lured back from Cantyre; and Montrose himself would go up into Gordon territory and reason with the sullen old earl and his perverse sons. In the spring he would deal with Leslie as he had dealt with Elcho, Argyll, Hurry, Lindsay and Baillie. We were making plans already.

We made our way by high and difficult ground through the middle Lowlands, and in three days were safe over the line in the hills of Perth; and so came to Struan by the waters of Garry. And there I am back to the morning of October when Montrose sent us on our own road.

He came riding out from the Castle of Struan with old Ogilvie of Airlie to where Tadg Mor, Ranald Ban and I had made a temporary hunting-camp by the banks of the Garry, on the edge of the bleakest mountain-land in all Scotland. We had come in the night before from a hunt up Rannoch way, and had just finished a breakfast of toasted venison when Montrose and Airlie rode up by the course of the brawling stream.

We were not in bad heart that morning. I do hope

273

come again, fair Ranald," he said, "but meantime you will guide these my friends the safest road?"

"I will do that, Montrose," said Ranald Ban.

Montrose said farewell then, giving us his hand in turn, and we gave him the kiss of fealty. And he turned away quickly so that we might not see his eyes, vaulted into the saddle, and rode slowly down by the stream and out of our lives. We never saw him again.

Old Maormor Ogilvie leant down to us from the saddle, before he turned after his leader, and the tears were running from his warrior eyes down his weathered cheeks.

"I was with ye when my son died at Inverlochy," said he, "and here we part. Your deeds will be remembered in Airlie."

I do not know who holds Airlie now. Perhaps he fought at Killiecrankie with Claverhouse Graham, and if so, he may be an exile like my grandson, but I do hope that he has tales of the Irish that fought with his forefather.

We three stood there by the camp-fire and watched them till a curve of the glen hid them from our eyes— for ever.

2

"We have a long road before us," said Ranald Ban, to make talk, "but we have no baggage to hinder us— and not an ounce of plunder for our year's work, as the Appin man said that went to Edinburgh to learn the ministry. Let me see now. We will keep well north of Loch Awe and the flanks of Cruachan, for the last time we were there we did not leave the Mac-Naughtons as much as the milk of a cow. Our best road will be across Rannoch into Appin and over the sea to Mull, where we will stay a while, and as long as we can keep you, with my father Ailin, and then down by the Sound of Jura to hunt Alasdair."

"I would like surely to meet the father you are always talking about," said Tadg Mor. "There is a thing or two I would like to tell him."

"And one or two you will not tell him."

"I mind the day well," said Tadg Mor ruminatively, "and you coming out of a tavern house in Aberdeen, a girl in one arm and a keg of ale in the other."

"You are wearing that keg on your shoulders this minute," said Ranald Ban. "It was the girl I wanted to part with, and I often wonder since how you persuaded me to give the keg to a shipman for his leather coat—against his will."

I left them bantering each other, and walked up by the course of the stream, and out into the heather. I stopped at the head of a lift of ground and looked around me over that very desolate country. The purple of the heather was past its glory, and all the hills were grey and solemn; and in the lifting swell of the great mountains northwards lonely patches of snow were already in the folds of the corries. Below me the river ran clear and fast over quartz boulders, and its sough came up to me as coldly aloof and lonely as the whisper of the wind in the dry blossoms of the heather. And it was then that a most devastating loneliness came over me in that austere desolate land, and I wanted to cower and hide and die like a wounded badger in its den. I lay down in the heather and sank my head amongst the stems; and the waves flowed over me like the wind that made the heather stir.

I was only a small, lonely, futile speck in this wide

cold lifting land, but small and futile though I was, that land was drawing its net closer and closer round me. Soon now it would be mouthing my bare bones amongst all the bare bones it loved to mouth. Montrose was gone, O'Cahan was dead; all the gay, rough, gallant men of the regiment were dead too; and all our poor faithful women scattered on the hills and dying, dying, dying. And Margaret Anderson! I would never see her again, never hear her high clear voice toning itself queer and softly to the depth of the Gaelic. Her lustrous eyes, her wide clean mouth, the hollows of her long neck were filled with dust; and life was dust in my mouth. Better for me to die too and be at the end of all struggle. I had only to hold my breath for a little while and my lonely soul would slip away from its useless body. I knew then that many men had died as I was ready to die in that pit: by willing it. I was in that very bottom slough of life where the terrible sin of Despair lurks to destroy the souls of men. And I did not know that if I moved at all I would have to move upwards.

I do believe that I would have died there in the wilderness if Tadg Mor and Ranald Ban had not come up through the heather and sat down at my side. Tadg Mor placed his hand gently on my shoulder and said nothing, but Ranald Ban bent close and comforted me.

"It will be all right, Maurteen. Fight it out. Men get taken that way before the road turns. I know. I spent two nights in the heather above Fordoun and the waves flowed over me."

After that Tadg Mor and he talked quietly together, giving me time to draw myself away from the abyss, and my foster-brother brought the talk round cunningly to the days of our youth below the Walsh Mountains. He told of a race to the top of Mount Leinster and back again, and how I won it against all Slaneyside; and Ranald Ban capped it with the story of a great race that he had once ran round the full circuit of Ben More in Mull.

"I would have won it too," said he with regret, "only four MacLeans and two of the MacBeths, and three MacDonalds and a young brother of mine got in ahead of me."

"How many were behind you?" Tadg Mor wanted to know.

"I had the whole place to myself," said Ranald boastingly.

And as Tadg Mor laughed, Ranald Ban came to his knees at my side, and a fresh interest came into his voice.

"Talking of races, here comes a man in a race of his own, and he making his last bid for the post."

I lifted my head and sat up. The famous droving road that comes over the height of land between Spey and Tay ran and looped below us by the Garry. A man was running doggedly on that track. He was not making much speed—just a bare jog—but it was his best. One arm was across his breast, the other helping to lift his weary feet; and his head was thrown back and sunk between his shoulders, like a man in a final effort for the winning post, as Ranald Ban had said. He swayed as he ran, stumbled once, shook his ragged head, and went on again.

He saw us on the head of the slope as the track swerved towards us, lurched, checked himself, and set a foot in the heather to come to us. But he shook his head against the steepness of the brae, and beckoned us wearily to come to him. And Tadg Mor swore mightily and leaped.

"*Tigearna!* It is Black Rab Fraser himself."

It was Black Rab Fraser, the servant of Iseabal Rose, who, in her quiet and steadfast way, had set her foot on a road that turned away from mine, and the thought of whom I had put out of my mind for my own peace.

The road had turned.

3

We ran down to Black Rab, and Tadg Mor put a supporting arm round him.

"I found ye," said he, and there was pride in his panting hoarseness.

"The race is over," said Tadg Mor. He looked fiercely up the valley, and his hand came to his hilt. "Was it Hugh Rose or Wat Dunbar was after you?"

"They were at the beginning of it whatever. Hae ye a bite among ye?"

"Not your size, but we will be seeing."

Whilst Tadg Mor supported him down the track, Ranald Ban and I ran ahead to where the camp-fire was dying down in ashes. I built it up and set it flaming with dry heath stems: Ranald Ban cut thin slices off a haunch of venison, and we had two of them toasting on forked sticks before Rab staggered in on Tadg Mor's arm and sank down in the heather.

Ranald Ban looked at me meaningly. "He was looking for us."

"He had his own reasons—or another's," I answered. "We will hear."

The man was nearly done, his cheeks hollow, his eyes bloodshot, his mouth loose. There was a bloody bandage on his head and another on his left arm, and one of his feet was bare and bleeding. Tadg Mor held a firm knee against him, and felt in the pocket of the leather coat.

"A case of need, anyway," said my foster-brother, and brought forth our own special flask of usgebaugh. We always carried an emergency one of the purest triple-run spirit for purposes of medicine and surgery. Now he allowed Rab one deep gurgling gulp, and drew the bottle away against the spent man's holding hand. That powerful spirit went through his veins almost visibly, and his back stiffened even as he cleared his throat.

"I'm all right," said the indomitable fellow. "There's nothing wrong wi' me—only the hunger."

"We will put that wrong right for you." Tadg Mor patted his shoulder.

"Nothing other than cold water crossed my lips since night before last. I'll hae that one now." He leant forward, snapped a slice of meat out of the flame, and stuffed his mouth full with it."

"If it sticks in your gullet," warned Ranald Ban, "your stomach will never forgive you."

Rab gulped and swallowed, and beckoned for another piece.

"Take it easy, Rabeen," advised Tadg Mor.

"Four days I am on the road—or is it five—but I aye knew I'd find ye. A strange thing—the second sight was given me two nights ago—my mother had it afore me—and I saw ye, the three o' ye together, the same as always, and ye lying round a camp-fire in a place like this; and Tadg Mor was crying to himself in his sleep."

"It was the second sight," said Tadg Mor quietly. "A dream I had—— Go on, Rab!"

"Before that, I had a mind to turn east to Aanside and across to Dee, but the vision I had told me to keep south by Spey and ower the pass. And here I am."

He looked at me then, not at Ranald Ban.

"Wat Dunbar has taken your *Roisin Dhuv*."

"There spoke his death-sentence, as God is my judge," said Ranald Ban fiercely.

"Wait—wait!" I stopped him impatiently. "We must get at this from the beginning. Let him eat first. Here is another slice, Black Rab."

He tore at the half-cooked venison with his white hound's teeth, and in a grim silence we watched him finish three pieces. And then Tadg Mor gave him a little more spirits mixed with water.

"You will get your fill of meat when your tale is told," said Tadg Mor. "Our *Roisin Dhuv*? Go on, Rab."

"Wat Dunbar has Mistress Iseabal hidden away," said he.

"Is she his wife?" I put to him.

"Na—as far as I know. It will be waur than that, I'm feart."

Ranald Ban sprang to his feet and sat down again, taking strong hold of himself.

"Tell us from the beginning," he ordered harshly, "from the time I left her in Aberdeen."

"Ay will I! We werena a sennight in her uncle's house. Maybe he wrote—I couldna be knowin' that—but Hugheon Rose came in himself with fower men and took her back to Fleenas. She went quiet with him—what else?—and he was quiet too, like a serpent. I followed to Fleenas, feart as I was, but he was quiet wi' me as well, and didna lift as much as his bare hand to me."

"He did not put her in the bell-tower?"

"No need, an' Wat Dunbar away."

"But Dunbar returned?"

"So he did. But he wasna welcome any longer. Wait till ye hear. Ye ken how bonny she was—ye saw the bonniness grow on her like the rose her name. Well then, ae day the auld Black Rose of Kilravock— her own blood, an uncle far out, and a man respectit— he came over to Fleenas with his son Iain to pree for the Covenant into her father's jaunt wi' Montrose. He didna get much out o' Hugheon Rose, but young Iain—a fine tall lad, and fair like his mother's people —when he saw our Iseabal his hert loupit out o' his mouth, and his twa e'en said as plain as words: 'Ye are the lass for me.' And, to make my story short, he said the same thing wi' his tongue in no time at all. And there it was. The auld folk were pleased fine, and why not they?—even if there was a word or two going the rounds about her riding off behind a black Irish devil—begging his pardon. The minister, John Balfour, put his thumb on that from the pulpit itself. She was a beauty, I'm tellin' ye, and fit for a king's bed, and Kilravock the strongest family in all Strathnairn, and well able to restore the Belivat name and lands. Ay! the auld folk were fine pleased."

"And Iseabal?"

"She said nothing, ae way or another. She was sad kind, and quiet in her ways—quieter than ever she was, but she was aye that since Alford. I said to her ae time: 'Will we rin for it again, *Roisin Dhuv*—you know where?' But she shook her head and shook it again. 'Nowhere,' says she. 'That road is ended. If I am to be sold, Rab, the bad bargain may as well stay in the family.' And then she took haud o' me and cried. Ay! she cried here on my shoulder. And I grat too. And so the match was made atween the cousins."

"And Walter Dunbar came home?"

"An' got the sour welcome, as I said. The sourness of it was plain as the day, and the reason for't. Moyness is only a small place bys Kilravock, and young Iain Rose had no bad name to put ahint him. And if Wat Dunbar had a bad name he soon showed how well he deserved it. He said never a word, mind ye, even when sly tongues paired him wi' a piece on a dambrod, but he up and acted like a king in his own right. Look now! Ae dark o' night, a fortnight ago, he cam' doon on Fleenas wi' his twenty men—ye ken the kind o' them—burned the steading to the ground, killed Hugheon Rose and five o' his men—I'm tellin' ye—killed Hugheon Rose dead, I saw him do it—and whippit off Mistress Iseabal without leave or licence."

"To Moyness?"

"No' him. Kilravock would root him out o' Moyness or the day was out."

"Where then?"

"Where? There's my trouble, but dinna blame me. I got the head and arm ye see on me fighting outside her door, and was lying for dead in my blood when they haled her off. I got twa o' the bloody rogues a' the same. As soon as I got my senses again I made Kilravock wi' a struggle, an' for three days we scoured the country. Wat had hidden her awa', and there are mony hidy holes up and down Findhornside. It would tak' a lone man a year to pree into them all."

"Not alone."

"Yes then. After three days Kilravock needed help himself. Lord Lewis Gordon, up from the killing in the Lowlands, made a drive into Moray and Nairn, burned out Brodie once again and made a ring round Lethen and Kilravock. I was fair desperate by that time, and I went across to see the minister, John Balfour, who was the only man in Ardclach no' afraid o' the Dunbars. It was he reminded me o' ye and what ye did for the Aberdeen lass. I wasna there when ye got back from Spynie, but all Moray was talking o' the daring and terrorsome deed. Is it true that ye cut off one o' Brodie's ears to remind him no' to listen to ill tongues, and left Kinnaird—worse off?"

"I knew fine," said Tadg Mor regretfully, "that we left something undone that time."

"No harm if ye did it whatever. Weel, sirs, when the minister reminded me, I says to myself, 'If they did a' that for an Aberdeen fishertown lass, what'll they no' do for a lady wi' the Gaelic tongue and the Gaelic blood—and bonny besides.' And to the minister I say, 'Whaur will I find them in a' the low Lowlands?' 'It will be a long road, indeed,' says he, 'for you and them, and a forlorn task at the end o't, but we will go down to shipmaster Alick Anderson of Lochloy and he may have word to shorten your road.' So down we went, but he had no word."

"Did he know that Margaret Anderson was dead?"

"He knew and was sair hurt. One of the Gordons brought him word." He looked at me underbrowed. "My mistress had a great respect for that tall fair one, though she mightna show it, an' I likit her weel. She fed me three days in Auldearn. I am sorry, Master."

"Go on with your story."

"He had no word o' ye, though the news of the loss of Philiphaugh was a week old. 'If they are no' dead,' says he, 'and dead they well might be, they will be

"It could never be," I cried to the dumb sky. "God would not let her be shamed."

"I will remind you," said Ranald Ban bitterly, "that the God that is preached in this land of Scotland is a chancy man and queer in his ways."

I flung my hand towards the desolation of the mountains.

"What can we do—four men lost in this wild land?"

Tadg Mor was on his feet, his hands firming on my twisting shoulder.

"Easy, little brother! Easy. The thing we will do first is to go down to Alick Anderson at Lochloy. That is what we can do. Black Rab had his vision for some reason."

His strong hands and his steadfast mind coming through them soothed me.

"We will do that," said I, and I was quiet now.

Black Rab Fraser shouted with all his might. "I never doubted ye once," he roared. "Gie me twa more skelbs o' meat and I'm ready for the road, and the Lord ha' mercy on Wat Dunbar's soul as little as He can."

But the road had turned.

CHAPTER XIII
ON THE ROAD

I

THE road we took twisted upwards of one hundred miles and, besides twisting, many of the miles stood on their heads. We covered that road in three days, for we were the finest marchers in the world, and that is tall boasting. We could have done it in less, but we had to go easy the first day with Black Rab, and give him an hour or two of sleep in the bygoing. We fashioned a deer's-hide pampooty brogan for his bare foot, and I will say for him that, good hillmen as we were, he was as good as any of us the last day.

We had been over many parts of the road more than once in our great marches behind Seumas Graham, and these parts were mostly friendly. Up through Badenoch, west of the snow-seamed scarred peaks of the Grampian Mountains, we were in MacPherson country, and that clan, that had fought with us in six battles, cherished us nobly as we padded through, and even hindered us with their hospitality. By the borders of the great forest of Abernethy, an old camping ground of ours, we swung away westwards to avoid the lands of Clan Grant. The Grants were always chancy—with us and against us. They had held the passes of the Spey against us in 'forty-four, sent three

A.N.Q.—10   289

hundred men to help us in 'forty-five, and now they might think it a pleasant day's work to hunt down what looked like a party of broken Irishers.

We were in MacIntosh territory now, and, there too, we had to move carefully, for that branch of Clan Chattan, in between reiving times, might be friendly with the lairds of Nairn—and sometimes was. But Black Rab knew the lie of the country hereabouts, and led us quiet roads where we were able to venture a lucky shot at a hind for our evening meal. Both Ranald Ban and Tadg Mor carried flintlocks. At one point going down into the Streens of Findhorn we were actually within a few miles of Iseabal's prison place, if we had only known it.

We crossed the Findhorn at a ford that Black Rab called Polochaig, and did not venture the last stretch until night came down.

"We might be safe enough with Lewie Gordon's men," said Black Rab, "but yon ahead of us is Cawdor land, and they crooked-mouths are the Campbell breed and used to slitting windpipes. The dark for us."

That last night, then, we went over the long tilt of the Cawdor moors, flanked the Hill of Ord, and passed within a mile of our old battlefield of Auldearn. We came down on Maviston of Lochloy shortly after break of day. And a quiet mood was on us—as quiet and as cold as the dawn.

The tide was in and a chill grey-green, but the hills of Ross across the firth had not changed from their blue and purple. The *Moray Quoine* was riding at anchor in her old place, and the reflection of her shook in the draw of the water. To my eye she was ready for sea, her cordage taut, and sails furled on all her yards. And I had a desolate numb pain thinking of the one that would not sail in that boat in this month of October. And I shrank from facing her uncle.

The hamlet was still abed—or the men might be out fishing—but a wisp of smoke, blue in the greyness, lifted out of the chimney of Alick Anderson's two-storeyed thatched house. He was an early riser, and opened the door for us himself.

It was less than four months since we had parted with him at the Ford of Gight on the Spey, but he had aged in that time and grown thinner. Still, the firm bones of him had not lost their strength, and his eyes could light up as they lit now. His hands welcomed us heartily.

"Come in—come awa' in," he cried. "I was looking for ye, but not for two days yet. Ye're a gran' chiel, Black Rab Fraser."

He ushered us into the big room with its oaken furniture out of Edinburgh, and a new fire of peat was beginning to blaze on the wide hearth. He bade us sit and went to an inner door to tell his housekeeper to flay a puckle more speldings for breakfast. I felt utterly forlorn where I stood by the fireside in that dark room that Margaret and Iseabal had once lit with their presence, and I did not know how to address the shipmaster. Neither did Ranald Ban nor Tadg Mor, who only cleared their throats and shuffled their feet. But Alick Anderson came to my side and placed his hand on my shoulder.

"I know, friend. I know it all. The lad of the Gordons you know—Myron was his name—rade down from Lethen to tell me. Dinna say a word. Montrose walked behind her at the head of his army, and ye three and a Colonel O'Cahan carried her on your shoulders. She was well lo'ed."

"She was loved." I met his eye then. "She had no pain, and at the end she said, 'Tell my Uncle Alick all my happiness.'"

He looked at me close. "Did she say that—my lassie?"

"That is what she said."

"It has meaning to me. I am glad." He straightened up and struck his breast, his eyes kindling. "I am prood she was acquaint of men and that her death was gallant. In her need I called ye, doubt in my hert, and ye smiled and came with debonair, and did a deed o' hardihood that shook all Moray."

"We did not do all the things Moray said," hinted Tadg Mor.

"I know. Myron told me. Ye did nobly, and now, at the word, ye are here again two days before time at the end of a terrible campaign."

"We are here," said Ranald Ban, and then quickly: "You have news for us?"

"Little myself, but I will take ye to a man that will have it for us by the time we get there." He put the subject aside with his hands. "It can wait a meenit. Ye'll brak fast wi' me first. Ye are meat-fed men, and I ask pardon for the poor fare I have for ye this morn."

His fare was not poor and, sitting to it, we found that we were hungry. Great platters of oatmeal parritch having the flavour of the live corn, piggins of new milk, oat and wheaten bannocks, fresh-salted butter that I had not tasted the like of since leaving Ireland, and for main dish a cured fish that he called spelding, which I think is a haddock lightly cured to an amber yellow over oaken shavings. Writing this my mouth waters thinking of the flavour of it.

"My hand!" said Tadg Mor, "meat and salmon

are a coarse diet by these. No more, Master Alick, if you want me to march this week—just that small one, then, and God increase your store!"

Alick Anderson was busy about us and ate but little himself, and as we busied ourselves he talked to us.

"It is no' easy or safe to get out and about Nairn the days that are in it, with the Gordons everywhere, and the Grants and Toshes reivin' awa' to themselves up-by on the borders. We did what we could, a' the same, John Balfour and myself. There is one thing we know. Wat Dunbar came in to Lord Lewie's camp below the house of Lethen three days ago, and was received friendly like. As ye ken, he was with the Gordons at A'ford fight, and still pretends to be on the King's side—and he on his own side all the time. He promised Lord Lewie twenty men to help the siege."

"There would be only eighteen maybe," said Black Rab, "for I killed two myself."

"Maybe you did not kill them dead, Rabeen," said Tadg Mor. "Was it on the head you hit them?"

"I hit them where I could, an' if they live I will hit them again."

"Eighteen or twenty, it makes no matter," said Alick. "It is not likely that Lord Lewie will refuse their help to offer us his against their master. That is my one bit of bad news."

"Dod Myron will help us," said Tadg, "and one or two more if they are there."

"And I know two or three that will be with us," added Ranald Ban.

"I hae fower men o' the Roses where I can put my hand on them," said Black Rab, "and they will cut any throat I point out to them."

"Keep your finger pointing away from me then," warned Tadg Mor.

"I have six Findhorn men in my crew," said Alick Anderson. "Hardy lads, trained to the boarding pike."

"Let us find where the lady is first," I hinted.

"Find her we will, and that soon," said the shipmaster. "A man I had up there followed Dunbar out of the Gordon camp but lost him at the top end of Dulsie Wood on the Findhorn. That way he rode and that way we are looking. And listen! John Balfour, the minister, sent me down word late last night. He is our man, and the man we are going to see. The message as it ran was this: 'I think I know. I will make sure to-morrow.' He couldna trust his messenger to say more. That is to-day. We will go up to Ardclach to-night."

"Why not now?" urged Ranald Ban.

"Because we hae to move canny. Did anyone speak ye on the road?"

"Not this side of Spey," Black Rab told him. "I made sure of that."

"Dunbar has his spies abroad, and if he found out that ye three were north——" He clicked finger and thumb. "It might go ill for the lady and for us too. No. We will wait the gloaming and go round about, for Moyness lies ower near the straight road. Moreover, a rest will do ye good."

There was a pause then and Alick Anderson leant his hands on the table and looked down at them.

"There's a thought has troubled me once or twice," said he slowly, as if speaking to himself. "What is to befall Iseabal Rose when we have her out?"

"Walter Dunbar will be dead," said Ranald Ban.

"And then?"

"There is her cousin," I hinted.

"Young Iain behind the walls of Kilravock! There is him surely." But he was not enthusiastic.

"I am thinking," said Tadg Mor, "that a lad of spirit would find a way out from behind a wall to try what good a clout would do Wat Dunbar—or is it from Wat he is sheltering?"

"My very thought," said the shipmaster. He looked from Ranald Ban to me and back again. "Mind ye, gentlemen, the *Moray Quoine* is ready to lift anchor any tide, and I am ready to risk Leith Port and the plague of Edinburgh for Mistress Iseabal's sake." He paused and finished slowly. "And I am ready to take her any place else she wants to go."

Ranald Ban made no reply and I had none to make. Tadg Mor stepped into the breach.

"Let us not be bidding the devil good-morrow till we meet him. *Roisin Dhuv* has a tongue in her head."

We left it at that.

2

It was close on midnight when we came to the manse-house in the hollow of Ardclach. We had come roundabout, across the Cawdor road, through a small place called Urchany, where a dog barked at us, and at last across a wide and treacherous moor with a stream to ford in the middle. The night was fine and clear, but without a moon, and Black Rab Fraser knew every inch of the road. The shipmaster had ridden pony-back as far as the moor edge.

"There is no crossing this place in wet weather," he had told us.

In a dry October of a dry year it was bad enough

in places, and we could feel the ground quake near the moss-hags. Going down into the hollow of Ard-clach we were amongst trees, and the fallen leaves rustled about our feet.

The shipmaster thought it prudent not to take us to the manse in a body. The small stone kirk stood apart from the township, and we climbed over the kirkyard wall, and made our way through the leaning headstones to the open porch of the kirk itself. Four of us waited in the deep shade in there, Tadg Mor making the sign of the cross as a safeguard against Protestant practices, while Alick Anderson went through the handgate and up the path to the manse.

We stood silently and listened. The manse was just in front of us and not forty paces away, a narrow house of two storeys, every window dark. We heard the shipmaster's knock on the door, a diffident knock for a house asleep. It brought no answer, and he knocked louder this time. In a little while a window lifted and we could make out someone in white in the black square of it.

"Who is't?" A woman's voice, but not our woman.

Followed Alick's murmured answer, and the woman said:

"Oh, it's you, shipmaster. I'll be doon in a minute."

"Auld Janet Calder, the housekeeper," Black Rab whispered to us.

In a minute, not more, the door opened, and after a word or two Alick went into the house, and the door shut softly. No light was lit inside that we could see. We waited.

A cold air was blowing up the valley, and the dead leaves rustled and whispered amongst the headstones. Tadg Mor and I moved closer together, for, toughened night campaigners though we were, a small dread of ghostly things stayed with us from a ghost-ridden childhood in Ireland. We sensed something unhuman in the mutter of the dead leaves against the stones, like the muted whisper of stone mouths. When the breeze died down the muttering stopped, and the strong sough of the river came up to us from below. The Findhorn is the most rock-torn river in the north, and the voice of it is never still—never weary and ever weary.

Alick Anderson did not keep us waiting long. In five minutes the manse door reopened and he was back amongst us.

"H-s-s-h!" he warned silence. "Come this way."

He did not lead us to the manse but round the back of the kirk to a secluded angle of the wall above the river.

"We can talk here." And then, "John Balfour is taken."

"The Dunbars?"

"Ay! three hours ago."

"Pity we weren't here sooner," regretted Tadg Mor.

"Well for us we werena. A strong party and all armed."

"He was taken by force?" I asked.

"He had to gang."

"If that was not force it was next door to it anyway," said Tadg Mor.

"And here we are——" began Ranald Ban bitterly.

"Wait—wait now!" said Alick Anderson quickly. "It is well that we are here, for I know the end of the road. Listen ye. Janet Calder is a faithful woman and in our trust. This is her story: John Balfour was out all day and did not return till nightfall. I know where he was. Three hours ago a strong party—a dozen or more, and two on horseback—came up to the door, and the horsemen went in to the minister. Wat Dunbar was not amongst them, but Janet kent them for Dunbars. She did not hear what was said in the parlour room, but when they came out she was standing in the door of the back-place, and her master saw her out of an eye corner. He spoke then, lifting his voice. 'I will go if I must,' said he. 'The man— or woman—must need me sore to call me to Lochindorb Castle this hour o' night.' One of the men growled at him, but Janet noted the way he paused before 'woman.' Lochindorb! That's the place he has gone, and that is where Iseabal Rose is hidden. I know it. Ye will have heard of Lochindorb?"

"A loch somewhere near, I hope," said Ranald Ban.

"Ten miles south of here. A big bit lochan lost in the moors o' Dava, mires and moors a' round it, and never a house or home within miles. But surely ye will have heard o' the Wolf of Badenoch?"

"I have heard of him," said Ranald Ban. "He burned Forres and the big church at Elgin."

"That's him. They speak of him hereabouts yet, and he dead two hundred years. The natural son of a Scots king, and the bloodiest robber outside Ireland—your pardon, sirs. He did not give up burning and reiving—and waur things—till, like ithers, he was ower auld for such like lusty amusements. He died in sanctity, they say. However, one of his strongholds was in Lochindorb, and it a powerful, strong stone castle near the middle of the loch, filling the whole of a sma' island. It was burned and its walls breached at long last, and no one has inhabited it for I don't know how lang, but there are habitable rooms still in some of the towers, and the reivers out of Cromdale and Badenoch might use it as a hidy hole once in a while. That is where John Balfour is gone and where Iseabal Rose is hidden. I might hae thought o't afore now."

"We will go there," said Ranald Ban firmly. "Is there a boat?"

"There will be. There used be a muckle flat-bottom for taking sheep and cattle in and out. But mark ye, if the castle is held, the boat will be moored at it, and that's four cable-lengths off shore."

"I am wondering to myself," said Tadg Mor, "why they took the parson. Our *Roisin Dhuv*—is she ill on us?"

"There might be another reason," was all Alick Anderson said, and, though what that reason might be we all knew, we did not talk about it.

"Well, soldier men?" said the shipmaster out of the silence. "This is where ye come in. Ye have been out with the great marquis and will have some of his stratagems—and there was Spynie Tower."

"I am thinking that the ablest head is the oldest one, shipmaster," said Ranald Ban. "Give us your own thoughts."

"Well then! this is how I see it. There are a score of desperate hard men to face——"

"Eighteen maybe," protested Black Rab mildly, and Tadg Mor made him grunt with a hard elbow.

"Eighteen or twenty, we must come at them in strength, and to get at them we must cross by boat and in the dark. Do you see any other way?"

"It is the best way."

"There are five of us——"

"Four," corrected Ranald Ban.

"Five, young man. I hae brought down a scarth at a hundred paces with a flintlock, and a Dunbar is an easier mark. Five I say, and my six sailormen —that's eleven; and Black Rab's four throat-cutters, fifteen."

"Enough and to spare," said Tadg Mor.

"I'm no' sure, and we must be sure. The Dunbars are fighting men. If yourself and Ranald Ban could slip friendly in amongst the Gordons and draw out the men of your choice, we could be doin' fine wi' them."

"We can try it," agreed Ranald Ban. "But the boat?"

"I will take up the ship's cobble. It can be done easy with two horses and six men. And it can be done most of the road in broad day. Only a matter o' my business taking a bit boat to the Earl o' Moray's loch near Dava. I mind me once, ten years ago, hoisting a twenty-foot whaling boat all the way to Loch an Eilan in Rothiemurchus. No trouble at a'. That's my plan—plain enough—and to-morrow night's the night if we can make the parts fit."

We talked it over there in the dark, and we could not better the main plan at any point; and the main plan was to get twenty men quietly to the shore of the loch in the first dark of night. For that we schemed, with all our wits sharpened by emergency.

"And that's that," said the rare Alick Anderson at the end, putting his hand on my arm. "There is one other thing in my mind. If we had a man lying at watch in the heather all day the morn it would be a great help when we are gathered——"

"That is my part," I answered the press of his hand, "if you tell me the road."

"I had you in my mind, Master Somers. We are mair than half-roads to the loch where we stand, and Rab Fraser could take you and choose a safe place where we could all gather to you."

"I know the place this minute," said Rab Fraser.

"And I could get a puckle scones and cakes from auld Janet for you," said Alick.

That is how it was settled.

Tadg Mor gripped me by the arm at the finish and brought his mouth near my ear.

"Whisper, Maurteen! Remember us stalking deer in Rannoch. Lie on your belly and keep your head down, and do not be thinking you can rescue *Roisin Dhuv* your lone. Are you hearing me?"

"I hear you. If you know me at all you will know that I will be too frightened to lift my head till you come."

CHAPTER XIV

THE ROAD ENDS

I

It was the long, slow day's waiting I had above the shore of Lochindorb.

Black Rab Fraser had brought me by an old reiving track over the shoulder of a hill he called Aitnoch that was difficult only at the end where the ground was boggy about a strong stream that flowed out of the northern end of the loch. This was his own country, and he knew it blindfolded. We had arrived there shortly before dawn, and he had posted me in a small grassy hollow on the eastern shore of the loch.

"The Wolf's castle is out there in front of you, as you will see," he had whispered. "This is the nearest point, but you are well hid. The bulk o's will come in over the ridge behind as soon's ever it's dark."

It was a long day. Luckily the curve of the hollow was deep enough for me to stand up and stretch my legs in without being visible from without. It was lipped on the loch side by a couple of low-stunted junipers, and, as soon as the dawn came, I crept up and made a spy-hole in the thick prickly bush of one of them. It was a desolate and lonely scene that I surveyed, but a bonny one too.

First of all my eyes sought the old castle, and there

it was in front of me, a full quarter-mile from shore. It was bigger than I had expected—a great pile of ruins indeed. The island that held it would square to an acre, and the grey stone outer walls, sound to the crenellations, rose from the water's edge. At three corners berstling towers lifted above the walls, two of them breached and in ruins, but the one at the northern corner farthest from me still showed part of a conical roof and a jut of chimney. That chimney held my gaze for a long time. If the ruins were occupied a fire would be welcome in these upland moors, and the chimney should give evidence. There was no curl of smoke over all the broken towers, but I would not yet be disheartened, for the morning was young, and rogues, as well as honest men, would still be in bed.

The loch also was a broader expanse than I had expected. I estimated it a mile in width from where I lay hidden, and I could see two miles or more of its length to the bristly bluff that jutted out into the water south of me. The breeze of morning rippled all its surface into cold silver, and I was near enough to hear the lap of water on the shingly beach. Behind me a strong limestone-ribbed hill rose in two steep shelves, but on all other sides there was nothing but a lonely sea of heather: great brown billows of heather rolling upwards and curving over and heaving up again to where, far in the south, serrated points were cold purple in the dawn. But that impression is not right. Those wide billows of heather were not flowing away from the loch, but seemed to be flowing and shouldering and converging down into the basin of it as if seeking to swallow it and keep it secret in their brown maw.

No doubt there were moorfowl and even deer amongst the hills, but that morning there was no sign or sound of life in all the desolation of the moors; no deer belled, no sheep bleated, no moor-cock crew, no eagle screamed, no hill-lark sang its morning song. There was nothing but a quietness of desolation that hid and hinted a strange austere beauty. That was Lochindorb as I saw it at first.

It was a long time after dawn before the ruins gave any sign of human habitation, and then the thing happened that I had been watching for. The smoke of a new fire curled from the ruined chimney of the berstling tower. The sight of that smoke gave me a fine stir, and set me to a keener watch. Now that the light was stronger I could pick out things more clearly. I was so placed that I had the whole eastern wall in view, and could also look along the northern or main front; and on that front I could make out the stern of a boat jutting from a bay of stone below the entrance barbican. More significant still, an iron helmet and a face below it appeared, presently, above the crenellations of the wall facing me, moved down to the breached corner tower, back again, and disappeared; and at regular intervals all through the day that head appeared, made its double turn, and dropped out of sight. The place was held and warded. We would have to move very carefully in the dark and finish with a burst. I took good care to move my head very cautiously.

The day passed slowly but not wearily. A sunny brisk day—but not cold—in the fall of the year, and a grand day for open marching, such marching as we had done one short year ago when we had put the fear of his own God in MacCailien Mhor. In that hard glorious year I had learnt to draw a mental armour about myself. My body was tough as woodbine though it was not powerful, and time and weariness I had grown not only to thole but to ignore. And so I could lie for hours below my juniper bush, no weariness on me, my mind, the force of living, sunk deep and resting, my eyes only alive and watching.

Some time in the day I slid to the bottom of the hollow, partook of buttered scones and oatcakes, and found that I was thirsty. But thirsty I had to remain, for I had forgotten to borrow Tadg Mor's flask, and I dared not crawl down to the shore so short a distance below. All the day after that I looked at the rippling water with a longing eye, but the discomfort was easily bearable for a man who had marched over stony Caol Ira in hot July.

The day passed. Occasionally small clouds crossed the sun, and shadows ran smoothly across the serenity of the moors. I was as quiet as those shadows. What I thought about, if I thought at all, I do not remember, but I do know that, for my own reason, I held my mind away steadfastly from the future. This thing I was now bearing I could bear; this crisis I was now facing I could face; this thing I had come here to do I would do; and after that let life take its own road. I was a young man in years, but that mighty year, packed close with life and death, had made my mind old. I was no longer a youth. I no longer dreamed and planned. I was in a bad way though I did not know it, for, unless life took a fresh start, life for me would be only a thing of irony.

It was close to sunset that things began to move; and then things moved quickly. Two or three men appeared on the stone platform in front of the main entrance, and the stern of the boat disappeared and was replaced by its bow. And shortly after that it began to fill with men. That startled me, and I watched with all my eyes. What I watched for was a woman, and I was near enough to distinguish one if one there was. There was no woman that I could discern. They were all men in the half-panoply of war, except one man in hodden grey.

The boat swung out into the open water; and under the drive of four long sweeps came towards me, but not directly. Some distance down the shore to my right the water had been deepened close in by piling the stones of the bottom to make the jut of a landing-place, and for that landing-place the boat made.

There were two men in that boat I knew well. One was John Balfour the minister; I could not mistake the pallid strength of his features. The other was Walter Dunbar. He sat in the stern, his head bare, with the low sun making it ruddier than ever, and he wore no steel on his breast. I looked back at the ruins. No one moved about it now, but the chimney still smoked. Was Iseabal Rose there all alone?

The big party landed, and I thought: "If twenty men were with me here this thing would finish now."

But Walter Dunbar did not land. He took his seat in the middle thwart of the boat, and grasped two of the long sweeps in his great hands. Voices came up to me but I could not distinguish words, except once that Dunbar said "morrow" or "morning." The squad fell into military formation, and it was then I counted them. Black Rab Fraser was right. There were eighteen men. Many of them I knew from the Alford campaign: rough, hard-fighting fellows unquestioningly attached to their leader. At a word they marched away northwards on the rough track winding by the shore, the track I had come in on. John Balfour was in the middle file and, once, he turned face to the island and lifted a hand as if in prayer or blessing. The man behind pushed him on, but not roughly. I did not spend any time watching them go. My attention came back to Dunbar, who worked the boat round, pulled slowly back to the castle, moored in the old place and disappeared.

The next ten or more minutes were bad ones for me. Walter Dunbar was back in the ruins. Was Iseabal Rose there? Were they alone? Why had John Balfour been brought, and what had he done? What was——? I stopped there and began again, and my mind grew more and more troubled. Was Iseabal Rose alone with Walter Dunbar? That question my mind dwelt on. I knew then how well I liked that small dark quiet woman, and I knew that the breaking of her quietness and her strength must hurt me too.

The sun was down now, but I estimated a full hour yet till the coming of my friends. "I cannot stand that hour," I spoke aloud to myself. And I went into the bottom of the hollow and stood looking down at the ground.

"I can never stand against that hour," I said again, and slowly unbelted my sword. I stripped off my broadcloth coat. A year ago it had been a good coat, but now it was stained green by sun and weather, and gaped at the elbows; and only one button was left. That button had been sewn on by Iseabal Rose on Gallows Hill above Alford. That thought made me hurry. I stripped off my shirt, braced my trews tight at the waist, took off my old brogans—I wore no foot hose—placed my flat leather cap on the little pile, and topped it with sword and targe. I stood up then stripped to the waist, and the evening air brushed its cool fingers on my naked back.

I climbed out of the hollow and walked down to the shore, the heather stinging my bare feet. I looked across at the castle, and for the first time it seemed far away, floating double in a dimension of its own; for the evening air was still now, and every ragged wall and tower was mirrored in the silver floor of the loch. A strange wan floor of silver, sunk here below moors that were now dark and sinister below a sky paler and wanner than the wan self-shining waters. And then a feeding trout shattered the surface of the mirror, and the reflected towers shivered in the widening rings.

I waded slowly out making no splash, and the cold tang of the water made my throat flutter. But I was used to cold. When I was waist-deep I cupped my hands and drank. The water was not peaty and had little white specks floating in it. And then I remembered a thing Tadg Mor always did before plunging in for a swim in the Slaney. I did that now, though I was not a Roman. I dipped my fingers in the water and signed the cross on my forehead. Then I lay out slowly in the water, holding my breath against the sting, and began to swim.

I was never a strong swimmer; that was why I dared not take a weapon to weigh me; and I was not sure, even then, of making that smooth quarter-mile. In Ireland I used to swim a hundred yards of the Slaney and back again, and pant on the bank, Tadg Mor laughing at me, for he could swim and dive like a wild duck. I set my mind against all impulse to hurry, sank my head low in the water, and struck out slow and steady in the breast stroke, the only stroke I knew. The water splayed back from my chin in long lovely ripples. The light was still strong enough for any watcher to see me from the island, but I no longer cared.

I do believe that, in the mood that was on me then, I could have swum the width of the loch. I made the ruins without difficulty. The water was cold, but I was warm enough, though not winded. I came to shore below the eastern wall where the water was deep close in. There was a narrow base of boulders along the wall, and I scrambled my way carefully over these to the corner turning the north side below an overhanging turret. I looked round the corner to where the boat, a big flat-bottom, was moored in its shallow basin. There was not a stir anywhere; and keeping close to the wall I slipped along to the boat. When I got there I found that on the within-side of it was a deep right-angled recess, paved roughly, with the main entrance at the back of it. That entrance was now only a ruined arch, and I could look straight through it to a wide patch of grey-green, mounded grass: the old bailey yard of the stronghold. The light was still strong enough to show me a big elder bush growing at the base of the far wall, and I could even distinguish the purple splash of its over-ripe berries.

I turned to the boat and considered it for a space. The thing I was about to do now took all my resolution. Then I untied the mooring rope from a jut of stone, slipped into the water, here only thigh-deep, pivoted the prow round to face the loch, and gave the stern a steady long push off shore. The water made a soft lapping ripple and that was the only sound. Any drift of air or water was down the loch towards the stream that drained it, and anyone who wanted that boat would need to swim for it or wait till it beached. I was alone on the island with Walter Dunbar and whoever else was with him, and I could expect no aid for nearly an hour.

I went through the arch, but I no longer crept or crawled close to the wall. I was fearful enough, but my mind was as stripped as my body, and knew that now no fearfulness could bring its prudence to my aid. I stopped at the mouth of the arch and looked across the bailey: a ragged half-acre of grass, crumbling stones peeping through it, surrounded by ruined walls that stood stark against the pallor of the sky, broken windows like eyes watching me. No one, nothing moved anywhere, and there was no sound.

And then from somewhere overhead came the murmur of a man's voice, low at first and then rising and growing vehement, so that I almost caught the words. The speaker was Walter Dunbar. The voice stopped, and after a pause another answered it. And my heart leaped and went on beating faster. For though the voice was only a murmur that never lifted, I knew it for the voice of Iseabal Rose: that low, slow-moving voice that I had not forgotten. It stopped, and the man laughed bitterly—or mockingly.

I strode out of the arch and looked up. The big corner tower had a broken window-opening one storey off the ground, looking into the bailey, and in the slowly gathering gloaming the reflection of a fire inside shone on the gapped stones framing it. There was no doorway in the base of the tower, but there was a broken one in the wall near-by it. To that I went and found a stairway open to the sky. Many of the stone steps were gone, but enough remained to take me upwards to the head of the wall inside the crenellated curtain. Facing me was the tower, and in it a doorway closed by a rough shield of planks. Through the many chinks came the glow of the fire within. There was silence now.

On silent bare feet I took the half-dozen paces between me and the door. There was no lock or latch on the outside, and I placed my hand softly on the wood and pressed. It gave stiffly for a few inches, and then jerked and fell back with a crash against the wall. And in the very crash of it a man exclaimed loudly, and there was Walter Dunbar on his feet, facing me from the fireside.

2

The room I looked into was a round stone room under the eaves of a tower. A part of the conical roof had been blown away, but the hole was roughly closed with a thatch of heather. A fire of bog pine blazed brightly in the open fireplace, and the dying light of the day came through the inner window. Other than a couch of heather and pinetops, a bench and a rough chair, there were no furnishings in that room.

Walter Dunbar had just leaped up from the bench.

Iseabal Rose sat very still in the chair facing round to the door. They had been sitting there talking to each other, and though his voice had gathered vehemence, hers had retained its old calmness. I thought then of the first time I had seen Iseabal Rose. That had been in the prison-room of Ardclach bell-tower, and, then too, she had sat in her chair and looked at me standing in the doorway, and her quietness had impressed its force on my mind for all time. She sat very still now too, the quietness of her unbroken by gladness or grief, her eyes fixed on me, and her hands clasped gently on her lap over my old war-cloak that was draped loosely about her waist. And again I was surprised by the soft dusky loveliness of her.

"Who is it?" asked Dunbar harshly, taking one stride forward.

He might well ask. Standing there naked to the waist, black-haired, black-eyed, black-chinned, I must have looked an outlandish savage out of an outlandish clime. Iseabal Rose answered for me.

"It is Martin Somers out of Ireland." Her voice was a soft bell. "Here in my heart I have been waiting for him this hour, his cloak about me. He always comes in my need."

I walked across the floor on silent feet, and Dunbar took his one stride back. He was in gallant dress, ribbons at his buckled knees, his vest ruffled, his fine red hair brushed back and held by a band. He wore no sword or dagger. A grand shapely man, tall as Tadg Mor, and even more supple than Ranald Ban in the swing of his shoulders.

I stood between them looking into the fire that flamed sibilantly, and he was near enough to put his hand on me if he wanted to. I felt the warmth of the fire on my bare breast and a little steam curled from my wet knees. And Iseabal Rose said softly:

"What strong clean bodies men have!"

That quiet mood of hers impressed itself on me—and on him too. There was no need to lose tempers and tear passions in this stark hour. Dunbar's voice was queerly detached.

"Martin Somers! and he is not welcome. No man likes to be disturbed on his marriage night."

I turned to her.

"Are you his wife, Iseabal?"

"I am not his wife, Martin. I never will be."

"Why do you lie, Dunbar?"

"This is my marriage night, nevertheless. Are you alone, Somers?"

"I will not lie to you this night. I am alone now, but twenty of my friends will be here within an hour."

"Why are you here?"

"To tell you that the game is played."

"The game has still an hour to run, and in an hour many things might happen. A man might die many deaths in an hour."

"One only."

"In an hour I could be out of here and hidden in the heather with my wife."

"I thought of that. Your boat is afloat far out on the loch. Until my friends come we three stay here alive or dead."

"You choose death very surely."

"No. The choice will be yours. Listen! You can choose death now or in an hour, or you can choose life; but if you choose life you lose Iseabal Rose."

"That is no choice. I have set all my will on one thing. You know that. And I have been patient. Have I not been very patient? I even brought John Balfour to marry us, and she would not. Do you think that the closeness of death will make me yield now? You fool!"

"All that is true," I agreed. "The choice is not a fair one for a man gone mad."

"Then I will give you two your choice; and I will trust you. You will hold your friends off and Iseabal

313

Rose will promise to be my wife in wedlock, or you will die, and the woman will be mine before I die. Choose!"

But Iseabal Rose leant to me.

"You are not afraid of death, Martin?"

"Not this night, Iseabal."

"Once you told me to hold my own soul against all travail. I have done it. Do you likewise. Be not afraid, Maurteen. Ranald Ban MacKinnon will do for me what I ask him, and my soul clean will be with yours within the hour."

I smiled at her.

"My dear, you will comb your hair white as snow, your grandchildren about your knees."

I turned to Dunbar then and took the single step that brought me close.

He crashed his mighty fist downwards at my head, but I fell close against him, and my hands found his neck where the deep veins were. And as my hands tightened a red spark crackled in my brain, and my eyes had a strange vision. I saw unknown trees slashing in a high wind, their trunks roped with knotted vines, and long beards of grey moss streaming from their branches; and cowering dunes where the sand blew in a brown haze over tossing narrow blue waters; and a clearing where tall corn shook its wide flags near a long hut of bark sheltered below swaying cypresses; and one big blue red-necked bird hurled itself from one tree to another. I never had seen that place in life, but I do think that the Indian blood in me was in control then, and I know now that what I saw in that vision was the mouth of the James River in the New World where my mother was born.

And once I caught a glimpse of Iseabal's face close

to mine and the flame in her eyes was the flame in the eyes of a fighting wolf bitch.

After that I knew nothing, I saw nothing, and I heard nothing but the turmoil of the wind as it blew in my vision. . . .

From a long way off I heard a voice that I had known in another life.

"Goad! we will never get his fingers loose without breaking them."

That was the voice of one Dod Myron, who had stood by Tadg Mor and me in Spynie Tower a thousand years ago. Were we back there again? Was I dead under Covenant swords? . . . And then another voice came nearer and nearer until it was within my ear.

"Maurteen, Maurteen! It is me. Can't you hear me? Whisper! It is me. It is me myself." And a big gentle hand smoothed down my bare back.

"Tadg Mor, brother!" I whispered, and all my bruised body relaxed.

He had me on my feet and whipped round the other way from the thing that lay on the floor, and his hand and sleeve were busy wiping the blood from my face —and from my mouth.

"Two fine black eyes you will have to yourself by morning," said he.

I saw Ranald Ban then, nostrils and eyes flaring, and Alick Anderson, his face strong and hard below a leather helmet, and Dod Myron the Gordonach, his mouth open; and I saw Black Rab Fraser, and he was holding Iseabal Rose on her feet.

"Iseabal!"

And she came to me. She was wearing her dark-green dress cut square at the neck, but the square was now torn, showing the hollow of her throat and the white of her breast; there was a stain on her lips and a graze above her black brows.

"I did what I could, Maurteen," said she.

I lifted her chin and looked at her face carefully.

"You will have a fine black eye your own self by morning," I told her.

And at that her face broke like a child's and her mouth was against my breast: and I held her and smoothed my hand through the soft dark of her hair.

3

Next day we worked the *Moray Quoine* over the bar of Lochloy, and spread sails north-about for the isles and Ireland.

And there my tale is told, and in a hurry at the finish. Not all my tale—only what was compassed in one year, but a great year. Some day soon, if God spares me, I may tell the tale of Ranald Ban MacKinnon in Ireland. It is a good tale.

.   .   .   .   .   .

These things happened fifty years ago, and I am finishing this writing by lamplight here in my fine new log house at the head waters of the Pamunkey River in Virginia of the New World. There is white in my hair, what is left of it. My wife is brushing hers by the fireside, and it is still plentiful but white as the snow we so seldom see in this pleasant land. Tadg Mor is sitting deep in the ingle-nook, smoking the tobacco of Virginia, and wondering when I am going to be done writing, so that I make for us our nightly compound of laced brandy-wine.

Tadg Mor and I are both hale and hearty, but anything more than thirty miles in the woods and hills tires us nowadays; we that used to pad at the jog-trot fifty miles behind Montrose and play a game of hurley thereafter to loosen our limbs. I am boasting a little. But why not I? We were not bad men in the days of our youth. Tadg Mor cries more easily than ever when he has the drink taken. I say to him now:

"Tadg Mor, do you remember Margaret Anderson?"

"Do I ever forget her, Maurteen," he answers soberly. "Do you think will we ever meet her over beyond?"

"We will meet her."

"And I will be jealous again," says my wife.

"Mind you, she was a bit of a Covenanter," Tadg Mor goes on, "and she might not be where we would be looking for her. Still, if she was in that other place I could be killing a man or eating meat on a Friday or missing Mass some Sunday. What do you think?"

"You did all these in your time. Trust to that."

"Very well so. I dreamt of her two nights ago. I was telling you. She came to me in Slaneyside, tall and bonny, and young, young; and she smiled at me, and I was young too. 'I am waiting long, Tadg Mor,' says she. 'I am waiting long for my belt of silver.' And then the tears were in her eyes and her voice weary. 'But where is Martin? I canna find my Martin Somers anywhere.' And I wakened myself with my weeping."

He turns to the fire now and croons to himself that strange, lonely lament that one will croon remembering beauty.